www.jjohnsonauthor.com

DIONIX

Evolve With Us

www.jjohnsonauthor.com

Come check out Dionix at www.dionix.ai , website developers as they have collaborated with www.jjohnsonauthor.com with his much needed and prodigious website. The website keeps all the author's inspirational manuscripts in-situ, in one place to make it exceptionally easy for his friends, family, loved ones or even reading fans from his previous works become easy to find, with new updates and new arrivals this season. To his readers, he has built his very own online library that's captivating, stories that truly inspire, resonate and empower, come check it out.

First Published 15/03/2025 In
Colchester, Essex, United Kingdom. By
Johnson Publishing-House.

Available On Barnes & Noble, Gardner's,
Waterstones, Amazon, Red Lion bookstore and

eBooks! My editors have been a huge help in hand, Amanda Johnson, Dr Pamela Campanelli, Andrew Jones, and Elle Willis. Supporting through the journey of my writing. Career so far, as any book writer or author would know the importance of having a third eye to help you go back over your work, to make your work fine works, and this takes time and patience. So, without the 'A Team' on standby things could be difficult.
A shoutout to our publishers, which was founded in 1986, OneDrive which is based in Cleveland, Ohio USA, and is owned by Tokyo-based Rakuten. Our books will be marketed as paperbacks and eBooks.

David had a Dream!...

Foreword

The riveting archaic history that had stomped through the grounds of Oxford University. Another nostalgic and pristine manuscript written in the author's very own unique, authentic style which draws attention throughout the twenty-first century. Whether it was academic integrity within pharmaceutical science, or playing catch-up study at the Bodleian Library, both nourishing and vitalised meals at lunchtime, with choices from baguette bar, or Christ church-cooked meals. The tranquillity set through the lunchtime daily walks throughout the University Park with acres of woodland to roam, retreat and find relief from academia. The manicured setting flanked the river Cherwell had brought a sudden serenity to one's wellbeing!   Amid the woodland and riverside was captivating flora and fauna which had brought natural life within the setting. The glorified botanic gardens kept a solace resonance, where many people would feel free and at peace, it was a funny thing the vibe that such a plantation would reflect upon one's emotions.

Preface

David came from a lower upper-class family from Oxfordshire, his favourite hobby and dream was to become a superstar at Polo. But he was having difficulties because he was left feeling rather perplexed, between his hobbies and education.
What would he focus on?
What would encourage him?
What is the inspiration that David desires?
David's, mother and father have been relying on their son to graduate from his university, with his Pharmaceutical Science BSc (Hons). So that David could expand his future with the family-run business at Mr & Mrs Smith's pharmacy in Oxfordshire. The question is, were Mr & Mrs Smith asking too much? David was merely still a teenager at nineteen years old. With a different diverse and flexible, and some might say a more vulnerable mindset to that of a wiser adult. David was a rather obedient empathetic, generous kind son to Mr & Mrs Smith throughout his younger years and has now grown to the age where his mind would want to start to explore some adulthood. What does that consist of? Partying up till late hours in the morning perhaps, engaging in sexual relationships with other females and guys, playing computer games, card games, smoking

pot, or just plainly over-exaggerating their hobbies and interests. But the truth be told, we all are living in this life paradox, with guidance from some formality whether that comes from paternal, maternal, or some authoritative figure, that tries to provide us with the moral sense of living, surviving, maybe religious guidance perhaps, many people would agree that we actually need someone to point the right direction we are heading or just encourage us when we start to do something well that we would rather enjoy? Could it be self-pride over one's own passion, or should we be left to follow our own chartered course to destiny?

What could be David's dream?

David was getting ready for his second-year term at Oxford University his second module is dated to start the Mon 2nd of October 2001, David will be nineteen years of age when he goes back to university his birthday was September 22nd, throughout the summer holidays, David had helped out around Mr & Mrs Smith pharmaceutical business with serving customers as the cashier. Overarching David's surroundings throughout his University for when he goes back to his second year at Oxford University which is the oldest

University in the English-speaking world, and to date one of the best and most prestigious buildings in the world, The University is made up of 39 independent colleges, many of the buildings can be found all over the city, visitors can explore the college gardens, the chapel and Christ church. As you can imagine David's parents had high hopes of their son graduating with flying colours with such an encouraging surrounding and archaic building, that's been well-known for high-profile educated professionals who end up becoming graduated students with a high pass rate... With so much encouragement, expectations, the archaic history of the building, and the professors that have passed on and graduated from this exact same institution, David had so much inspiration that surrounded him. What could possibly drive him off course to graduation? Even David's parents were quite literally banking on him, as they had paid his three-year tuition fees. Mr & Mrs Smith were very proud parents to David, like most parents who take their teenage kids to Oxford University, they have high hopes for their children, with all of them being High School A-level students and previously in their GCSE'S. They also needed a very good proposal letter to get granted acceptance into

Oxford University, stating their reasoning for why they should be accepted? what are their aims? what achievements do they expect? their study progress? and why should Oxford University accept them as students? You must remember Oxford University is a first-choice University for thousands and thousands of kids, not just locally, but overseas and all throughout the United Kingdom. It was a high-school dream to be able to graduate from High School and then walk straight into Oxford University, it was a pinnacle part of any teenager's life. The end of school has the thought' What direction is one actually going to head, into adulthood and future aspirations for the self?

Introduction... Sunday
1st October 2001

One Sunday evening David was getting his school academic essentials, and accessories ready. Pens, pencils, stencils, rulers, pencil cases, and notebooks, in preparation for his new year of study ahead of tomorrow. Most teenagers seem to find it very daunting with feelings of anxiousness and depression from the fear of not remembering the strain and stress from all the written assignments and exams that they have to face at the end of each module. I don't think you can find that one student who is highly excited to go back to university, whilst many students would be looking forward to finishing their BA (hons) or master's degrees. The thought of doing a three-year degree, after six years of primary school, and another six years of secondary school, and some students may have attended two to three-year college courses after high school, so either twelve or fourteen years of schooling before another three very dedicated years left at University trying to expand your academia. Many Students were gluttons for punishment and others just found the fascination about broadening their arisen. In the lightness at the depth of the long-distance future, those many traumatizing lonely winter cold nights, there isn't much comparison or better option. I mean what else could you possibly be doing that is much better or even near equivalent to broadening your future, giving yourself better advancements to higher and better education would only amount to higher-paid job prospects. When realistically only one should long for a brighter and better future. Although like many students David was not just anxious about going back to university, it had become momentous with the methodical practice, studying, taking notes, and assignments which sometimes can become rather strenuous, giving one hope that there could be a distant breakaway. One thing was for certain David was looking forward to being with his studying partner and best friend, Jasper Flynn, Jasper was a tall stocky gentleman, with ginger hair. He was maturing out from his teenage years into his twenties. David and Jasper had so much in common, they had studied the same academia with a pharmaceutical science PhD and they both had enjoyed the same hobbies. They loved to watch polo the sport of kings. Very soon they were both about to discover the sport on a new level. They aspired to start being able to go and participate in person. This would have taken some research throughout the local area or possibly looking through the University sports teams, as they may have a polo team already. After both the lads David and Jasper had been students at Oxford University, they had thought it best to get a piece of inside information from the background of the University, by looking through the blueprint. Not quite out of the extraordinary being an Oxford University and the most prestigious University in the United Kingdom, as Polo has dated back as far as the 6th century and was often referred to as 'the sport of kings', and ironically enough they had later found out that Oxford University had their very own polo team. David and Jasper were gearing up for their first day back at university tomorrow morning where they'd both meet on campus. They'd both been messaging back and forth about their newest hobby, they had always spoken about the matches they watched previously on the television, but now their interests had begun a bug as David and Jasper had started to endeavour their aspirations into a reality of actions. They thought the cost of Polo wasn't going to be cheap, the cost of a horse, the stick they use to hit the ball with, this wasn't just any kind of stick, very similar to a hockey stick, but in the sport of polo, it was called a mallet. Both their parents were middle-class, business owners, and paid for their three years PHD, degree. Although David had helped Friday evenings and Saturdays at his parent's Pharmacy, I don't think they'd be best pleased with forking out the extravagant costs of David's new adventures. It was very unlikely that David could bring back a solid income from a hobby. Like any hobby, unless you have got a supernatural talent you don't stand a chance to make anything big, if at all. The problem was David had no ancestors past or present that had participated enjoyed or even understood the sport. Therefore, David's tactics of trying to persuade his parents about the sport and him being exceptionally good at it would have been a fine thing if they already had been a natural talent in the bloodline. The outlook for David's future was that his parents, Mr and Mrs. Smith had looked into the longevity of David's well-being, wealth, and vitality while paying for his Oxford University Scholastic journey. David's parents had known what was best for him already with Mr. and Mrs Smith's pharmaceutical company, and a shop that was open six days a week down Oxford Road, open 9 am-6 pm, mon-fri and Saturdays was open till 9 am- 1 pm, a half-day Saturday. The family-run business was only an eleven-minute' drive, which was approximately from Wellington Square, the Oxford University to Oxford Road, the family's pharmacy was Eight miles apart. The distance travel was rather convenient for David and his parents not having to pay him to have digs at the

University also, as that comes with extra extortionate costs. Over time his parents could have happily retired from the family business and let David when he is settled down have an extended family with his future wife all possibly set up in line with the pharmacy business. The trouble any parent would face is no matter how obedient a son or daughter may be now and the narrow path you would like them to take is not always as perfect as one may seem. As young adults or late teenagers are still going through change, and so many other influences and different paths they could take. Could David and Jasper become influenced into the wrong adulthood, or could they take the right path by making the right decisions set out by the parent's guidance?

Chapter I Monday 2nd October 2001

It was David Smith and Jasper Flynn's first day back in the second year at Oxford University, with both their parent's setting hopes for their sons. Jasper Flynn and his family had come from Hertfordshire, Welwyn Garden City this was distance learning away from his family home for Jasper as he had to stay on Campus. Which for Jasper was more convenient as he had his best friend David only a few miles down the road. Jasper's benefit was being on campus due to the further ambience from such a prestigious inspiring University building which was surrounded by libraries and students both young and old, full of charisma, wisdom, and a passion to study and share knowledge. David would often meet Jasper Flynn on campus at around 9 am before their first study session had started at the pharmaceutical science studio, Their lecturer was Professor A.David Smith, as cited in… (Deborah Loeb Brice, 2001) Professor Smith was no relation to David's family ironically enough, Smith was a rather common name as we drew into the twenty-first century. Professor A. David Smith the lecturer of the Department of Medical Sciences at the Pharmacology studio of Oxford University, was in his mid-sixties, he was always dressed rather formally in either a black or blue suit. If he wore a black suit, he would generally wear a red tie and a white shirt, although he would wear a blue matching tie depending on which shoes he had worn, Professor Smith had spoken very vibrantly when he gave a formal discussion to his pupils with an element of sternness. The attire became an important part of any lecturer's appearance as that alone would show morals, principles, and charisma to show that you can direct your students with competence, after all, Sir A.David Smith was a professor who came equipped with an academic lecturer within the Department of Medical Science. It had been noted along with his smart, formal attire that he had worn some bifocals, and that had given the impression that he had sat previously hours on end looking through assignment after assignment marking the academic papers. Either that or the Professor had been playing around in the chemistry lab with various pharmaceutical ingredients, trying to formulate a new artificial drug that our bio-chemical mechanism might react to better well-being. Being David and Jasper's first day back at University walking into their second year, that Longley dreaded feeling, of getting your Module textbooks, Pharmacy and Pharmacology, Volume 53, Issue 6, Published June 2001. As cited in. (Oxford Academic, 2001a) They had all of a sudden started to feel bombarded with an overload of information about what this year had in store. David flicks through the textbook with that look of trepidation as he slowly feels swamped under academia. David reads through a research paper to try and get to grips with this year's modules, Triton X-100 is a non-ionic detergent that interacts with cell membranes to reverse multidrug resistance (MDR). Nevertheless, it causes cytotoxicity through its non-specific interactions with cells. The goal of this effort was to create polymeric chemosensitizers that could reverse MDR and reduce harmful side effects. Compared to the free detergent, the polymeric chemosensitizers may also have longer retention periods in tumours after being administered there. Inulin (T-IN) and Triton-X-100-immobilized dextran microspheres (T-MS) were made and described. They were compared to free Triton X-100 solutions in terms of their cytotoxicity against Chinese hamster ovary cells (CHRC5) that are resistant to drugs. The products' in vitro impact on CHRC5 cells' accumulation of 3H-vinblastine was ascertained. When compared to free Triton solutions at equivalent concentrations, T-MS and T-IN both demonstrated a considerable reduction in cytotoxicity. In the presence of T-MS or T-IN, CHRC5 cells' drug accumulation increased by more than two times. These findings imply that immobilization of chemosensitizers may be used to create polymeric drug carriers with MDR-reversing potential and reduced cytotoxicity. ‘This formula is well above my pay grade, as I am just a historical researcher and author, but from what we can gather looking at the different medical ingredients, chemicals, and some of the concoctions mixed, comes with varied concentrations which had caused cytotoxicity to the cell walls, this is why they had used many of these formulae on pet animals such as a Chinese hamster. It appears they are trying to formulate something that can help break down the cell wall to allow the drug to activate through into the cell body. Although David and Jasper's faces are concerned, if they take their time, participate in tutorials with their tutor, and study all the module materials they may start to enjoy their study. Getting some background knowledge, is wisdom you can bring forward to your examinations or assignments. David, Jasper Flynn, and their friend William Macintyre. William was from Liverpool and like Jasper he had stayed on campus as his mother was a nurse in the NHS and his father Paul Macintyre drove a great big arctic lorry for Hunts Transport, serving haulage & logistics serving all geographical regions of the United Kingdom. With both parents bringing in around 60-70 thousand pounds between them per annum, it hadn't seemed like a lot of earnings seeing as they had to pay for their son William's Degree in pharmaceutical science. William's father, Paul Macintyre, didn't want his son to struggle through early adulthood, as he knew full well what it was like being a young father to William. When William started to progress from a child to a mature teenager, things were soon to turn a lot harder. Finding work without qualifications, even with exceptional qualifications, many graduated students still had difficulty finding the work they needed, they ended up taking not-so-meaningful work. This wasn't to make these three boys have a lack of encouragement as no doubt they had a variety of different aspirations between them. Like many humans, the breed, the specimen, always has many interests and hobbies to fall back on if plan A doesn't work out. Many ungraduated students, change their minds about their academic studies halfway through finishing their degree. Then these undergraduates would be studying pharmaceutical science one moment, then the next moment they would be speaking to the student support team to try and find an alternative academic study so they could progress with something else that they were keen on. It would have to be with another similar study in science, perhaps biology, or physics perhaps? They're all a form of science in some shape or form. It was the student's first day back at University with Professor A. David Smith, there were twelve students, six boys, and six girls. The first opportunity day back in the second year was known as the refresher's week, the first opportunistic day to refresh, research, resonate, and observe what is lying ahead of you for the remainder of the academic year. William Macintyre, Jasper Flynn, and David had already made friends with one another. While David had taken a liking to this rather vibrant uptown girl from the city, her name was Daphne Johnson. Her family came from The Royal Borough Kensington and Chelsea, as you could quite imagine such an elegant sort with a voice that would coax you to a peaceful slumber. Her family had worked at the local medical centre. William had the hots for Verity Page, she was a blonde lass from Bristol, with a tremendous southwest highly spoken accent, where the letter S is always pronounced with a Z. That she must have inherited from her upbringing by her parents or grandparents.

Verity's parents part-owned the Wapley riding school, it was just off Wapley Hill, Westerleigh, Wapley, Bristol. BS37 8RJ, As cited in.. (© Wapley Stables Ltd and Wapley Riding School Ltd, 2001) It had become evident that Verity Page's customer service skills had come from her family's horse-riding business, it wasn't quite clear what Verity's passion was to be studying pharmaceutical science. Maybe her interest was to learn new medicine that can cure sick animals perhaps so she could take her career that one step further, after all, Verity and her family were rather empathetic with looking after and caring for horses. They had such prodigious stables, at the Wapley riding school, and many residents and riders from near and far would come to visit or participate in the riding school, from teenage to adult years both boys and girls. Some families would bring their horses for a run out around the assault field, where the horses could practice their jumps, and the rider gets to know their horse better. It was highly beneficial for the rider to get to know their horse's flaws, anxieties etc. Some horses may find certain jumps a struggle to another, many other horses may take the jump better by running around to their left-hand side, rather than running around to their right-hand side and taking the jumps, this was all dependent on each horse's preference. This is known as a silent conversation with your horse, getting to know it in the motion it desires best, rather than physically waiting for the horse to speak aloud. Once Verity Page graduated from Oxford University, she and her family would have the full work, at the Wapley Riding School in Bristol. They would then have a horse stable where they could give medical treatment and look after the well-being of the horses, and that would be a phenomenal achievement for when she graduated. Already she and her mother provide the standard care and grooming of the animals, but to be professionally medically trained you needed to get some decorum from somewhere, and Oxford University it was! William and David had labelled their best friend Jasper Flynn a carrot top, at first Jasper had found it nothing but ironic and annoying. But like most ginger-haired people they get used to the fact that the majority of people just act like ginger people are just vilified, and after a while, Jasper Flynn just answered to anything. After all, they were his foolish best friends for the next two years at least. Jasper Flynn was fairly a shy boy, but he had the hots for a girl who wore glasses with jet black hair with freckles, her name was Eldora Jenkins. Eldora Jenkins was autistic; she had such a beautiful character. Her family had come from Cardiff, Wales, her ambition was to become a clinical research associate, which is nothing short of surprising to know, if you know of anyone who is autistic then you would know that is a very formal and wise choice. The brain functions very in-depth and deep, they will not miss an ingredient as they will understand everything to perfection quite literally. The job description of a clinical research associate, they run clinical trials to test new and existing drugs for their effectiveness and run risks and benefits to ensure they are safe for the intended use or not. Eldora Jenkin's bifocals give the impression that she is a deep reader and researcher, her observational skills are phenomenal, and her listening and understanding, also her analytical skills were important for her so she could understand everything bit by bit until she gradually mastered it. Once you get to know Eldora Jenkins, you will see her for who she is by her character. For she empowers people with her intelligence. She was not one of those girls you could try to reason with or be little, as she always knew what was right and wrong. And just like so…

That was the first day finished at the Oxford University refreshers day with teacher, Professor, A. David. Smith, as a full-time Student, had thirty study hours per week. Today they had a two-hour academic study that helped the students from Professor A. David. Smith's classroom allowed the students to set a precedent for the rest of the week. Over a few weeks, they can start to schedule a routine, and then their mind and body will start to settle into a therapeutic regime. At first, they will find their academic studies an absolute strenuous catastrophe, causing anxiety and depression to many students' well-being. It was highly important for students to find their feet early on in their academic studies, so they could settle and start to process the module that they had started. This would give them plenty of insight into what to look for as part of their future assignments and exams. Whilst leaving the pharmaceutical science classroom, David, Jasper Flynn, William Macintyre, and the three girls, Daphne Johnson, Verity Page, and Eldora Jenkins had all decided to go to the Oxford University Library, The Pharmacology was located at Mansfield Road,

Oxford 0X1 3QT, So the six of them had all decided to analyse their study week within the iconic archaic Bodleian Library, this was the main research library within the University of Oxford, the building and library were founded in 1602 by Sir Thomas Bodley, and recorded as the oldest library within Europe.. Cited in. (Wikipedia, 2001) They could probably find the previous year's academic study books from the pharmacology class and cross-reference their research. As they opened the door of the library and walked in David and Jasper Flynn were always overwhelmed by the old-fashioned rustic smell, it almost smelt like dust and cobwebs, plus the varnished bookshelves within the library which held the books together in the right section and column, in situ, with the genre, from fiction to nonfiction, the full spectrum sciences, history, geography, dictionary, encyclopaedia, French, German, Spanish different languages, etc. The library was always relatively tidy and clean after all it wasn't cobwebs and dust, it was just the smell of the ancient books with weathered pages. After years and years of people reading them and taking them home back and forth to the library, it had resulted in the pages which had tended to turn colour, an off-white, to sepia.

Eldora Jenkins was overwhelmed too with the library, she had gone straight to the pharmaceutical science section which was the near left-hand side to the front desk of the library, no doubt she had wanted to research some new medicines. She had always liked to explore and expand her horizons. And eager to devour and explore every new paper or publication that she could lay her hands on; she had always enjoyed putting herself in-depth with further research so she could be slightly advanced to the rest of the students in her classroom. Her friends and her tutor had often questioned her intellectual side, they were either left inspired or just plainly discombobulated by the information that she could absorb. Like most autistic people, they tend to go above and beyond to further research their academic studies. Professor, A. David Smith, wouldn't be frowned upon, his students going above and beyond. Like most tutors, they would encourage it. It was highly important to see their students flourish. While Eldora was happily further researching medicines. The other five students, David, Jasper Flynn, William Macintyre, Verity Page, and Daphne Johnson, were just happy to be going through their module book and taking some notes to get themselves ahead for the week ahead. The library was a prodigious place for students to get some inspiration, with pure tranquillity and hardly any noise disturbance. Apart from the odd person walking up and down the bookshelf Isle to either find the book they are looking for or replace the book they had borrowed. The six of them, David, Jasper Flynn, William Macintyre, Daphne Johnson, Verity Page, and Eldora had planned only to spend time from when they arrived at the library which was just after 11:00 am up until 1:00 pm then all head to the canteen for lunch. The first day back at Oxford University and already they had set forth a positive appraisal if they could all encourage one another to carry out their academic studies like this for the remainder of the academic year, then they would all flourish with flying colours. For some students, it was exceptionally hard to maintain structure to their studies as unforeseen circumstances can and may occur, such as sickness, illness, or any bereavement throughout the families which can force students to pull out from the academic year until further notice and things have settled down which would then become convenient for them to return. That sweet rustic library smell brought a positive aroma that gave the encouraging vibe of becoming inventiveness within their research, and a positive reflection to their studies. The similarity to a superstar football player walking onto a freshly cut lawn at Wembley Stadium during a cup final was very much the same to an academic student walking into an archaic, historical, library, with the rustic sweet smell of literature. You could smell the tall oak library bookshelves too, it smelt like they had just been varnished. If you ever wondered how anyone could reach the top shelf if you ever did need a book for research or academic study purposes. That was important to the Librarian at the Bodleian Library, Sir Appleton the Librarian had his wooden steps to reach the top tier from the library's bookshelves.

It was approaching close to 1:00 pm with time approximately 12:45 pm, Jasper Flynn's stomach had started to rumble, so with himself being the first one to retire for a spot of luncheon. Everyone else, David, William Macintyre, Daphne Johnson, Verity Page, and Eldora Jenkins had begun to gather their module books and academic study essentials as they too were ready to go and source some much-needed sustenance to fuel body and mind. They had all decided to eat at the University

Park, as recorded in. (Oxford Mosaic, 2001) The University Parks consist of around 70 acres of beautiful parkland, bordering the River Cherwell, including sports areas, a duck pond, and a large collection of plants and trees in landscaped surroundings. In the summer, you can visit a refreshment stand run by the local sandwich shop Jimbob's Baguettes, selling snacks and drinks. They had picked this location for their lunch break today as it was such a beautiful landscape, the surroundings with such authentic scenery from one of Oxford's finest landmarks. David had often loved the B.L.T. Baguette with the chocolate topping flapjack from Jimbob's Baguettes, Eldora Jenkins had enjoyed Tuna and cucumber sandwich and a rather succulent Green Granny Smith apple, Jasper Flynn always liked egg mayonnaise roll, with cress and a Mars Bar, Daphne Johnson had bought Cheese salad take-away bowl, which contained green leaf salad, carrots, croutons, tomato, pomegranate seeds and Caesar salad dressing and a peach for dessert, Verity Page only had wanted something light to eat, she grabbed a vegetable rustic soup and a jam & cream scone for dessert, and William Macintyre had bought the breakfast baguette, sausage, egg, bacon, smothered with brown sauce. He bought a caramelized yoghurt for dessert. They picked the right location to unwind from their morning study, looking at this beautiful place, which was originally owned by Merton College, it was incidentally purchased by the University in the 1850s and then first laid out as a park for sports and recreational purposes in 1864. It had then become available for the enjoyment of the members of the University, its residents, and the visitors who came to visit Oxford Park, and it is open to the public pretty much every day of the year until nightfall. (the only exception being Christmas Eve) with many walks to choose from, with a large collection of plants and tree space for informal games and picnics.

And for many of those who enjoy sport here's the opportunity, which depends on the seasonal conditions and the time of year, whether you would be catching a game of cricket, lacrosse, tennis, football, or rugby. And just as you imagined you may encounter the younger generations pretending to fly/run around with broomsticks between their legs playing what appears to be a game of witches or Quidditch. As they were still at the beginning of October they had a good couple of weeks for some average warmer climate, then the temperature would start to drop as they were nearing the winter climate change. With darker mornings and getting darker earlier in the evening. After David, Jasper Flynn, Micheal Macintyre, Daphne Johnson, Verity Page, and Eldora Jenkins all had finished their lunches they had often enjoyed the wonderous sights from the sight-seeing around the most prodigious of landscapes and being at the beginning of October, the 2nd to be extra precise, the falling of the trees leaves, Autumn. It was just only a few weeks into the start of Autumn and what a beautiful sight, the crispy leaves that fell from the deciduous trees from under those passers-by feet, the crunching sound as they had tread them into the tarmac footpath and in between the expanse from those leather shoe to the pavement, the foot trodden down to the crisping wafer of those russet leaves that had crumbled into smithereens. The temperature had slowly dropped but not enough for those squirrels to go and hibernate they too would be having tremendous amounts of fun with all the last of the falling acorns, abundant everywhere, over the footpaths and across the playing fields. The squirrels would have ample fun collecting all of those acorns just in time for hibernation. Nothing unusual amongst the habitat from an open playing field with acres of land, you often see deer, rabbits, foxes, and squirrels, but as per-say when the sporting activities throughout the day commence many of the larger animals tend to run for hiding. The University Park was an exceptional place for everyone, not just for those hard-working students but many visitors who would also like to come through here to see the awe-inspiring views as it was one of those Universities that had so much archaic history here it had become a Worlds famous landmark, not just the University but the landscape surrounding the vicinity gave the University that distinctive feature compared to the rest, it was magnificent. You would often see many Oxford University students taking selfies, pictures with their friends with the beautiful scenery in the background from the outstanding views within the landscaped grounds of the University Park, or even pictures with squirrels gorging on their usual feast of nuts. There was never anything not fascinating about enjoying still photos with some of the amazing animals and other wildlife that the park contained. No doubt even the observers from the social media posts would appreciate a good example of someone enjoying the amazing wildlife that this privileged world has to offer. David had thoroughly enjoyed his lunch break catching up with Daphne Johnson, David was fairly shy, but it was rather clear that he had fancied Daphne. He had spent a lot of time asking her for some wise counsel to help David make exquisite decisions about his future. This was rather ironic as any person making a note here would think if you asked that same specific in-depth question to the opposite sex, it had become quite clear he was almost trying to involve her in his plans. Even more so, his incentive had become clear, he wanted her to help him make that kind of decision. It was quite normal for an introverted person to show their affection extraordinarily but rather try their utmost hardest to include them as much as possible in every deed. But for David being so shy and not so full of himself had liked to plant the seed slowly, to show his affection and dedication. It is an important part of males and females slowly getting to know one another and not rushing things. Daphne Johnson, the brunette slender, vibrant city girl, who came from The Royal Borough of Kensington and Chelsea. Daphne conducted herself with such an elegant vibrant tone of voice. She had brought a red bashful smile upon those rosy cheeks of David. They were both enamoured with one another as the academic study persevered the days into months, you could see they enjoyed being in each other's company. Finding the right connection that can help encourage you through your academic study

is just as important as enjoying your time being single and finding your own feet within your very own journey throughout your academic study. But many students both young and old had preferred it best to reflect and encourage a person of interest perhaps. but it wasn't mandatory.
David's mother had called him on his mobile telephone, as his mother was just passing Oxford University which was only fifteen minutes away from Mr and Mrs Smith's pharmacy, "Hi, David" "Hi mum": David and his mum conversing back and forth! "I am outside son, I can take you back home before I head back into the pharmacy, would you like a lift?": Says Mrs Smith. "Okay mum just finished my lunch, and I am just standing chatting with my friend Daphne, but ermmmm, I'll come now": said David. You could kind of hear it in David's voice he didn't want to leave Daphne. "So sorry Daphne that was my mother on the phone, I have to leave. But I'll see you tomorrow"? David says, as he hugs and then waves as he wanders away from Daphne. "No problem, David, argh": as she waves David goodbye. Daphne Johnson goes back to the park to find the others, Verity Page, Eldora Jenkins, William Macintyre, and Jasper Flynn. Jasper Flynn was fascinated by Eldora Jenkins, with her jet-black hair and her black framed bifocals, they say girls with black hair tend

to be intelligent. In Eldora Jenkin's case, she was not only just intelligent she was autistic also. They shared a common rarity interest as Eldora Jenkins was autistic and Jasper Flynn was ginger. They both had the same understanding, as some people would treat them differently, although they are a tremendous representation of Oxford University's finest. William Macintyre was conversing back and forth splendidly with the Bristol Boujee blonde lass, and that was our Verity Page, Daphnee had caught up with the others, and then they had all decided to head back to their university lodgings. The boy's lodgings were separate from the girls for health and safety reasons and more so they could focus on academic education. Leaving Daphne, Verity, and Eldora, saying their goodbye to William Macintyre and Jasper Flynn, "Bye boys": says the girls as they part ways towards their side of the campus, "bye girls, we will see you tomorrow": said Micheal and Jasper as they walk into the boy's block, they head straight into the entertainment room as it was still relatively early. At 3:45 pm, within the entertainment room they had table tennis, a pool table, and a dart board. The University had provided well for the students on campus, giving them plenty of entertainment and being able to manage their mental health and well-being. It was highly important to look after the welfare of the students for those who were working away from home. Jasper and William had started to play table tennis, pinging the ping-pong ball back and forth whilst gossiping about the girls in their classroom. Specially Verity Page and Eldora Jenkins, "net": exclaims Jasper. As it had appeared William Macintyre had lost his concentration on the thought of the blonde Bristol accent with the suppressing beauty, of Verity Page. These young boys didn't know how to play the game when it came to showing affection to the girls. Those gentlemen had better not take too much time to let those girls know they were something special before it was too late and lost forever. 'The trouble is with both boys and girls alike, although they are deemed so eager and passionate about the opposite sex, they also have the fear of failure with their lack of achievements, such as their academic studies' What do they chase after first, Their pleasurable things or their future? Jasper was highly struck by Eldora Jenkins, he was telling William Macintyre over the game of table tennis, how her superior intelligence brings the best out within her personality and that he liked the fact she wore glasses as it gave her that maturity look, it gave Jasper that comfort for his future crush to feel stable and inspired by the girl of his dreams. After playing table tennis for a couple of hours, they would end up in the lounge watching television or often they had listened to music to unwind for the evening. The girls were back at their lounge area on their side, doing girlie things like straightening each other's hair, Eldora would sit in the evenings reading some fiction books and on other occasions, she would be reading her academic module books. Daphne was straightening Verity's silky blonde hair to perfection, both Daphne and Verity were catalogue girls, as they had not one blemish they came complete dolly birds, Daphne Johnson had such a slender athletic figure, she had elegant brunette hair with a short fringe and its length was just to the small of her lower back, with a touch of summer tan she was glowing. Eldora enjoyed playing a more simplistic kind of lass, she was very pretty but rather casual with it. Don't get me wrong all three young ladies were highly intellectually intelligent, but Eldora would rather rely on her personality than her cute looks, so she intended not to spend so much time trying to look like a princess. Daphane and Verity were gossiping, whilst Eldora was sitting on the lounge settee, (a chaise longue) flicking through an OK magazine weirdly enough. Maybe Eldora was trying to find some scientific health-related factors, as I do not believe otherwise that OK Magazine

has much else to offer other than gossip in and around celebrities. “So, what do you think of Jasper Flynn”, kindly says Daphne.
“Eldora replies’: “you know what Daph, he is a cute ginger lad, what I like about him, is that he is different and not like all the other guys, he is not full of himself and comes across as shy but also slightly affectionate, and I like the thought of getting to find that out. If my thoughts are true or not, it is all in the chase, right?”
“Yeah, you are so right, Eldora, all of us girls need to focus past all the masculinity, who is the bravest, who wears the best clothes etc. We need to start focusing on what can bring more comfort to our hearts, not just desires”.: Says Daphne.
Verity chirps up, “I like a man to be macho, a little bit cheeky, and intelligent. I want a guy who can protect me and support me in all my needs both mentally and physically otherwise I'll be out here all alone trying to pay the bills, sort all the paperwork out, and do all the DIY jobs in and around the house”. “Trust you”: Verity says to Daphne and Verity, “you can’t have it always, that is just greedy. I’ll have it anyway way I like it girls”.: Says V.

Chapter 2

Tuesday 3rd Oct 2001

It was 5:45 am, and the sunrise had just begun to appear amid the midst of darkly grey-blue skies. There wasn't much movement around the University at this time of the morning, although many students would have set the alarm to start getting ready for the second day back at university, with some students visiting the gymnasium or going for a jog around the local park, as many students would feel ready and refreshed after exercise. It seems to alert the brain from functioning whilst others believe it tires them out too much to study. Daphne, Verity, and Eldora had woken up to their alarm that was set, they had needed to set the alarm early doors, as girls like to take their time getting ready. Women have an elegant touch of class, with doing their hair and makeup. They would go together down to the shower cubicle, but before they had packed their wash and clothes bag. They had intended to look outside to see what the weather had in store for them, so they could make a wise choice rather than become unstuck having to get the wrong attire on and then having to come back in to get changed as they had made the wrong choice of clothing due to the weather conditions. But as it happened, it appeared to be a clear sky, although the sun had just started to rise north of the campus block and just above the house in the distance. There wasn't much movement within the trees, the branches and leaves weren't blown around by any wind. You could hear the birds happily chirping away which is usually a good sign of either lots of scrap food left over from yesterday's lunch break, pigeons splitting open the black bags with their razor-sharp beaks, or the weather with clear sky and the sun was coming out without a wind or breeze in sight perhaps as that was the usual occurrence with happily chirping birds outside the window. The girls could happily take an hour in the shower as they had set the alarm purposefully to enjoy and take their time getting prepared and primed up for the day. A lady's dress code wasn't just about shampooing the hair, drying it, straightening it, and then applying the makeup. These Oxford University Student ladies were an eloquent kind, they were cut from a different cloth, and they wore, smelt, and looked differently, they had styled the new 21st Century of high profile, highly sophisticated women to this generation. Daphne Johnson was the first girl from out of the shower room, she was by the sink basin, drawing on her eyeliner with a towel wrapped around her head in a cone, dome shape. Then out came Eldora. "Hi Daphne, that shower was toastie and warm, wasn't it?" "Yes, the showers are beautiful first thing in the morning aren't they Eldora": replies Daphne. "Can I borrow your hair dryer please Daphne?" "Of course, you can" Daphne has said! The girls had a bundle of time, it was nearing 6:00 am and they didn't have their first lesson until 9:00 am, still with plenty of time to get ready and have a light snack for their breakfast. Verity Page was the last of the girls to finish in the shower, as she waddled into the sink basin where the girls' mirrors were located, with her towel tightly wrapped around her bosom, and tightly firmed around her gluteus Maximus. All three girls had fine figures with both Daphne and Verity Page taking their beauty preparation to the next level, as a picturesque glamour model. Do not get me wrong Eldora Jenkins was a very attractive young lady, but she withheld herself differently with slightly more sophistication, she drew glasses which gave her a different eloquent angle to look at her character with such charisma, wisdom, and intelligence, she had a whole lot more going on than just a pretty face. And that is not to say that Verity and Daphne weren't intelligent because undoubtedly, they were, otherwise, they would not be attending Oxford University! But for Daphne and Verity, if plan A hadn't planned out so well for them, they always had plan B to fall back to they were never short of opportunities.

6:00 am The boys had woken up on their side of the campus, William Macintyre and Jasper Flynn were also roommates which worked well for them both as they could resonate, compare and contrast study notes throughout the evening and talk about

what they had learned through the course of the day. David Smith, their best friend would get a lift into university the majority of the time by his parents. If not, he would use public transport to make the short journey to meet his friends at the University.
It wouldn't take so long for the gentlemen to get in the shower and groomed, although some men do like to look their best. But they'd usually get the best parts done at the local barbers, as they are the experts, they can shave your eyebrows, nostrils, and ear hairs, and shape your hair back, forth, and sides. The difference is that the men didn't wear make-up. As long as they showered, wore pressed, ironed clothes, combed their hair, shaved their beards, and moustaches, or even trimmed them neatly, that is what is known as a neatly groomed gentleman. Just one last touch of aftershave and they were pristine and good to go. Good for a dog's dinner. The ladies had appreciated a nicely presentable man looking rather suave, with his shiny shoes, moccasins, brogues, loafers, chino trousers, nicely ironed shirt with a rather fetching matching tie to go with the shoes or the trousers, and a fine blazer to finish off, the real gentlemen look had polished off nicely right in the view of

the ladies. One thing was for sure, without a shadow of a doubt it would be David who drew the girls' attention the most, as he wore that exact description of which he had gained the morals from working in his family-run business, the pharmacy of Mr & Mrs Smith. Working the shop floor and being at the forefront of customer services at the till, he needed to be presentable for serving customers throughout his weekend. So, setting standards, speaking vibrantly, dressing modestly, and serving the customers appropriately helped the business speak for itself in volumes.
It was an important role to maintain customer services with a proven track record, of high diligence, and it was an equally important role to maintain a fair professional experience for all customers.
It was fairly warm outside today so William and Jasper both had worn black chino trousers, white shirts, and black ties, whilst Jasper had worn his black leather brogues and William had worn his brown suede loafers with tassels. They both look smart, casual, and comfortable, that was a very important part of the day because a happy man with the equipment he brings to the task can help make the task a lot more bearable. Rather than

feeling overwhelmed by having an uncomfortable amount of clothes on, one can make light work seem strenuous. But to be honest with you, it wouldn't have been a terrible thought to have worn a blazer either, as you have the option to take it off if it is too hot, or if it is too cold or starts to rain, you'd be far glad to be overdressed then underdressed. It concluded a double-edged sword' damned if you had and damned if you hadn't despite the weatherman.

William and Jasper Flynn had sat in the kitchen sitting room eating porridge and cinnamon, it was a recipe that Eldora Jenkins had given the boys since she had told them the ingredients they could not get enough. You could find cinnamon down any herbs and spices aisle in any shopping centre usually, the favourite porridge was ready brek, smoothly textured, and went down a treat with the cinnamon added flavourings with hot warmed milk. It was one of those cereals that were rather more-some, wholesome, it would sit nicely on the tummy, and a great feed just before you head off to bed as it would sit nicely on your stomach to help you ease into a nice deeply peaceful sleep. It was loaded with carbohydrates enough to give them the energy they needed for the academic study they had ahead of them today, Carbs is a superb source of energy along with fructose such as fruits. Fruits also have many vitamins and minerals that would support your vitality and well-being. These boys knew they needed `five a day`, so they often took some fruit with them to their study. Daphne Johnson, Verity Page, and Eldora Jenkins had fruit for their breakfast, Eldora and Verity also had some fruit loaf as well as a peach and some strawberries. These girls, as you can imagine were very picky with their choice of foods, the fast carbohydrate, fructose was a quicker source of energy boost which more than likely heightened your metabolism. Daphne Johnson had picked out a banana and Granny Smith's apple, they were rather succulent and the purest green apple out on display. It was coming up to 8:15 am. Both boys and girls would generally meet each other outside their dormitory, which students like to call university accommodation or even digs. Their dormitory was only a short distance away from the main entrance of Oxford University, and of course, being on Campus many amenities were within the distance, while some study blocks may have been a bus ride away. But all within around 14,250 square km radius. Both Jasper Flynn and William

Macintyre had finished their breakfast and were ready to go and meet the girls outside the girl's dormitory, which was only a block away. After they had met up with Daphne, Verity, and Eldora they would generally go and meet David by the main entrance waiting patiently for his mother or father to drop him into university, they had an outstanding friendship their little sixsome groupie, they hadn't lacked any encouragement between them. This was the importance of finding legitimate friendship as you could coast through any struggles together that you may face in the foreseeable future, the encouragement and support from one another came to help you through some of life's most strenuous situations.
William and Jasper welcomed the girls, like two young gentlemen and held open the girls' dormitory front door, Daphne Johnson, Verity Page, and Eldora all looked extraordinarily modest, hair straightened and brushed, Oxford Uni Dress code was a black dress, trousers, blazers, and white shirt or blouse. Daphne and Verity had often worn a midi black dress with either skin tights or black tights this time of the year as it was the end of summer, Eldora Jenkins always tried her utmost best to be a little more extravagantly

modest by wearing a longer dress, while still trying to bear the heat with a blazer on top. Plus, she had liked to cover her skin up from being sunburnt, although the other girls hadn't minded too much to show a little flesh to gain a tan from the beaming sun. The girls were often happy to see the boys both William and Jasper, as they had always shown loyalty and commitment, and being methodical shows how compassionate and gentlemanly they can be. Both boys and girls liked it to be amicable and reciprocated, as the boys had always greeted the girls in the morning at the doors of their dormitory and had always shown their full adherence back.
"Right then shall we go meet David by the gate": says Daphne.
David was her Oxford University heartthrob. A few of them give Daphne the nod, whilst Jasper, Eldora, and William reply "Yes of course". Out from the dormitory, they walk toward the main entrance into the Carpark where University Staff, lecturers, cleaners, chefs, and visitors come into the carpark or drop-off point for parents with students. It was 8:45 am and they were standing at the drop-off point, David's mother had just arrived in her blue Renault Laguna. David mum's pulled

up slowly by the kerbside to the drop-off point as she could see David's friends all smiley and waving toward David and his mum, David's mother was very friendly and supportive of David and his friends, she had always engaged with such zeal and compliance with the other youngsters at Davids University, she acted and treated them all fairly and had always shown encouragement and always asking them how they were getting along with their academic studies. She knew full well what it was like once upon a time to be a University Student. "Bye David. By Kids": waves Mrs Smith, as she says her goodbye.
"Bye Mrs Smith, have a good day": say the others.
"Bye Mother, see you later this evening,": said David. And just like so… The Oxford University School gang was back together again to start their second day on campus with yet another dreaded day with their tutor Professor A. David Smith. It was dreadful in the sense that they had to engage their brain to get the knowledge and wisdom that they needed to become better prospects for their future. But once they had graduated, they also knew it would be worth it, so for the matter, it was worth fighting for.

So, the group was walking down toward the Department of Medical Science block, and on their way the boys, David, William, and Jasper were having that discussion again back and forth about the 'Polo Sport' they had wanted to look into for a short while now. So today after their academic studies they were going to arrange to find out what were the Oxford University requirements for their school team, training or trials etc.
Their Pharmacology science tutor Professor A. David Smith had his session nicely planned out for his Students today, lightly letting them into something that they will be getting themselves prepared for in the distant future within the near end of the academic year, he had lightly prepared some examination papers for his students to have a brief analysis. He has no intention to scaremonger his students but rather let them in slowly to what will be laid ahead within the forthcoming academic studies, hoping that it will give them some more focus in the coming weeks as to what kind of knowledge will be expected to draw upon. A, David Smith greets his students by the front door of the classroom with a unique but gracious smile, this brings a sudden warmth feeling to his students which indicates that they're in good

hands, “Please do come in and take a seat” gently speaks the Professor A. David Smith. “Good morning, Professor Smith” replied the cohort, as his understudies they have to call their tutor by their consulted full name, but “Professor Smith” was enough as he had preferred. “Please do take a seat, I will give you five minutes to settle in, get your academic stuff ready, your pens, pencils, rulers, calculators, and study notebooks, before we start. As I wanted to show you a few things before we roar off like headless chickens”: Said profoundly Professor A. David Smith.
David was in a rush this morning to get a lift to Oxford University with his mother, he had totally forgotten his academic Pharmaceutical Science module book. David raised his hand above his head, with his index fully stretched to the sky into a pointed motion into the air, Professor A. David Smith had noticed David’s signal, “Yes what is it please David”? : Said the tutor
“mmmm I am ever so sorry, I am not sure what to do as my mother was in a rush to drop me into Uni today and I mistakenly left my module book on the edge of my bed, as I was up reading through last night, I don’t suppose you have a spare module book please, for now”? : Implies David.

Professor A. David Smith rightly explains to his students, "although it is not good practice to not be taking good care of your module academic books, we do have a few spare books that we have over ordered as we understand that some of you would misplace one or two by mistake, alternatively if we come unstuck it can also become beneficial to work in two's so we don't all end up misplacing them, here you go, David, come and collect it from my desk" "Thankyou": says David with a grin on his face. "Right then, now you are all situated comfortably in your allocated seats, we will begin this session. Let us just take a look at page 1207 in our module booklet, underneath the headline, Colon-Specific delivery" exclaims Professor Smith, of budesonide from microencapsulated cellulosic cores: evaluation of the efficacy against colonic inflammation in rats as cited in.. (Oxford Academic, 2001b) "Now just for a moment let us break down this headline by ciphering through the text, what does it tell us?": Said Professor Smith, " Eldora Jenkins placed her hand up "Budesonide is a medicine used to treat mild to moderate active Crohn's disease, and inflammatory in bowel disease": Professor Smith was in awe by Eldora Jenkins response, "you have been doing your homework, Eldora, well done": implied Professor Smith. "So, in response to this headline as Eldora had noted the use of Budesonide, they have been using this to try and prevent inflammation that occurred in this rat as stated. Throughout the course of this module some of our practical work will be using other forms of medicine on animals to see if we can formulate a cure" explains Professor A. David Smith. Looking back through the module paper, Strong corticosteroids like budesonide (BDS) have significant effects on the pharmacotherapy of inflammatory bowel disease, particularly in the management of Crohn's disease and ulcerative colitis. Enteric-coated formulations of BDS are available on the market. Nevertheless, these medicines are not selective enough to treat colonic inflammatory bowel disease, just as other site-specific dose forms that are now accessible. This study set out to assess the effectiveness of a novel BDS-containing microparticulate system in treating experimentally induced colitis in rats. To combine pH-sensitive and controlled-release features, this microparticulate system was made up of hydrophobic cores containing BDS that were microencapsulated in an enteric polymer that solubilises at pH values higher than 7. The colon/bodyweight ratio was used to measure colon damage and inflammation. Measuring macroscopic and histological damage in colitic rats, as well as myeloperoxidase (MPO) activity. For four days following the production of inflammation, rats were given oral BDS, which was a component of the established system, once daily. The experimental design included two control formulations: a BDS suspension and enteric microparticles containing BDS. When compared to the administration of control formulations, the colon/bodyweight ratio was considerably decreased by the new BDS delivery technique. In a similar vein, when the BDS formulation was used instead of the oral drug suspension, there was a considerable decrease in MPO activity as well as in the macroscopic and histological damage of the inflamed colonic segments. However, when the novel treatment was contrasted with the control formulation, which consisted of basic enteric microparticles, no notable differences were seen. So Professor A. David has read out the day's module study, and now he wants to guide, reflect, and for his students to take notes so they can go home and analyse what they have just been

reading, He then talks about enteric coating, which is a polymeric coating for the active medication which stops the disintegration of the active in the patient's stomach acid. He talks about the microparticulate system, which encapsulates the hydrophobic cores containing the medication. So, we can get our understanding that our scientists in pharmacology have carried out an experiment on live rats with colon issues using an empirical study; in doing so they have carried out three different varieties of the experiment.
From the author, there was no specific number of how many rats that they had with colon issues and also there was no significance to how many procedures had improved with x amount of rats, although it had said experiments were an oral suspension, i.e., a liquid that would suspend the micro particulates to enable an even dosage to be administered.
The enteric-coated capsule containing the microparticulate system is again, to be administered orally, also the author's notes stated how often they were administered, which was once daily.
Finally, a placebo of enteric-coated inert micro particulates, the findings were that the novel

enteric microparticulate system administered once daily by oral route decreased histological and enzymatic activity.
Professor A. David Smith was particularly overwhelmed with the amount of academia that they had covered today, researched, analysed, and reflected on. It has been insightful for his pupils within his pharmacology science class, to give them something to meditate on when they get home back into their dormitory. You will see that studying medicines and science is a whole new language on its own and some of the Professor's students would usually go to the library to do some further research to get some well-equipped and needed knowledge on most of the terms used in biology and medicines which are derived from classical languages, such as Latin and Greek.
"Right then class, you may be dismissed from your study, and go out and enjoy your afternoon break, but please do make sure you reflect on what you have learned today as we have covered a lot within the two hours, I am grateful to have you all here, see you all again tomorrow": Says Professor A. David Smith. As usual, David, William, Jasper, the girls too, Daphne, Verity, and Eldora want to go into the library for an hour before they head off to

break, like before, they had gone to the Bodleian Library (Wikipedia, 2001), they had other modern libraries on Campus but like many students, had preferred the archaic historical feeling as they approached the library store as it gave them that rustic emotional sense, full of optimism and wisdom. Some of the world's most famous study researchers, historians, geographers, pharmaceutical scientists, architects, etc have all gained their scholarships from this same precise building over the many years it has still been withstanding... But this time in going back to the library even Eldora had also wanted to go back and reflect on what they had just been reading from the module of today's textbook. It was headlined, Colon-Specific delivery of budesonide from microencapsulated cellulosic cores: evaluation of the efficacy against colonic inflammation in rats. Basically, in a small nutshell, they were carrying out medical experiments with rats, which had inflamed colon, from what we had noted earlier they had carried out three different medicine procedures to see which chemical would react either faster or slower breaking through the membranes and cell walls. It was highly important for the students to thoroughly understand the use of both Greek and Latin words, they would generally research the Oxford Dictionary for the meanings and definitions (etymology) of either biology or pharmaceutical explanations that needed to be interpreted into their own words so they could understand a fair bit easier. As they were coming to the end of their study session, they had just noticed three other pupils from Professor A. David Smith's class, Darius Silva, was a half-Brazilian lad who was brought up in Tottenham Court Road, in North London, he was born in the UK, and His parents were Brazilian. Samantha Hutchinson was fairly tall with a slim figure and ginger hair, anyone would've thought she and Jasper Flynn would make the perfect match, with both being red and fair-haired, but Jasper Flynn was engaging his time with Eldora Jenkins. Samantha and her family had come from Liverpool, and Paul Barrera, was a short lad and half-Italian, he and his family had come from Bournemouth, and his parents were both Italian. They were just about to converse and engage with some different study theories, as they had just turned up to the library whilst Jasper, David, William, Verity, Eldora, and Daphne were all gasping to get some well-needed energy, food, and drink after their gruelling day, of three and a bit hour full-on study and going through academic papers. Darius Silva, Samantha Hutchinson, and Paul Barrera will be going through the same stuff as they had just done, and for them to go through it together would have been overdrive. Sometimes over-studying can overload the brain and cause mind block. So, it is best to gauge your studies by having regular breaks and finding some hobbies or other interests that you can enjoy along your academic journey, it is also important to find a release and not just intend to do full-on study all day, as after a while it can become momentous. It was important to the students to find the right balance, so they could gain knowledge and wisdom but still enjoy some entertainment, hobbies, and interests as they need to look after their eudemonia. The Mental Health Support for Students was highly engaging, with many pupils being fully aware that they had support groups on campus, some students had anticipated the help and tried to persevere. The foreign students that had come a long way from home, such as abroad from African, Asian, American islands etc, had found it extremely hard to acclimatize and also take time to get used to staying away from their parent's home as just young adults. The group was now off to get some lunch in their break, with David, Jasper, William, Daphne, Verity, and Eldora, the boys had been talking about finding out about the University's Polo team, so they could find out about training information and what else would be involved in registering their interest. So, after they had finished their lunch, that was the boy's next plan of action. (Oxford Mosaic, 2001) Back to the same location as yesterday, with the glorious weather, sunny blue skies, and hardly a cloud in sight. With plentiful beautiful agricultural landscapes, fields, parks, and green space that stretches out and opens your lungs to fill them up with fine air. Free from contamination, it was a place of solace, The University Park, where all the students let their thoughts transcend into oblivion to be set free for a while, at least before they had to head back to academic study. Some students finished for the day, and many went back after the morning break depending on the module and study consistency. The group had gone back to the same local sandwich shop, Jimbo's Baguettes. David wasn't overly hungry today, having only brought cheese and onion walkers and an apple, whilst Daphne got the egg mayonnaise roll, and prawn cocktail crisps. William Macintyre had brought the B.L.T. with pickled Onion Monster Munch crisps, whilst his friend companion, Verity Page brought the Cheese and Tomato sandwich in tiger loaf crust and a banana. Jasper Flynn then brought the Tuna and cucumber roll and the dried bag of apricots, a rather ironic concoction for Jasper, probably had many observing his strange choice of fruits. This may have had people thinking he was trying to hold back some weight, maybe a weight loss plan he was thinking! Last but not least; Eldora Jenkins chose the Chicken mayonnaise lettuce baguette and a pear.

When the weather was on their side Jimbo's baguettes had always seemed to bring home a nice revenue. No doubt he would have always been earning right through the winter months, with all the outdoor sports played in most weather conditions, like rugby, football, and athletics, I very much doubt there was hardly a dull moment at Jimbo's baguette place.

The group was heading somewhere with a nice peaceful view to sit together and enjoy their wholesome lunch break before the boys headed off to find the Polo University team's info. They had crowded around near the River Cherwell bank edge, finding a picnic bench that overlooked the flowing river. However, there was a slight movement with rather clear water as you could see the stream of weeds and sludge at the bottom of the river, The river verge was banked up with tall leaves, long grass, and lily pads were grouped in the middle of the stream, ducks and swans swam neatly in their flock up the stream. It was a luxurious place to sit, easing the tension from a hard few hours' slog at university. Letting those thoughts unravel, mind replenish, let go, and rebalance for the night's rest. It had been noted that over the years with population growth, the quality of water, and no doubt sewage over-waste would have spilled into the River Cherwell, already in the student newsletter and local papers, people had been told not to swim in the river as the PH levels had started to drop below 6.5, over time this gradually would decay towards nature's tremendous, beautiful habitat. After they had enjoyed their lunchbreak with the most refreshing, breath-taking views, the boys, David, William, and Jasper Flynn had wanted to go and find out how to get involved with the University Polo team, and if they had needed trials or some kind of training lessons before they qualified to be able to jump on horseback. Many Students were inspired by the sport; Polo, as throughout the 13th Century many Kings and Emperors played their version of Polo. It was a sport for the hierarchy such as noblemen and even some women of high class had started to play it, which is more and more common in today's times. It had been noted. (The University of Oxford, 2024) that the school university did have a Polo team, their rival was Cambridge University. The sport: Polo, to these students that had put themselves onto the course of studying pharmacological Science, had wanted to try and set themselves apart from the average society by participating in an aristocratic socially elite sport, which was funded for the rich.

However, could these students afford the University's hire fees for the horses and equipment required to play polo? Well, they were on the brink of finding out, and no doubt if there was a will or a must, these students would most certainly find a way.

If they hadn't had enough savings or University subsidies they would soon be on the telephone to their parents, or grandparents pleading about poverty. The vast majority of teenagers and young adults know how to play the part of their parents, as you can imagine, David calls his parents, "Mum, Dad, I would like to play for the Oxford University Polo team, but the fees they are asking for are £675 for a student to pay for the hire purchase, while representing the Uni team" if his parents would have had said no, he would've no doubt gone and said. "Well, William and Jasper's parents supported them", or he may have said, that he would do extra hours in the pharmacy on weekends to help pay for some of the costs. You could put nothing past these students, as they have become very wise before their time, knowing full well their parents would've treated their grandparents the same, the offspring just observe and follow suit, in situ.

So, the gentlemen got the bus to the Kirtlington Polo Club it was a thirty-five min bus journey from Oxford University to Kirtlington polo club where the University Polo Team had trained, whilst speaking to the Oxford Polo sports recreational ground receptionist. It was David who spoke to the recreational ground Oxford Polo sports receptionist, and also one of the many trainers for Oxford Uni Polo team, his name was Hector, and he had played alongside Cameron Walton Master, who was a captain for the Oxford

University Polo team in 1995. Hector speaks “Hi gents, welcome to our Oxford Polo team, and how could I assist you today”? David and Jasper both have the urge to step forward to speak, Jasper opens his mouth and expresses his thoughts first on this occasion “Right so, we are wanting to find out some information about how we can try out polo as beginners. But we want to train and play together as a team. Is this something you can help us with”? “Right of course, let me explain a few things”. “We have our complete novice team for those who have zero horse riding experience, which you would undergo a six to eight-week riding school basic training, before we put you on an intermediate riding class, which can take a further eight to twelve weeks”. The boys nodded in agreement. “After that, you can start to play a beginner's light training session as a polo player, learning some basic teaching points. How to move with the ball, pass the ball, shoot the ball, defense, offense, basically start to teach you the rules. After you get to grips with that you can start the advanced horse-riding school, by the time you have finished all the training you will have hopefully become a competent Oxford University Polo player. Then we can start putting you into

tournaments and University leagues etc... We charge £675 a year for University Students that are staying on Campus, which is relatively cheap considering that is the hire price for the horse, coaching, and enjoying yourselves in the process": Says Hector.
Starting with a sigh, as David begins to speak, "Thank you Hector, which sounds very reasonable and perfect". Although David seemed convinced, I don't believe he or any of his friends were overwhelmed with the price, £675 was not a huge amount considering what they get in return. Still, any University Student wanting to pursue a hobby as a sideline dream, they've had to pay the price. These boys would find a way to pluck a few Sir John Houblon's from their great fathers' skyrocket. Sir John Houblon's was the representation that appeared on the rear of a £50 note. And notably seeing as they were rather high scholars, they would've used a dialect that was extraordinarily different to the average culture. The students would frankly use that phrase to impress their parents as they had known what was embedded on the rear of a plush £50.00 note, and they had just needed over thirteen £50.00 notes to cover the course of a term to start their hobby

playing Polo. As cited in.. (Horse & Hound, 2001) the boys were overwhelmingly happy to be coached by Cameron Walton Master, he was one of Oxford University's advanced players and one of the highest prospects in his
division.
Later that afternoon when the boys had arrived back from the big red bus ride from Kirtlington back towards Oxford Uni.
David, Jasper, and William had headed back onto campus before David had to be picked up by one of his parents, they were planning how the conversation was going to be dealt with when they approached their parents later that evening. But before David had to leave and be picked up, they had wanted to meet up with the girls, Daphne, Eldora, and Verity to tell them about the exciting news. Jasper and William had opened up the conversation with the girls, as you could imagine 'all puffed up with pride and broad shoulders' "Girls, girls we are so excited to start our new adventure, polo": Said William, "yeah we just need to pluck up £675 a term for training and competition" says Jasper Flynn, "are you girls going to come and support us while we entertain

you with our new hobby"? : David says to the girls.

Daphne, Verity Page, and Eldora Jenkins were such supportive girls, and they had seemed very amicable and reciprocated with those boys," of course": says all three of the girls at once, "it would be our pleasure": Says Daphne. The faces on those boys, David, William, and Jasper were overwhelmed with extraordinary excitement. As they were walking back toward the main entrance to drop David to his usual pick-up point, they jumped into the air fist pumping the sky whilst clapping heels at the feet. This had the girls in hysterics, it was so lovely to see the friendship and attraction both these boys and girls had between them, as it was all rather endearing. Wherever the boys had gone the girls would follow and vice versa. When the girls had gone somewhere the boys would follow. Besides Verity Page had a lot in common with horses having her family's riding school based in Wapley, Bristol. This was another strength to all the girl's reasoning, and why it had become so easy with those boys, as it was very similar in interest. Most girls like animals, especially horses, and if they hadn't enjoyed riding them then they would most certainly like feeding them, whilst others also just liked taking care of them, grooming them, or clearing the stables. You would be surprised how people don't have to like horse riding to love and take care of the horse, as they are one of the most beautiful, alluring herbivores, with such elegant features and muscular physiques, so bold and so strong. Yet, they are the softest creatures on earth in comparison with their size. They like to eat fruit and straw right from your hands, the size of a horse's jawline and teeth, you'd think would cause some damage but yet take food so gently from us humans.

"Right guys my mother is here, I have to go. We`ll catch up tomorrow and I will let you know the outcome if I can swindle the expenses to the Oxford Polo team or not, past my parents": remarked David

" Great idea David, why don't you ask to see if they can at least pay a part of the expenses" : stated William

" not a bad shout William, yes if not, I'll ask them to at least lend me the expenses and ill work them off at the Pharmacy on weekends" : replied David.

"Right, I best be off, mum has arrived. Bye for now": Says David. "Bye

David": as they all wave goodbye, William, Jasper Flynn, Daphne Johnson, Verity Page, and Eldora Jenkins. Later that day, before they had separated both into their dormitories, the girls had wanted to organize an evening with the boys so they could spend some valuable time together one weekend. They needed to take some time away from routine studying, so planning a night at the cinema, and something to eat would be good, and the attraction they were growing closer together. Spending more and more time together, working, studying, walking, and supporting one another side by side they had an awesome sixsome, `the extreme six`. The only time they were separated was nighttime when they had to enter a separate dormitory, other than that there was no restraining from them. Eldora Jenkins noted that the University had a movie night for the students on campus, which would've been a whole lot cheaper if not free, then they could go out an eat. Next weekend they were screening 'There's Something About Mary` featuring some of the girls' all-time favourite Cameron Diaz, the high school sweetheart. Ted tried his utmost hardest to track down the dashing elegant blonde, aka Cameron Diaz. This Movie is based on a college high school crush, ironically in comparison to a very similar situation these boys and girls all feel in and around the sixsome groupie they have gathered together. It is these kinds of films that they can observe, impersonate, review, reflect, and enjoy with such fun and laughter. Daphne Johnson and Verity Page 'were like, "That was a great find, Eldora, I guess we will have to locate the cinema room at some point in the week": expressed Daph and V. Both William Macintyre and Jasper Flynn weren't exactly jumping for joy at the thought of the choice for the movie, but they knew they were in favour to those wonderful supporting girls, so they wouldn't dare decline the offer. Those three pretty, tasteful girls would soon replace those boys. Handsome or not; respect works both ways. "Ok girls we shall tell David tomorrow, but we would like to accompany you"; sheepishly says William Macintyre and nods the head of Jasper Flynn in agreement. And it was just like so...... the three boys and the three girls all partaking in one another's choices of entertainment. Before they had left each other to disperse into their dormitories, Jasper Flynn had been dying and eager to ask for Eldora Jenkin's contact number. So, as it was, they were exchanging contact details so they could text throughout the night and when they were apart, that is if you could pull them apart from the hip as it were already. In doing so, this had given the signal for William Macintyre to get enough fortitude strength to ask Verity Page, the dashing blonde dignified, elegant Bristol bombshell for her contact details. As you can see, she was highly striking to the eye, you could see why William, although a handsome strapping chap himself had needed the urge to pluck up the courage. He would've no doubt crawled back inside himself like a little tortoise' if Verity had turned him down. But likely has it, she fancied him and gives her number politely with ease and vibrance in her voice, "Of course William, take my number": Verity Page says. "Wow, my, thank you said William bashfully with happiness. Both boys are stunned and happy and the girls too, Verity and Eldora Jenkins. When the evening had come, Daphne Johnson had always felt a little left out with this lot as David had always got a lift home with his parents. But she was happy and willing to wait for David to swap contact details, as she knew how much in common, they both had. It would've been only a matter of time, and Daphne was confident at that. William had noticed Daphne was left out, “Don’t worry Daph, I will speak to David tomorrow I’ll get him to swap both your contact details between you” “Bless you, William, thank you, yeah that would be nice”: says Daph. That had made Daphne feel a whole lot better with reassurance from one of David's male friends.

It was time to leave the girls by their dormitory and walk back to the boy’s room. William and Jasper Flynn were overwhelmed, hugging Verity Page and Eldora Jenkins goodbye, and saying goodbye to Daphne Johnson. With not so much amusement for her as David had already left, but with thoughts into the hopefully near future as William had promised Daphne that he would get David to ask her for her mobile number, just so she hadn’t felt left out. “Bye Daphne”: said William Macintyre and Jasper Flynn, “Goodnight boys,” said Daphne. The girls walk happily into their dormitory front entrance.

As the boys headed back to their dormitory they noticed Darius Silva, the Brazilian chap who was also in their pharmaceutical science class walk right up close to them, “Hey you two, where are you going?” Darius said as he slowed the pace of his walk toward the boy's dormitory, “We`re headed back to our room”: explained the boys, William and Jasper. William Macintyre had just thought of a cunning idea, and also rather calculated as they had needed one more polo player in their group to make a team of players, so William had asked Darius to join them in the polo training. “What do you think about joining me, David, and Jasper in the Polo team Darius?” exclaims William, “You know what, that doesn’t sound like the worst idea” Darius had said in response. “Just to let you know Darius there is a joining fee of £675 a year, which entails, horse hire, horse riding lessons, and polo training sessions which is significantly cheap considering what we can get in return”: explains William. “It is worth it”: convincingly said Jasper Flynn. “Rightly so and I agree with the pair of you”: murmurs Darius. Right then, this evening within the gentlemen’s dormitory all the lads would’ve been pleading poverty to their parents, and for some support to help them fund their new profound profession, polo the sport. Jasper Flynn calls his parents, “Hi mum, hi dad I miss you both, I just wanted to let you know study is going well in my first week”

"Oh hi Jasper, so lovely to hear your voice, and we are overwhelmed to hear study is going okay" : says Jasper's mum, and grumbled his father in the background.

"Mum, I have been taking extra study sessions with my friends in our local library after the sessions at university to help me improve and to pass the time. My friends and I have come up with another alternative idea alongside the study, which can benefit our welfare and well-being mum, and dad" said Jasper "Okay Jasper tell us what it is? We are glad you're working hard towards your studies as that is important": says Jasper's parents. "Well, me David, William Macintyre, and Darius Silva have all been wanting to join the Oxford University Polo team, what do you think?" Jasper Flynn's old man, his father grumbles again, mrrrmmm well boy you're asking now. I know polo the sport is a wonderful game as me and your mother like to watch it from time to time, but it's a game that the kings used to play, now followed in suit by the rich folk. Well, how much is it boy"? "£675 a year dad, I have most of it in Mum's savings and once I graduate, I can help pay it all back, I swear Dad. Please": pleads Jasper. Mrs. Flynn speaks to the father, in the background,

then back on the phone to Jasper, "Go on let him, he is a good boy after all and he's our son and priority" "Thanks so much mum": happily answered Jasper to his mum "coughs his father, your lucky boy as I may have thought twice about it if it wasn't for your mother. Now go on lad get gone before you ask us for anything more"
"Thanks Mum, Dad, I'll call you again soon. Love you, bye". Says Jasper. "Bye boys, let me know when and how you need the money and we will sort a way of transferring the funds, but we need a receipt?" "No problem mum, will do, speak soon," says Jasper.
Well, Jasper had appeared to convince his parents almost effortlessly. This had left William Macintyre in awe, as now it was his turn to contact his hard-working father, Paul Macintyre who worked for Hunts Transport, driving gigantic artic lorries serving haulage and logistics. But as luck had it, his mother already had a lot of empathy and compassion for others and was very hospitable as she has worked within the NHS sector. It was quite like Jasper`s mother had given in to her beloved son. We will note a very similar reaction with William`s mother.
Phone rings, "Hi William, nice to hear from you

son": happily, says Paul his father "Hi dad, how are you and mum? I have been studying full on the past few days": explains William. "Me and your mother are fine thanks son; we are glad to hear your studies are going well" You could also hear Mrs Macintyre in the background yelling from the kitchen 'Hi son! `. "Dad, could you please speak to Mum, as me and the boys have found a new hobby. It's for the Oxford University Polo team, but we need to fill out the submission form and pay the fees. The fees are £675 dad, what do you think"? "Well son, me and your mother work hard all year round to make ends meet and pay for your bursary fees, but you do have some money put by that your grandma has for you when you graduate".: Said Paul, William's father. "Oh, wow thanks Dad, please speak to Mother about that as that would be phenomenal": voiced William "Dad, you know what, I will make it up to both you and Mother as soon as I get home": again exclaimed William.

"Okay son, you don't have to get all soppy on me to get your way. Just promise me that you will carry on methodically with your academics"? "Most certainly pops, you are the best. Catch up soon Dad": as William says goodbye. "No problem boy. Take good care of yourself, don't forget to give me some reference to the payment and I will arrange a bank transfer," says Paul the father. Paul, William's father walks over to the olde iron chest in his and his wife Mrs Macintyre's living room to turn the key to open the olde iron chest and then to reach in and count the few thousand pounds that he has saved up. And some of the money that his wife's mother had granted them to help support William whilst taking his further academic studies. In total, he recounted seven thousand four hundred and twenty-five British Sterling pounds. Paul couldn't remember how much his savings was, and how much was supposed to be for William as it was not kept separate from the other. Now that had left Paul to negotiate it with his wife. Mrs Macintyre had no recollection of the amount, as this was something she would have to ask her mother about, trouble has it her mother has dementia and most likely does not remember the amount either. All they can vaguely remember was putting in quite a fair few hundred pounds that her mother had put by for William. Now this has left them in a position where they will just have to accept William playing polo and leave them paying for it, without

any arguments or questions about it.
After Jasper Flynn and William Macintyre had gotten off the telephone with their parents, they wanted the joy to begin, so they both messaged the girls. Jasper Flynn messaged Eldora Jenkins via SMS messages, “Hi Eldora I am so glad we have finally exchanged phone numbers, I just wanted to tell you how pretty you looked in Uni today” The message was received. Edora Jenkins was sitting in the sitting room with Daphne Johnson and Verity Page, “What’s that Eldora? your phone keeps making a bleeping sound. Who is it?” Verity says teasingly to Eldora. “Excuse me why I take this message girls, as it might be important” Exclaims Eldora.
“Right go ahead answer it, Eldora, don’t mind us”: Daphne explained vibrantly. “Ooh, it is only Jasper Flynn asking me how I am that’s all”: Says Eldora. Eldora Jenkins sends a reply to Jasper Flynn by SMS “Awee thanks Jasper, that’s so cute. You looked adorably handsome today; I am so happy we can text and write to each other too. You know what, nighttime gets lonely. So, it is nice to have someone to talk to in the evenings” Jasper Flynn’s phone bleeps, as a message is received. Jasper Flynn had the Ericsson T66 mobile phone, in 2001

mobile phone devices hadn't advanced a magnificent deal considering what was always being aired within the media, with faster and better internet coverage and browsing. (Google, 2001) It was only in the 1990s that mobile phone devices started to get popular, with the first mobile device being brick-like built (Jamie Spencer, 2001) But in 1973, Motorola created the first portable cell phone. This portable gadget weighed about 2.4 pounds and was brick-like formed. It was known as a DynaTac 8000x and is regarded as the first cell phone. It had signified the stark difference, with no greater advancement rather than just a simple mobile device, which had become more and more popular and feasible to use. It had then become more and more of a simple way to connect with society, and the vast majority of people were holding onto a mobile device. In many cases a lifesaver if you had broken down in a vehicle or local transport. Jasper Flynn tells Eldora Jenkins the magnificent news, he sends her another SMS, "Eldora, guess what, me and William both had our parents agree to us playing Polo for Oxford University. We are so thrilled and look forward to seeing you tomorrow". Ping-Ping! Eldora's phone goes off again, vibrating on the

armchair in the sitting room. Verity Page grins at Eldora. "Are you talking to lover boy"? stirringly says Verity
"None of your business V" chuckles Eldora.
With that Eldora sneaks in a reply SMS message back to Jasper, "That's fantastic news Jasper, I am made up for you. I will be there to support you every step of the way. Ps, I best go as Verity Page in trying to nose in on our conversation, she is a ruthless intruder. Text you tonight"
As you may have already noted Eldora was a very sufficient writer when it came to sending a simple text message. Rather than trying to use shorthand texting, she could simply only write a short story. Eldora had to be authentic and
precise.
Jasper Flynn sends one last SMS message until later that evening. "Okay was nice talking with you Eldora, I know how that feels, someone watching over your shoulder. Me and William are going to get a take-out pizza for our little celebration tonight, as our parents have accepted us playing for the University Polo team. PS. Speak tonight." Meanwhile, David is back home with his parents, Mr and Mrs Smith in the kitchen. Mrs. Smith is cooking the family meal, whilst Mr

Smith, David's father, is sitting at the dining table. Mrs Smith calls David down from his bedroom, as she is ready to dish up their families evening meal. With the whole family being pushed busy-wise, with the family-run pharmacy and David at Oxford University, Mrs Smith had prepared a nice and easy Spaghetti Bolognese.

"David come down please, I am ready to dish up your dinner," shouted Mrs Smith. "Okay mum, just coming; just switching my television off," said David. Most students when they had finished a strenuous day's study would relax in their bedrooms, and many other students would play computer games, but not David. He enjoyed catching up with reality TV programs such as 'Pop Idol' and similar that were on television. Other times David tends to scrivere, analyse, or reflect on what he has or is going to study shortly. The study was not only important to him but also to his family business. He liked to doodle on his sketch pad and a great hand he had, rather artistic.

David would always find something to keep him occupied that was therapeutic, this had helped his mind stay preoccupied with positivity.

They were sitting at the dining table; which was in the kitchen area. As you can imagine, a rather Victorian Oxford townhouse with high ceilings, oak skirting boards, and an olde pine cornice that margins around the perimeter of the ceilings. You could smell the wood from the pine or the oak, the varnish too that coated it for protection.

The marble dining table with the plush velvet chairs is set and ready for a king. Mr and Mrs Smith had run a successful pharmacy in the local constituency of Oxford. The locals were accustomed to Mr and Mrs Smith's Pharmacy as it was very convenient and was one of the better pharmacies inside Oxford. They had always aimed to give customers satisfaction by working in a timely and sufficient manner, speaking with customers in a friendly but passionate manner to let the customers know that they are cared for and make sure they are completely satisfied. One of David's roles was to come in at the weekend to help with maintaining the pharmacy throughout with cleanliness, renewing and ordering new stock, and preparing for the week ahead. Mr, Mrs Smith, and David all sat at the dining table with a fresh but scrumptious-looking spaghetti Bolognese with a stick of garlic bread in the middle of the dining table to share between them. A garlic stick, with melted garlic butter at the centre core of the bread, was delicious dipped in the Bolognese sauce. Also in the middle of the dining table was a jug of fresh orange juice, Mrs Smith had liked to look after her two favourite boys. She knew garlic was good for blood circulation and the heart and orange juice had a lot of vitamins in it. She had noted a simple meal had many benefits to it rather than being a quick and easy meal, it had handsomely squeezed a lot of nutritional value to it. Whilst sitting around the table enjoying this rather tasteful delicious dish that Mrs Smith had prepared, David says anxiously "Mum, Dad study went well today. We studied in the library after our class with Professor A. David Smith" David trying to ease into the conversation. "That is awesome David if you keep this methodical pattern, you will have no struggles in finishing your assignments and exams" Explains Mr Smith, David's father. "Also, Mum, Dad, me, and the other boys, William Macintyre and Jasper Flynn have been wanting to join the Oxford University Polo team, is that okay"? "MMM interesting David, but there must be a catch. Playing a sport on horseback isn't going to be free is it, so tell me what are the requirements, prices etc"? Embarked Mr. Smith "I

don’t believe it is too expensive considering what it has to offer. The price is £675, a yearly term which includes: horse hire, training sessions throughout the year, and when we become competent enough, we can play for the Oxford University Polo team, all for the same price” David bargains with his mother and Father.
“That’s a fair price David, and I agree you do get a fair bit for your money’s worth, I tell you what your mother and I can do, we can let you work it off at the weekends and even help out in and around the house; cleaning the cars, helping me clear the garden etc.” Says David’s dad,
“Brilliant thanks Dad, Mum, that’s fantastic I am overwhelmed and I will most certainly work for it with great dignity and gratitude” politely says, David. The three boys so far, David, William, and Jasper were all in awe at the distant future Oxford Polo team photography shoot, possibly for the new 2002 team play-out season. As they had been looking through the Oxford University’s Hall of Fame Polo team album. The immense feeling that must have been felt by those boys as their loving care providers had agreed on all terms possible. But let's have it right they were also very lucky young adults to

have been supported and brought up in and around rich lavish families and just being able to attend Oxford University, let alone play Polo the Sport that was only played by the hierarchy and kings of old age. They had carried on at the dining table enjoying this flavoursome and succulent spag bowl that Mrs Smith had prepared, almost scoffing up the whole of the garlic stick in moments of the dinner being served. Saving strawberries and cream for dessert, the care was there, the love was there, the taste was most certainly there, the nutrition was there, and the five a day was there. Mrs Smith was in subjection in the most meaningful way and was the structure for her family. Mr Smith and her beloved son David were spoilt.

Later that evening, right after David had finished his tea, he left the dining table where he was urging to tell his friends about the fabulous news that his parents had offered to support him with funding towards the Polo team training. Like a herd of sheep that had just galloped up the long stairwell to his bedroom, you could hear every foot pounding each step as he took a dash of excitement to his room, to tell Jasper Flynn that his parents had offered to support him for the Oxford

University Polo team. He got into his bedroom to get comfortable, sitting on his bed all wrapped up in the quilt covers, his mobile phone device was on his bedside chest of drawers. He overreached to grab his device, sending an SMS to Jasper Flynn, "Hi Jasper have you and William had much luck with both of your parents yet for the Oxford Polo Team fees that they're asking for?, Both my mum and dad have agreed, I am so overwhelmed" Ping-Ping goes Jasper Flynn's phone back at his Dormitory with William Macintyre, he reaches for his pocket, noticed the SMS by David, sends his reply "that's fantastic news, David, yes both me and William have got the funds for the Oxford Polo team also, our parents had both agreed to help us with the fees" David receives the reply, "that is superb, so happy all three of us get to stick together, see you both in the morning" Jasper Flynn replies once more "Brilliant David, look forward to seeing you tomorrow". David was all cosy relaxing in his bed, where he would spend the rest of his evening, in rest.
Jasper Flynn and William Macintyre were heading to their room inside the Boy's dormitory on campus where they stayed, which is also known as `student accommodation`. Before they headed

right off to sleep William Macintyre had wanted to send an SMS message straight to Verity Pages mobile device, he had planned this promptly and made the lady wait. The best time to send the first text message to a female was right before bedtime "Hi Verity it's me, William. I have been yearning to send you the first message, but I had wanted to wait to the time was right, reflecting on the past few days. I am so happy we have become close acquaintances as you are so pretty". Ping-Ping vibrated Verity Pages device, she too was huddled up inside her duvet with her dressing gown on, she replied to William by SMS message, "Awe William that is the cutest thought, I was wondering why you hadn't text me all da. Eldora Jenkins and Jasper Flynn have been pinging each other back and forth all day, I was starting to get jealous, any way handsome man it is getting late, and I am exhausted after today, I will see you tomorrow outside, xx".

Chapter 3 Fri 12th Oct 2001

A week has passed by at Oxford University, and David, William Macintyre, Jasper Flynn, Daphne

Johnson, Verity Page, Eldora Jenkins, Darius Silva, Samantha Hutchinson, and Paul Barrera started to build a closer relationship. Although Samantha, Darius, and Paul Barrera had kept in their little group of three the vast majority of the time when they had felt it necessary. It wasn't long before Darius Silva would be joining the boys in the Oxford University Polo team anyhow. So, with all being said and pushed extremely busy-wise, as it were, with academic studies in and around the same classroom. In and out of the library throughout the weeks, and now the boys are going to begin training for the Oxford University Polo team. Samantha Hutchinson, the pretty ginger-haired girl with legs eleven, had some firm lengthy legs. She hadn't blended in so well with the girls although they spoke between them and preferred talking and hanging out with the boys more. She had two younger brothers back home in Liverpool, so all we can guess is that she just felt more at ease with the boys. So, they have nearly finished their second week At University with already so much planned just for this year alone.
The boys, David, William Macintyre, Jasper Flynn, and the Brazilian Darius Silva have all paid the receptionist for the Oxford University Polo

team, Hector, the £675.00 each for this year's term training and were due to start the training. After University this evening, the boys and girls were planning on spending the evening together watching a movie and having something to eat together, their friendship was better, and their bond was even closer. The Movie they were watching, was the Movie Eldora Jenkins suggested last week, 'There's Something About Mary' which stars Cameron Diaz. But after some thinking and further research, Eldora Jenkins found out that on campus they only had a movie theatre that didn't screen movies but rather theatre plays. She found the nearest cinema that was only a short bus ride away, as cited in. (Herd, 2001) called the `Ultimate Picture Palace`, it was in the centre of Oxford, Jeune Street, Cowley Road. OX4 1BN.
The gang was excited to adventure out as a group, and Daphne was excited to be spending the whole evening with David, Eldora was extremely excited to be sitting with Jasper Flynn and likewise with Verity Page, she was overwhelmed to be sitting in with her handsome man, William Macintyre. No doubt some endless, not-so-guilty consciousness canoodling will be taking place on the back row. The other three were invited along in their trio. It

was an odd number, so they would've just mingled in.
The movie wasn't to be screened until later that evening, at 06:45 pm, so first, they had to get through today's session at Uni, with Professor A. David Smith, their Pharmacology Scientist specialist. David had intended to sneak into one of the dormitories on campus tonight, whether he was going to sneak into the boys or the girls, he would have to be very vigilant just in case any staff members were on night crawl. And we all know David would have preferred to stay in Daphne Johnon's bedroom, however he would be a rather smooth and fast mover if he did. They were all on their way to meet young David from his usual drop-off point by the main entrance from Oxford University, and as per normal, the boys; William, Jasper Flynn and this time Darius Silva too as he had now signed up to play on the Oxford Uni Polo team, and had thought it was best to start bonding with the group. They had met up with the girls outside their dormitory before heading to meet David. Samantha Hutchinson, the ginger-haired girl and Paul Barrera had shifted back a little. They liked to be in smaller groups some of the time, and speaking privately was sometimes a better option

than airing your daily routine, struggles, anxieties, or just plain worries perhaps. So, they had thought it was best to start walking to the Pharmacological science units and hang about nearer to the classroom. Many a time their conversations would end up getting somewhat deep. The amount of complete nonsense they would speak about in a short spell, they were disgracefully talking about some sort of segregation, or something cultured, the usual kind of uncomfortable topics that these students would have pangs and distresses about, so it was better to get it off their chests than to keep it in. Samantha had often spoken to Paul about how awkward she had felt around the other three girls, Daphne, Verity, and Eldora, as it had all seemed so very clicky-clicky, as if they already had their chosen boyfriends. It was very awkward for her. Jasper Flynn was also a ginger lad; he kept grinning towards Samantha as they both had something in particular in common 'red hair'. Samantha felt as if she couldn't smile back towards Jasper, as Eldora Jenkins may have got the right hump and may have thought that Samantha was flirting with 'her man', this had made things a whole lot more uncomfortable for Samantha Hutchinson. By the time Samantha and

Paul Barrera had been conversing back and forth, David had arrived, his mother dropping him off on her way through to work. David, William Macintyre, Jasper Flynn, Darius Silva: the four boys, Daphne Johnson, Verity Page, and Eldora Jenkins all came stomping their way through the corridor to the pharmaceutical science classroom. Standing proudly at the classroom door entrance, with a blue suit, brown brogues, and brown and chequered cream tie was Professor A. David Smith who looked extraordinarily dapper today, "Good morning troops, please come in and take a seat," says Professor A. David Smith with a warning smile. David, sat with William Macintyre, and Jasper Flynn, while Darius Silva, Paul Barrera, and Samantha Hutchinson sat just in front of them, right at the back of the classroom and to the right-hand side. In contrast, Daphne Johnson, Verity Page, and Eldora Jenkins sat opposite the left-hand flank of the classroom. Noticing the group had stuck closely together, they had all tried their utmost hardest to keep on inspiring and encouraging one another through their academic studies, with a few of them staying a long way away from home, they needed to give each other courage and edify one's morals. Professor A.

David Smith provided the students with the short abstract of information that he wanted them to focus on. By analysing and writing down some feedback and a conclusion, in their own words, the abstract was cited in. (J Howard Rytting, 2001) This study sought to determine whether ondansetron, an antagonist of the 5-HT3 receptor, could be administered trans-dermally to treat chemotherapy-induced vomiting. Several enhancers were evaluated to increase the very poor permeability of ondansetron from an aqueous suspension through shed snakeskin as a model membrane. At a concentration of 40% or more, ethanol enhanced the flux. As the concentration of ethanol rose, so did the solubility of ondansetron. After the shed snakeskin was pretreated with azone, oleic acid, or lauryl alcohol, the permeability coefficient rose. When ethanol was mixed with other enhancers, the permeability was further improved; this was most noticeable when ethanol and oleic acid were combined. Ondansetron's partition to n-hexane and shed snakeskin was significantly enhanced by oleic acid. Oleic acid may increase ondansetron penetration in two ways: directly via the stratum corneum or through the creation of an ion pair counterion. It appears that the greatest flow that may be achieved by combining ethanol with other enhancers is sufficient to produce a therapeutic effect. Professor A. David Smith breaks down this abstract, so the students can understand it better in layman's terms and identify the key terminology. "This study investigates the effectiveness of various preparations of ondansetron; a drug usually in tablet format which is taken for chemotherapy-induced vomiting. This experiment was to bypass the tablet and make the preparation into a topical cream to be applied to the skin to prevent it from being vomited. The experimenters had used shed snakeskin to mimic human skin and to see how well the cream passed through the skin membrane. They had three experiments. 1) Ondansetron in aqueous suspension 2) Ondansetron in aqueous suspension with 40% ethanol 3) Pre-treatment of skin with a topical fatty acid, followed by treatment with Ondansetron in aqueous suspension with 40% ethanol.

The results of experiment 1 had minimal effect. Adding ethanol increased the absorption rate in experiment 2, and pre-treatment with a topical fatty acid and the addition of ethanol achieved the best therapeutic results for experiment 3. It was coming up to the end of the academic week for the University students in Professor A. David Smith's class studying pharmaceutical science. Many of the students hadn't planned for extra academic study within the library, such as Eldora Jenkins, Daphne Johnson, Verity Page, Samantha Hutchinson, William Macintyre, David Smith, Jasper Flynn, Darius Silva, and Paul Barrera. They were planning to have a study-free weekend to recuperate, refresh and unwind, as it was just as important for students to look after their wellbeing and mental health. Eldora Jenkins had found a local cinema that was screening the latest movie they had all wanted to go and watch, so they all intended to venture out that evening. Back in the classroom, Professor A. David Smith; at the end of the week's study session had given a run down and reflection from their study week. He felt overwhelmed by his students' dedication, and the progress they had made, he also suggested to his students that they do not try and overload themselves with too much knowledge and over-study, as only so much information can be stored, and it is best to study for shorter periods over and over again until it sinks in. The teacher had thought it was best for his students to have some weekends to find a muse, as studying 24/7 can become relentless and deteriorate someone's well-being.

Part of the curriculum of the Oxford University students was also to prioritize their own welfare, hence why the University has multiple variations of hobbies and interests, such as different sports, athletics, reading classes, chess, debate clubs, poker clubs, yoga classes, religion culture clubs and many other things to find tranquillity away from study.

The cinema they had intended to go to later wasn't showing the film until 6:45 pm and was called the 'Ultimate Picture Palace'. It was located in the centre of Oxford. But for now, they had just finished their study week, and they were off to find somewhere different to eat rather than the usual Jim Bob's baguettes. Even though it was surrounded by acres of tranquillity, awe-inspiring sightseeing landscapes, green land, and a river, they had thought it was best to try something new and flavoursome. Daphne Johnson had noted the Christ Church was located on campus (Christ Church Oxford University, 2001) the hall was allocated for all Students to have a sit-down cooked breakfast or lunch, this was more appropriate for the students to chat and reflect on their week while enjoying a freshly cooked nourished meal. The Christ Church had catered for everyone, with allergies of all sorts, from vegetarian dishes and breakfast to main meals, soups, and pasta dishes. The students could walk around the canteen and choose any heated dish they wanted from the heated griddle, and the chefs would place the item they had chosen onto their plates. The students would then pay a small fee to the dinner lady at the cash desk. David had chosen the lasagne, he also grabbed a side salad, coleslaw, lettuce, cucumber, tomato, and some buttered French stick. Jasper Flynn had wanted the English breakfast; you could pick your items. William Macintyre only wanted tomato soup with some French stick, he must have been losing his appetite, Daphne Johnson had chosen a salad and some pasta as her main, Samantha Hutchinson had the Spag bowl, Eldora Jenkins had the chicken and pasta with a Caesar dressing and vegetables, Verity Page had chosen the plaice, peas and fries for her main meal, Darius Silva had a home-made Minestrone soup which was made with fresh vegetables, pasta, and looked rather tasteful, fulfilling and delicious soaked up with some tiger loaf and butter, it was a dream meal. Paul Barrera the half-Italian, had fancied spaghetti and meatballs for his main meal. The students were all prepared and ready to sit down together to enjoy a fully nourishing meal. As you can imagine sitting in the National Heritage 'Christ Church' left them feeling empowered by the archaic history. What an exceedingly impressive historical feeling from the Romanesque-Gothic architecture. The long oaked pew that had been used to seat the students whilst eating their lunchtime convivium alongside the elongated oak dining tables. With the Gothic revival chandeliers overarching the tables, it was very almost like something set up to dine the Kings and Queens. They had such a prodigious layout, which had been set up for the Oxford University students. The boys were conversing back and forth over their lunch, as they were excited to be starting Oxford University team polo training on Monday. David, Jasper, William, and Darius were all paid up, ready to start their basic training. Boys will be boys and ready to impress those girls. The girls, Eldora, Daphne, Verity, and Samantha were just as happy to be watching the 'chick flick at the cinema tonight with the boys supporting them, they too were happy enough to support the boys at the polo. Paul Barrera was the odd boy left out from playing polo, but he wasn't amused by the sport, he'd have rather been a spectator with the girls. Polo the game itself doesn't look that complicated while watching it until you must realize that you need to get used to your horse, learn how to ride it, and then get the horse to gallop then chase, all the while taking a huge swing at the same ball while seven other players are all chasing the same thing. While the boys were cavernous in discussion about the sport polo, with all things set aside now for when they start training in the week. They were overwhelmed and in deep thought about this movie night with the girls this evening. At first, they were like 'It's just a chick flick', but thoughts had started to go a bit deeper. They were spending the night with the best bunch of girls, Daphne Johnson, Verity Page, Eldora Jenkins, and Samantha Hutchinson. These four stunning and sophisticated girls weren't your average girls, they were all higher-class, very well-spoken, and highly maintained and these girls were not about to settle for no less than gentlemen. So, David, Jasper, William, Darius, and Paul were now paying some attention to the thought of spending a romantic

evening with the girls, with David sitting with Daphne Johnson, William Macintyre was just as eager to sit with Verity Page, Jasper Flynn although some may say he was best suited for our new ginger girl Samantha Hutchinson from Liverpool, he was already taken by Eldora Jenkins as they have been sending SMS back and forth. That had only left Samantha Hutchinson, which made perfect moral sense to sit with both her boys Darius Silva and Paul Barrera. They met the others in their little groupie a bit later in their academic studies so made sense for them to sit with one another. The boys were contemplating what to wear this evening, as they reasoned they had better have worn something formal to impress the ladies, as it was their first official date night.
David had thought it may be best to wear a suit; he said, "What do you boys think about wearing a tuxedo, to the cinema dinner date"?
Jasper and William were like "A tuxedo is a high-profile wedding dress code". Jasper then went on to say: "It is best to wear something a little less over-dramatic like a casual but formal suit".
William too agreed: "That makes perfect sense, casually smart as we are not getting married. Even if that's your future intention, no need to show

you're rushing things like a desperate child".
David Smith laughs: "Yeah your right boys, just a casual suit, tie, and some nice brogues will do the job".
Both boys and girls were sitting at the extraordinarily long elongated oak wood dining tables still inside Christ Church's dinner hall, it was only 2:45 pm they were in no major rush as they hadn't needed to get to the local cinema, the Ultimate Picture Palace at the centre of Oxford. It was only around a fifteen-to-twenty-minute bus ride from outside Oxford University and the movie didn't start until 06:45 pm, they still had four hours to go. Daphne and Eldora had suggested to everyone about taking a nice brisk walk around the University Park, as it was such a beautiful solace place, with over 70 acres of parkland to enjoy the end of the summer. Autumn leaves would've just started turning colour getting ready to fall by the end of the months of October going into November. The University Park was bordered, with the River Cherwell running through the park, and giving the students the absolutely blissful and peaceful sounds of the constant running of the stream. It was a place to ventilate and motivate your welfare and well-being and was an

extraordinary place to set your spirits free. Free from anxiety, worries, or distress. There was no place like the University Park and its complete open space. The whole woodland environment with natural habitat, and a place for everyone to enjoy. Without a doubt, everyone was overwhelmed with Daphne Johnson and Eldora Jenkin's idea about going for a brisk walk through the university woodland park (Oxford Mosaic, 2001). It was a place that many students would go to take and eat their lunches or even visit Jimbos Baguettes like they have, many a time. Or even just go to read a book of any genre, anything specific, often reading poetry, their favourite love story, Roald Dahl, Charles Dickens, William Shakespeare, stories from their favourite author. There were acres to sit and enjoy your favourite book, anywhere within this wonderful spacious woodland whilst nibbling away at a delicious fruit, or even a salad garnish, anything healthy that you packed away for daily nutritional indulgence. I mean if you were more analytical about what an absolute treasure of heritage this place was to the University then you would know that these students come with a high I.Q, and they would make sure they would look after their welfare, well-being, and vitality. As soon as it had become a lunch period, hundreds of students would gather through the University Park, just to unwind, relax, meditate, reflect, stretch, chill. You would even see some girls take a blanket and practice yoga. Yoga is a tremendous exercise to do to release aches and pains, it is a perfect way to destress the mind from strenuous days of studying. Both boys and girls had enjoyed their afternoon stroll up and along the River Cherwell, the girls enjoyed listening to the running stream, and watching closely as the baby ducklings surrounded the mother duck as they swam up to the shore. The boys David, Jasper, William, Darius and Paul were throwing stones down-shore, not to upset the girls whilst they were happily enjoying watching the ducklings swim with mother duck. The boys were highly focused on skimming stones in the opposite direction. I am not certain as to why this was such an addiction for boys and men, as soon as they saw a flow of water whether it be the seaside, a river, a lake, or a pond they would have the urge to throw stones in. I don't know if it was a masculine thing, macho thing, boredom thing, or whatever it was, boys would find a way or a reason to do it. To some, the thought may have become slightly perturbed, and to many, it may have become thought of as perfect normality that had set the differences aside from both male and female, whereas boys had liked more destructible things and girls had liked more beautiful things of nature that were more reserved. Isn't it ironic that you think about the purposes of males and females from a sociologist's point of view looking through a lens at both males and females and how they act? A female is rather more reserved than a male, I am not trying to be stereotypical here but in contrast to the majority of how females and males act, a woman does act more reserved to a male whereas a male will be slightly more erratic, like the enjoyment of throwing stones down the river, or giving each other a dead arm walking along. This isn't ordinary behaviour in how a female would act, it becomes stranger that women tend to be attracted to males when they act inappropriately to show off their masculine side to prove themselves as a man in front of a female or to get their attention. Likewise, the females like the strangest of things, ducklings swimming the river with mother duck, or like they'd get upset over roadkill, or go all squeamish over spiderwebs catching a butterfly for supper. It is almost like they are two different species. However, they had highly enjoyed each other's company and engaging with one another's attractions and were distracted by their 'weird' variety of tastes. You could see how hard David was trying to impress Daphne by throwing innumerable amounts of stones and rocks up the river Cherwell, as he kept running up beside and brisking past her right shoulder, skimming the water as the stones ricocheted upriver cascading along. I bet David would've been much preferred to grant the fortitude strength to cascade his lips up closely past Daphne's soft lips as he stroked past her, but he hadn't had the minerals to do that just yet. The slow-growing affection that these students had, boyfriends and girlfriends, was like watching a sunflower seed fully bloom to the great length of a full-grown sunflower, taking its time to reach its full potential. This evening could make all the difference as their first full date night approaches, it would be nice to see how William Macintyre and Verity Page get along as the two have been a long time coming, texting each other back and forth for a few weeks now. Same as Jasper Flynn and Eldora Jenkins, it doesn't leave much attention for Darius Silva and Paul Barrera, as they only have the lovely Ginger scouse girl, Samantha

Hutchinson to tussle over.
Samantha Hutchinson still had some secret attention with Jasper Flynn, eye contact from time to time, and although she knew that he was taken by Eldora Jenkins, this hadn't stopped the pair from making eye contact. It was almost like every occasion they were trying to make eye arousal with one another, they were undressing each other with their eyes from time to time. Jasper Flynn would've acted very inappropriately towards Eldora Jenkin if he did go there with Samantha Hutchinson, especially as she had the choice between two different boys that had been left on the market. Darius Silva and Paul Barrera, I mean what more could Samantha want with these two strapping lads to choose from? Knowing how much of a powerful and independent woman she had been, she could quite manage both of them if she were to choose that option. She could eat them up and spit them out like tangerine pips, she was a girl in high demand and always went after what she had aimed for.
It was 3:35 pm and they had started to take a stroll back towards the University Campus, this time David didn't need to get a lift home with his parents as he was staying over on Campus that

weekend and he had brought along with him the formal wear for the evening and some civvies for the rest of the weekend so he could stay comfortable throughout his weekend stay on campus with the others. So, they had all gone back to their dormitories, Daphne, Verity, Eldora, and Samantha were about to steer off to the girls, and David, Jasper, William, Darius, and Paul had started to walk towards the boy's dormitory. Eldora Jenkins murmured: “We will get dressed and meet you outside guys at 5:10”. Significantly they were all to meet up outside at quarter to six, so this would give them extra time, an hour to get to the cinema and to sit down before the film started at 06:45 pm. This would give them all plenty of time to catch the local bus into the town centre of Oxford, where the bus route ended right outside the cinema. You could see the excitement on the girls' faces, to be having a date night with those handsome boys, grins like ‘Cheshire cats’, you know the grin that was so distinctive and mischievous. Any onlooker would’ve thought these wicked witches were about to cast a spell on those young boys. Not a devilish thought within their innocent souls, such good-mannered and highly intellectual girls were just so overwhelmed

to be having a truly deserved date night with the boys. Seeing as the girls were going to speculate the gentlemen whilst they were going to start playing polo Monday week and from there onwards.
Eldora Jenkins was making an extra effort tonight to make sure she put Samantha Hutchinson's nose out of joint, trying to look extra glam for 'her' Jasper Flynn. By doing so she took some tips from the girls, Daphne Johnson and Verity Page as they helped her choose her outfit and helped prepare her makeup and hair. She still wore her bifocals, but with her long thin pencil skirt that was tight fitted, and showed her curves, thighs, and tightly clenched buttocks, and a black and white blouse which perfectly showed the curvaceous rounded breasts that she covered, being so modest. This had drawn a highly sophisticated elegant woman that Eldora Jenkins was, she wore black and white flat plimsol shoes which made her stand her usual height at 5ft 4 inches tall. Samantha Hutchinson was in for a challenge tonight to pull the attention away from Jasper Flynn and Eldora's Jenkins. I Don't believe anyone would be as smoking hot, more so, as it were a surprise from her usual get-up-and-go outfit. When Samantha Hutchinson had

walked out of the shower, to see the girls Daphne and Verity doing Eldora Jenkin's makeup this had led her to feel discombobulated, as she now knew she had a lot to compete with. She had already drawn out her blue knitted midi dress from her wardrobe, which she had wanted to wear with her high-heeled boots on, to be fair, any kind of blue had matched girls with red or ginger hair as it had tended to blend well together. Possibly because they are very opposites in the colour spectrum. To be honest with you, all the girls had started to look stunning this evening, just as the gentlemen were making an effort for the girls, as it was their first proper date night. Who would have thought that the girls had taken the longest to get ready, shower, put makeup on, and all of them nearly all dressed and ready to go? The boys were still fluffing around in their dormitory getting ready, Jasper Flynn was still to iron his white shirt. He had his trousers and shoes on, tie ready, and blue Blazer at the ready. It was just his shirt, then brush his hair then he was ready. David and William were pretty much good to go, they just needed to put their shoes on, David was wearing brown brogues and a dark navy-blue suit, a light blue shirt, and a light brown tie. Paul Barrera and

Darius Silva were both ready, Darius was wearing a silky black suit and looked rather dapper as his suit was very dressy. As soon as Jasper had hurried up and finished ironing his shirt, they were good to go. David and William were pacing up and down the hallway, "hurry up Jasper, you're like a woman!" exclaimed David.
"Ok I am coming, just doing up my shirt, putting my blazer on and tie then good to go, wait by the door, I'll be down in five minutes": Said Jasper.
"About time, your absolute girl" mockingly said William.
David, William, Darius, and Paul Barrera were all ready to go, all of them waiting down by the front door. Jasper Flynn was just putting on his shoes then he was coming.
Daphne Johnson, Eldora Jenkins, Verity Page, and Samantha Hutchinson, the awesome foursome was ready to leave their dormitory and to meet the boys. The girls had all looked like high-end fashion models, and all the students in the University were turning their heads observing these stunning beauties. At long last Jasper Flynn had come down, and now the boys were all ready to leave the dormitory to meet the girls. David, Jasper, William, Darius, and Paul, had dropped

their jaws as they finally approached the girls. "Switz Swoo", William gives them the wolf whistle of encouragement. "Look at you boys looking handsome," Flirtatiously says Samantha. That has only put pressure on Eldora Jenkins as she clings onto the arm of Jasper Flynn. Eldora was not having Samantha steal her man from her. To be honest I think Jasper Flynn was highly taken aback by how Eldora Jenkins had looked, she looked stunning with her black satin long, tightly fitted pencil skirt which showed off her thighs and curvaceous buttocks, black and white plimsols, her black and white blouse that hugged tightly up close to her breasts, covered although not leaving much to the imagination from the dirty mind of Jasper. Eldora Jenkins wasn't just an autistic brainiac, tonight she was stunning. The majority of neuro-divergent people are so lovely, and once you get to understand that they view and process things differently than neurotypical people, the quicker you can get to understand what their day-to-day struggles can look like and help to support them. You begin to realize they deserve to be treated with empathy, care and compassion, many neurodivergent people have the most beautiful imagination you could think of. I mean who wouldn't have liked to be inside Eldora head for a day? It must have been like an Oxford dictionary, she had seemed to know everything. Darius Silva was telling Samatha how stunning she had looked with her knitted blue midi dress; it had made her ginger hair stand out and very well matched with the light blue dress. It had seemed a superpower for the girls that they could choose a different primary colour that could make something else shine with elegance such as Samantha had done with her dress. Samantha no doubt would've been saddened by the thought that Eldora Jenkins and Jasper Flynn were already close with one another, this had led the only options left to be Paul Barrera or Darius Silva. They had all carried on their journey to the front main entrance as there was a bus stop, adjacent to the University which had bus routes into the Town centre. Samantha Hutchinson's demeanour came across as rather insidious as she drew a jealous hatred toward Eldora Jenkins, she had kept trying to evolve a certain pickthank from the boys both Paul Barrera and Darius Silva it was like she needed some emotional support and gratitude as she hadn't got her own way with Jasper. William Macintyre and Verity Page had looked like such a suited couple, they were clutching hold of each other's hands as they walked toward the bus stop. The perfect couple. The same as David Smith and Daphne Johnson, another couple of sweethearts. The evening was still young as they awaited the bus. The bus was coming at 5:15 pm but they had arrived fifteen minutes early, by the time they had got to town they had plenty of time to grab something to eat before they headed into the cinema. They would've got into town by 5:30 pm on the bus. William Macintyre had noticed the air to turn a slight bit chilly, not forgetting it was the ending of the summer and nearing the Autumn months. The temperature had slightly started to drop casually from what had been mid-summer months, it was 11 degrees C early that evening, so with that, William had wrapped his arm closely around the shrug of Verity page's shoulder to enclose her to a warmth. Samantha Hutchinson had sat tightly between Darius Silva and Paul Barrera, so in that sense she was luckiest to have the warmth coming from both directions. Many a time you would come to think that Samantha Hutchinson, although she was a rather stunning red head, she had no levity when it had come to choosing a date for the evening, I mean in all

seriousness she had the options of both Darius and Paul, but with her red-headed devious ways, she had much preferred chasing after something that she wasn't allowed.
Their bus was arriving outside the Brasenose College, as cited in.. (Website by, Passenger, 2001) It was the U5 bus and was heading to town from the 'high street.

It wasn't a bus shelter, as you had imagined later in October, they would drastically all huddled close together. After all, it was their date night, so they were aiming their best to cling to their date partners. Daphne and David both give the hand signal 'the classical hand wave' to the bus driver, just to indicate that they are awaiting a bus ride into the city's town centre. The driver from the U5 bus had put on his air brakes to gradually slow the bus down to a stop right up next to the curb side. The bus driver had to park relatively close to the curb at all bus stops just in case anyone who was disabled wanted to enter the bus, by doing so would have enabled him to be able to lower the ramps that led up to the bus entrance. The bus ride into the town centre was only 75p, Oxford University into the Town Centre. The bus stop was very convenient for students to be able to head into the town centre with all the amenities and essentials that they had ever wished for so close by. By the time the bus had stopped at the town centre the time would've been 5:30 pm meaning that the cinema film was being screened at 6:45 pm, in theory, they would have had about an hour realistically to spend before they had to ensure they were seated, which would have given them fifteen minutes before start time for the movie. In total that was one hour and fifteen minutes from the time they got off from the bus when it arrived at 5:30 pm. Jasper Flynn, Verity, and Eldora were discussing that it would have been a better idea for them to get some fast food for dinner before they went into the cinema, and with that, they had ended up in agreement. It had become more convivial and convenient for them to get some fast food now, so they could spend more quality time together on their date night. These quality times hadn't come around very often, so they had wanted to make the most of it. While there was adulation burning within the hearts of these young students it was a time to keep prodding the stove from the furnace of one's aorta, to keep that young admirable dream alive. They had arrived at their stop, and they were gathered up near the exit doorway of the bus, Daphne, Verity, Eldora, Samantha, David, Wiliam, Jasper, Darius and Paul had all given the bus driver some gratitude, as he had driven them safely to their destination on interest, “than-you driver” as they had all alighted off the bus one by one. They continued on their journey by walking down Cornmarket Street they could see in the very near distance, a Kentucky fried chicken opposite side of the road from the bus stop. cited in (Mr Kentucky, 2001) Jasper Flynn had noticed, the fast food restaurant, and inside the KFC they could sit down and enjoy some nice southern fried chicken, that was finger-licking good. Their orders hadn’t taken long at all to be cooked. After Jasper Flynn had noticed the fast-food chain, it hadn’t taken much convincing to get his friends to accept that it was tasty, it was cooked in a rather expedient time frame to ensure it would give them plenty of time to head on to watch their movie. And KFC was a rather succulent meal, chicken on the bone, boneless chicken, and sides such as coleslaw, Corn on the cob, chips, and beans. Nearing the KFC, they were now under no obligation not to walk inside and enjoy some fast food. It was one of Jasper Flynn’s all-time favourite fast-food chain restaurants, he was salivating! Jasper, David, Daphne, and Eldora Jenkins were going to get a chicken on the bone, box to share, which came with four portions of chips, eight pieces of chicken, two sides and a 1.5 litre of Pepsi, the sides they had chosen were beans and coleslaw, they had placed their order and it had come to £7.99. They sat down, Jasper Flynn had asked the customer service man for four plastic cups to share the Pepsi, and then he sat back down at the table. William Macintyre and Verity Page had wanted the BBQ ribs, and chips to share, they had chosen twelve pieces of ribs and a large portion of chips to share between them and a large Pepsi, which they had asked for two straws to share the one large Pepsi. Honestly, this is what first dates are made of, two straws and one cup, the romance from bonding time had started to become more relevant here with William and Verity setting the new vibe and trends. Samantha Hutchinson only wanted corn-on-the-cob, coleslaw, chips, and an orange Fanta, Paul Barrera had wanted a chicken breast/fillet in a bun with chips, and Pepsi, and Daruis Silva, wanted six chicken wings, two pieces of chicken on the bone, chips and a Pepsi. Some of them left feeling rather perplexed at Samantha's small appetite had them questioning whether they had thought that she was losing her appetite, while a couple of them thought maybe she was just trying to control and maintain her figure. The vast majority of young adults at this stage of their lives have started to pay a lot of attention to how their appearance may project in front of others, leaving many students feeling anxious. Most of the time seeking the approval of others while waiting for some kind of engagement, or encouragement, this was the importance of males and females giving one another lots of compliments on how they looked. At this moment Samantha had noted she wasn't going to be getting any compliments or encouragement from the man she was eager for, Jasper Flynn as he was taken by the stunning Eldora Jenkins. Let's face it she had made the extra effort by letting the girls Daphne and Verity do her makeup, she looked stunning with the nice fitted long pencil skirt and black and white blouse that hugged her figure. Eldora Jenkins wasn't your average super-hot-looking woman, she had a bundle of intelligence too. Jasper Flynn would be absolutely mad if he hadn't chosen Eldora Jenkins over them all. And if you were taking a girl/woman home to meet your parents with their head screwed on then you wouldn't have any problems, worries, or other thoughts about taking her to meet the parents the first time, Eldora Jenkins had always ticked all the boxes. I mean she had looked half decent at the best of the times, even when she made zero effort. Just her casual, lazy day, no makeup, hair loose and wavy like she doesn't care. Her intelligence had seemed to mask her which only accentuated her allure, she was a gorgeous specimen. You could see that Jasper Flynn and Eldora Jenkins were enjoying their 4 pieces of chicken on the bone between them, while David and Daphne had the other four pieces they had come together in the chicken box of eight, four fries, and 1.5-liter bottle of Pepsi, sitting right opposite one another, David and Jasper Flynn one side of the table, and Eldora Jenkins was opposite Jasper, and next to Eldora was Daphne sitting opposite David. The little romantic awesome foursome. The succulent chicken on the bone, you could see the grease on each of their lips, it had looked like lip gloss. Jasper Flynn was talking to Eldora about the movie, and how exciting it was for them to be getting away from the University. It was nice for them to escape the dormitory, stuck inside just with the same girls in their block, and the same boys inside their block. It was nice for them to be set free this evening, free from any formal study work, free from all the anxiousness. Letting their thoughts go transcending into the depths of a nice chick-flick, with convivial like-minded people. And being a chick-flick there was bound to be some sort of romance, or boy crush, possibly a happy ending and they had taken their favourite person along with them as their date tonight to the cinema. The evening was only going to end in one way. After all, enjoying a rather extravagant food for choice, fast food takeaway, they had enjoyed their stroll down to the Ultimate Picture Palace, down Jeune Street, Cowley Rd, OX4 1BN. It was 6:15 their movie was about to be screened at 6:45 pm, it was always far better to enjoy a movie at the cinema with a full stomach, rather than an empty one. As that can cause an unsettled feeling and trouble with concentration on the film. Eldora Jenkins had already pre-ordered all their tickets online, so they had fast-forwarded the queue, as they only had to show the email that had the receipt from the online booking. Daphne, Verity, Samantha, Jasper, David, William, Paul, and Darius would've had to square up the payment with Eldora throughout the rest of the evening or the very next day as it was rather kind of her to make sure she had booked all the seated area together so they could all sit next to one another. There were five boys and four girls, nine number in total seats. They were watching screen room 1 for the movie 'There's Something About Mary' with a poster of Cameron Diaz, with blonde shiny hair and bent over wearing a red dress, the poster was displayed right next to the screening front entrance doorway. Eldora Jenkins had looked at her email to see the location of the seated area they had got for seats, Row 3, seats 123, 124, 125, 126, 129,130,131,132,133, this had made things slightly awkward although they weren't so far apart, Daphne and David sat together, Eldora Jenkins and Jasper Flynn together, that was the first four seats taken 123, 124, 125 and 126, William and Verity sat with one another,. That had left Samantha Hutchinson sitting next to Darius and Paul Barrera, so she took the last seats between them, with William and Verity sitting in seats 129, 130, and 131 was Samantha sitting by the right shoulder of Verity, as she hadn't trust Samantha sitting next to William. 132 and 133 were both Daruis and Paul's seats. They all sat down promptly, to get comfortable, relaxed and reclined as they possibly could. David had taken Daphne's hand while they sat nice and cozy about to watch the movie trailers before the main feature began at the cinema. What was this movie about? As cited in… (Trending on RT, 2001)/ There's something about Mary, it is a 1998 American Romantic comedy film directed by Peter Farrelly and Bobby Farrelly, who co-wrote it with Ed Decter and John J Strauss. The Film features Cameron Diaz as the title character, while Ben Stiller, Matt Dillion, Lee Evans, and Chris Elliot all play men who are in love with Mary and vying for her affection. Jasper Flynn was overwhelmed with how alluring and prepossessing Eldora Jenkins had looked this evening, he took her by the hand and leaned over his chair to give her a smooch/kiss on the cheek to say thank you, he also complimented her for how beautiful she looked. While William had already made the first move with Verity. The opening credits bellow with a joyful sound, as the movie is about to begin. Then William places his hand on her thigh as he clenches his manly hand across her quadricep with a sensual squeeze. Verity makes a comforting sound. "Mummy this is nice William". And David was left rather cosy with entwined legs with Daphne's. Daphne had far stretched both her legs over the thighs of David trying to indicate some attention coming from David perhaps. David was so naïve and never got the hint. It wasn't until Daphne had indicated that he had noticed. "Rub my thighs please David, be a gentleman" mockingly said Daphne. "Of course, not a problem beautiful one," said David. The movie was about to begin.

Ted Stroehmann, a 16-year-old high school student in Providence, Rhode Island, is getting ready to go on the prom with Mary Jensen, his ideal partner when he gets his testicles caught in his zip in 1985. He manages to unzip it painfully and ends up in the hospital, missing their date. Ted then stops communicating with her.
Throughout the start of the movie, Jasper Flynn is rather thankful that Eldora Jenkins came up with the idea, so he goes on to say, "Eldora thank you ever so much, for inviting us all to the movies, I feel overwhelmed and you looking rather stunningly beautiful this evening" : Jasper says rather beguilingly.

In 1998, thirteen years later, Ted is still in love

with Mary and works as a magazine writer. Ted employs Pat Healy, a private investigator, to find her on the recommendation of Dom Woganowski, his best friend. Healy learns that she and her brother Warren, who has an intellectual disability, reside in Miami and work as orthopaedic surgeons. After a few days of monitoring her Healy also gets obsessed with her. When he gets back to Providence, he tells Ted false information about Mary, claiming that she is overweight and has four children from three different men. In order to pursue her, Healy leaves his work and goes back to Miami. In an attempt to win Mary over, he starts stalking and lying.
Halfway through the movie, Paul Barrera asks both Samantha Hutchinson and Darius Silva if he can be excused while he needs to dash to the toilet and just like so…. Squeezing past their legs in the tiny cinema chairs, then he needed to walk to the opposite side of the cinema hall, as the toilet cubicle was located three-quarters of the way up the opposite side from the steps, from the bottom to the top.

Ted drives to Florida to visit Mary after learning that Healy is lying about her. He picks up a

hitchhiker who puts a dead body in his car while they are driving. After the hitchhiker confesses to the murder, Ted is wrongfully jailed for it and is released on bond by Dom. After a few weeks of dating, Healy's British architect friend Tucker reveals his deceit. After Tucker falsely accuses Healy of being a suspected serial killer, she breaks up with him. Furious, Healy approaches Tucker and learns that he is actually Norm Phipps, an American pizza delivery kid who is also smitten with Mary. Norm had purposefully hurt himself years before to become her patient and to be close to her. To keep close and turn off potential suitors, he acts as though he is still crippled. Healy and Norm work together to push Ted away when he and Mary start dating again.
Samantha Hutchinson had soon become rather amused and comfortable to be sitting in between both Paul Barrera and Darius Silva. After all, they were her friends for the longest within her Pharmaceutical Science Academic class.

Mary becomes outraged and dumps Ted after reading an anonymous letter that says he paid Healy to find her. After Healy and Norm deny mailing the letter, Ted approaches them aggressively. Later on, Dom—who turns out to be Mary's ex-boyfriend "Woogie"—arrives at her flat and confesses to composing the letter. Prior to Ted finding her, and despite being married and having children, they find out she had a restraining order against Dom because he had developed an obsession with her.

Coming near the end of the movie, 'Something about Mary', the happiness, zeal, and look of enthusiasm and joy this had brought to all their faces. It had become evident that a chick flick was the only way to go to bring them all closer together as a group, as friends, and as a company, one could keep as future companions. Studying any sort of academia around the opposite sex, it was important to find your soul and study mate to sometimes share, resonate, and reflect ideas. As you know, studying is a long haul with many of these students being away from home and away from family, they need to find a bond to support their mental health and well-being.

Outside, Healy and Norm listen and go in to protect Mary from Dom. Then Ted shows up with Brett Favre, whom Mary broke up with after Norm made up a story about him making fun of Warren. Ted says that since Favre is the only one who doesn't use deceit to win her over, he should be with her. Ted departs in tears after rejoining Favre and defeating the other men, but she follows him outside and declares, "I'd be happiest with you." Magda's boyfriend uses a sniper rifle to attempt to shoot Ted for kissing Mary (as he is also infatuated with her) but hits one of the band members instead. The end of the movie trailers had come up on the huge cinema screen, then all of a sudden music gently playing in the background, the actor's names appearing on screen, movie editors, movie producers, and movie makers, the lights had suddenly flashed on. Rather striking to the eyes making everyone feel rather discombobulated. The majority of people at the cinema were dazed by the lights, as throughout the whole movie they had been sitting in the darkness watching a lit screen, so when the full room had become lit again it had become a shock to the system. When they had begun to try and stand from the folding chairs, as they had startled to their feet, holding the chair with the opposite hand, grabbing their coat, the gentlemen trying to support the ladies, by holding onto their arms, with the ladies not only grabbing hold of their coats but miraculously trying to do their coat up with both hands while they hold their handbags in the other. ‘It was like a sudden catastrophe, a moment of madness. Today at the movies there were many families together, wives, husbands, mothers, fathers, and young teenagers, and as you can imagine although they had watched an entertaining joyful movie, they were all dashing for the main exit to get home. Jasper, David, William, Daphne, Verity, and Eldora had all looked together to find and locate Darius, Paul, and Samantha, they had spotted them as they were walking out from their aisle, they had just seen Samantha waving and smiling. There were only a few seats between them all but as suggested after the lights had come on, everything had all become a bit confusing and there was a loss of the coordination of arms, feet, and eyes for a short moment. So, this had people left feeling a little betwixt in knowing where they were, whom they had come with, where the exit was, ‘from the same entrance they had walked in’, but most notably it had taken a few moments to figure it out. Going to the movies’, the cinema was a place for complete insouciance by letting your thoughts transpire into the depths of the visually scripted Movie ‘Something About Mary’. It was a well-chosen movie by Eldora for their friendship and companionship, this would have manifested some alluring compassion between them, bringing them closer together. Now they were all gathered outside together, all happily in each other's company, with happy smiles from the entertainment and the rather stimulating conversations they had been having amongst their couples. Samantha, Paul, and Darius in their groupie of three, all of them together have been rather flirtatious and consensual with each other as the movie progressed, they all snuggled up on the chairs as they recumbered at the back of the Ultimate Picture Palace cinema's folding seats. The holding of hands, entwining of legs and feet. A lot of canoodling going on while they were watching a romantic film, the film lasted for one hour twenty-seven minutes, and it started at six forty-five minutes past the hour 6:45, so that's 6:45 + 1.27hr = 8:12 pm past the hour. Their bus was arriving at 08:45 to head back to Oxford University, the night streetlights had come on, the night sky had become misty, marl grey with a mixture of black, and you couldn't see any stars in sight. The temperature had dropped a fair bit from when they had arrived in the town centre, and the girls had goosebumps and hairs standing on end as they were more dressed-down to impress the gentlemen. The boys were in suits and blazers, so the gents being rather macho and gentlemen-like had decided to comfort and cuddle their ladies, enclosed to try and keep a warmth captured between them, from the male's bodily heat absorbed to the females, trying to keep them warm from the chill within the late summers night. The rain had started to pour down, just as they imagined from feeling the cold moisture throughout the air. But to be fair, David and Daphne seemed extraordinarily overwhelmed as David smothered her to keep her warm. Daphne was also delighted as she knew she had David later that evening, and how he was going to try to sneak into her dormitory. They hadn't yet wanted the others to know, otherwise, they'd all be trying to sneak their partners into the girls' dormitory, and they would soon get caught red-handed by the staff members if they were all to make exceedingly too much noise. Their bus was arriving any moment, and they were taking the U5 bus from High St, in Oxford Town Centre, back to Brasenose College which was adjacent to Oxford University. Back in the distance behind four or five cars, they could see a big red bus, with a lit-up digital screen that shone a yellow letter from the alphabet, with the letter U and numerical, number that shone 5, so U5 was showing in the distance. It had come to the girl's amazement that they would shortly be inside the warm away from the cold weary night and out of the rain. Paul Barrera had overreached his hand to a wave, so he could signal the bus driver who was gradually getting closer to the bus stop.

The high street bus stop had some shelter from the rain, but the way the wind was blowing across still seemed to reach the legs and arms of the girls. The bus driver from the U5 bus had slowly hit his air brakes as he pulled up to the curb side at the bus stop. The bus driver was the same man as before on their first trip into town, as they were all reaching for their return tickets, the bus driver not only took into consideration it was raining and to let them all get in the warm, he had remembered them all from earlier to he had said “Come on you lot, don’t worry about your ticket, get in the warm”: explains the bus driver. “Thanks driver”: these were the words of both David and William, as the whole group was happy and glad to be getting out of the cold and wet weary night.

They all happily got on the bus and were thankful

they had an amicable and reasonable bus driver. They all gathered to the rear of the bus, Samantha Hutchinson sat down and was surrounded by her boys, Darius Silva and Paul Barrera. They stood around her while she sat down on the seat, holding the handrails and balancing with the strength, core, and balance from their arms, hand grip and legs. Samantha was like... "thank you, boys, for accompanying me this evening at the cinema, it meant a lot".

Both Darius and Paul were like. "No problem, it was all our pleasure". Verity Page, And William Macintyre were sitting in the back seat right next to Daphne Johnson and David, while Jasper Flynn and Eldora Jenkins were just in front of them. They were all commending Eldora for the fantastic choice of movie they had just watched at the cinema, with both Verity and Daphne saying, "That was a splendid choice of movie Eldora".

It had brought a vibe of romance to the group, and spending some well-needed time together was great for the eudemonia. The boys shaking their heads in agreement, David, William, and Jasper, "Absolutely marvellous choice of movie Eldora" stated Jasper

Flynn. Reminiscing and reflecting on the overall day they had enjoyed, is not a bad ending to the gruelling weeks of studying. David, Daphne, Verity, Eldora, and Jasper were all reflecting on their day and evening and how straight after their academic study Friday afternoon, they had ended up trying a different place to eat their lunch; The Christchurch, which had catered for everyone with allergies of all sorts, from vegetarian dishes to breakfast, main meals, soups, and pasta dishes, they were catered for like Kings and Queens, even more so with its heritage, the building, decorations, surroundings and architecture were phenomenal. The Christchurch itself was a Romanesque-Gothic architectural building, which inside was struck with elongated oak dining tables and Gothic revival chandeliers, after they had eaten their lunches at the Christchurch, they then went for a walk around the University Park, the 'woodland area' as they had like to think of it. They thoroughly enjoyed their walks through the park, as many students go there to unwind, relax, enjoy and have lunch, and read books. The fields had many sporting events going on throughout the year. The University Park was a place to free yourself from all anxiety, stress and

worry. And for these students, their weekend had just begun.
Later that evening all nine of them bonded together at the movies for one hour and twenty-seven minutes, as you can imagine the friendships drew closer, the romancing, it was a movie that projected a lot of adulation and admiration all for Mary' who starred as Cameron Diaz. David, Daphne, Eldora, Verity and Japer Flynn, had finished fondly reminiscing on the day.
They were just about to depart from the U5 bus, from Oxford Hight Street to Brasenose College, which was right outside their university. David and William thanked the driver, and Jasper Flynn yelled "Thanks driver!" Daphne and Verity with such generosity went on to say, "Muchly appreciated driver", As Samantha, Darius, and Paul Barrera hopped off the bus they murmured "Cheers driver". Eldora Jenkins hadn't felt the need to commend the driver as all her friends had already done the job for her.
The time was nearing 9:00 pm as they got off the bus outside the college. The day and evening when they ate dinner, watched Something about Mary, and walked in and out of fresh air made them all feel exhausted.

David had needed to make a plan of action to sneak into Daphne's room this evening, so he had planned to go back with the boys into their dormitory for a bit, then when they had got into bed he was going to sneak out and meet Daphne by the girls' entrance when it was safe to do so. Verity Page and Eldora Jenkin were looking forward to getting back in their bedrooms anyway so they could message both William Macintyre and Jasper Flynn a few flirtatious SMS's, some mischievous moments and good night messages no doubt. Samantha was also exhausted and looking forward to her bed tonight, likewise with Paul Barrera and Darius Silva. They carried on walking towards their dormitories, still in a dark, raining chilly night. David, William, and Jasper had walked the girls back, holding onto them to wrap their arms around their shoulders to keep the girls warm. Darius and Paul had carried on walking up to the boys' dorms while Samantha Hutchinson had carried walking with the others. As Jasper Flynn had walked Eldora Jenkins to her dormitory door, he had then applauded her for such a superb night that he had. With that, he cascaded a kiss on her soft velvet red tender lips by surprise, "Thank you, Jasper, you made my heart miss a beat"

Squeamishly said, Eldora. By a similar sequence William Macintyre had walked Verity Page to the girl's Dormitory, he hugged her goodnight, and a cheeky squeeze of her pert tight buttocks, you could see by the gesture on his face how enjoyable that was. as you could only imagine she had a rather firm gluteus maximus from all the horse riding.
Verity said:" Good night William, I will text you when I get into bed" "Ok Verity I will look forward to your message, Goodnight" : Overwhelmingly said, William.
And that was like so. Both girls, Eldora Jenkins and Verity Page had gone into the girl's Dormitory, and both boys William and Jasper had started walking back in a hurry to the boy's dormitory as they were excited to be getting into bed to text the girls until they had fallen asleep no doubt.
Samantha Hutchinson wasn't far behind them to go inside the girl's dormitory next while Daphne Johnson and David had purposely held back a little bit as they were to make a plan of action.
Paul Barrera and Darius Silva were just walking into the boy's dormitory. You could hear Darius whistling along while he was walking up the way, his usual happy habit, he wasn't so sure if it was a

sign of madness, or it may have been a coping mechanism that people often used when they were anxious, they can feel the need to whistle perhaps to take their mind away from something.
They have all gone into their dormitories apart from Daphne and David. Daphne explains:
"Right David, if you either hang about for a short while outside our dormitory or better still go sit downstairs in the boys' dormitory until I text you, the way will be clear for you to come in, okay?"
"You know what Daphne, which sounds like a great plan, at least they will be in their rooms by then": pleasingly said, David. David kisses Daphne on her left cheek as she sniggers back at him.
David then goes back to the boy's dormitory, but as luck has it for him, all the boys have gone straight up into their rooms, as both Paul and Darius are shattered, while William Macintyre and Jasper Flynn are more than likely lying on their beds texting the girls for a while before they go to sleep.
David had the joy of feeling openly free as he waited in the lobby area until Daphne Johnson said it was clear for him to sneak up to her room for the night. While they had both waited patiently for everyone to drift off to sleep, Daphne had sent an SMS message to David asking him to creep over

into the girl's dormitory. David had to appreciate that it was his first night over at Daphne's room and the only canoodling they would be getting up to would have been naïve, at the most some kissing. David and Daphne were both very introverted and reserved people.

No doubt if David had a dream, it was merely a wet dream' over the endearing thought of canoodling closely with the stunning blonde Daphne Johnson. It was around 9:43, David had been waiting anxiously for Daphne to text him to come up to the girl's dormitory and he was sitting restlessly in the boy's lobby room of their dormitory, with his legs up and crossed on the single armchair, a nervous twitch in his legs, he was eager to spend the night cuddled up to Daphne.

Beep-Beep goes David's mobile phone, the great big grin on David's cherry chase was enough to endure enough happiness inside a full opera house of spectators. He was overwhelmed, "I'll be right over Daphne, see you in a moment" was David's reply to the SMS invitation that Daphne had sent, he ended with a smiley face, and sent the old-fashioned way of SMS,).

David had started to creep over to the girls' dormitory. Leaving through the main entrance from the boys, by being ever so quiet as he gently stepped out from the lobby, and out of the main entrance door. Opening and closing the door as gently as he could, trying to not produce any squeaking sounds from the door as it opened and shut, all the while avoiding his jacket blazer, legs or shoes brushing up against the door or door shut so he would make minimal sounds on the way out. He walked gradually towards the girl's dormitory but was mindful of his step, using an effortless heel-to-toe motion as he stepped along the way. There was little light that had shone the way along the path of the University's walkways, they had started to lower the light levels out of hours. The lights from the lamppost had simmered to a vague yellow and there were only about eight lampposts along the 500m distance between the boys and the girl's dormitory. Just like the description, the light had barely shone the way, just enough to find your tread on the footpath along the way. It was still a dark and cloudy night, with a marl grey tinge smearing through the night sky but now the rain had stopped.

Daphne Johnson was enduring her heightened

emotions as she was waiting and holding the girl's dormitory main entrance door wide open for David to come to her peacefully and gracefully. The smile of happiness and magnificent gratitude as David walked into the girl's dormitory, holding hands as they slowly crept up the stairs to Daphne's room. Walking up the staircase to the girl's room, David was holding onto the railing with his right hand, and Daphne's right hand with his as they both gently took each step as it came, with the tips of their toes. Slowly placing their heels on every step as they walked up towards the neck of the stairwell.

They hear a creaking sound!

It must have come from the fourth or third-bedroom dorm, on the left-hand side.

They had come to a halt. Daphne whispered "David shhhh, did you hear that noise?"

"Yes Daphne": quietly whispered David.

They await until they hear another sound, which sounds like a flushing sound. "Must have been one of the girls getting up to go to the toilet in their room". The doors on the left went up in odd numbers and Daphne's door was number 13, it was six doors up from the left. So, the noise was

coming from either numbers 5 or 7.
They had crept as quickly and gently as they could, hurrying to Daphne's room. Daphne was holding the room key in her hand, so she could burst into her room a lot easier. She held it in the opposite hand as she met David at the door, she knew she had to be as vigilant and as efficient as possible. Daphne was well equipped for the kidnapping of David into her room, and they both had done a tremendous job. The nicest thing about this moment was they were the most innocent, loving and youthful couple in the University. Two very introverted hearts with shared tenacity in their hearts. It could end a Romeo and Juliet love storyline; you could almost see their names written in the skylight David+Daphne-
forever.
David was stunned and drawn in as he crept into Daphne's room, with her extraordinary, summer flowery bed, yellow tulips, and red roses printed all over a lightly cloudy blue coloured background, with four matching pillows, and two plain yellow pillow covers at the bottom, six pillows high in total, fit enough for a Queen. Daphne had added some extra fluffy cushions that just remain as a feature to the bed decorations.

She had one double window at the end of her bed to the right, which overlooked the pathway and main entrance that David had just walked. On the window, she had her own blinds fitted and some nice red drapes around the frames. The smell that lingered through her room was the same perfume fragrance that Daphne had worn throughout university.
David was so happy to be here, he could feel the comfort and was like his New Haven. His new love story and companion were about to start making dreams happen. David and Daphne had emerged onto the bed, but first Daphne had to go in the bathroom to get changed into her bedtime robe, David just unchanged into his underpants; his boxer shorts, and an undershirt which was the plain white t-shirt he had worn under his suit garments. While Daphne was getting changed David had folded his garments, laid them over the back of a chair and gotten under the duvet so that he had felt comfortable. Daphne took a while longer as she had to remove her makeup first, then squeezed into her mauve silk night dress and baby pink nightgown. If Daphne had worn just the mauve silk night dress, I could tell you now, it wouldn't have left much to David's imagination.

Daphne was an introvert and so was David, they were in no rush to break the ice in that department. They were happy just to have some flirtatious fun this evening as they both had a lot of academic study ahead of them. And for the case of having one good time, it could ruin the fun of one another's future if it were to go wrong down the line.
Now that they had both peeled back the bed sheets and climbed into the bed, they both would prop their little heads softly into the six soft pillows. They then engaged in eye contact and were anxious in thought and emotion. At this point both were experiencing feelings of nervousness although they were both sensible young adults, in their late teens. It was humorous not knowing how to make the next move, a cuddle, a touch of some sort or even a soft kiss, at this point not even any leg or foot engagement between them.
All of a sudden and without warning, David put his outstretched left arm over Daphne's right shoulder. The sudden stare had become fascinating as if they were waiting for one or the other to say "Well, who is going to hold who first?", or make the first movement. At this point, if you are waiting for any serious adult content to start, you have walked into

the completely wrong bedroom from the two most introverted couples alive at this point. Daphne was saying how happy it made her that David had come back with her into the bedroom, as Daphne knew David was a gentleman and would respect her wishes by treating her like an innocent lady just as he was an innocent young man. From the innocent thought and rather reminiscent moment, Daphne moved in closer with a soft kiss to David on his lips.

"Thank you for taking care of me David, I hope we can continue to grow together": Tenaciously says Daphne.

"of course, Daphne, I knew you were the one since the first day I had set my eyes on you, in our pharmacology classroom": pleads David.

"That's so sweet David, you are my one, my only": Smile-fully said Daph. David crosses his left leg across Daphne's right thigh,

"your leg is so tender, soft, and smooth Daphne" : David said.

"You know David us ladies have to do some self-care, and skin care": Daphne remarks. As they lay deep into the pillow, allowing their bodies to fall deeply into the mattress comfortably entwined, both arms and legs enlaced between them, their

eyes can barely gaze back and forth into each other’s beautiful innocent softly glazed blue eyes. David's left arm had dropped down over the duvet cover, down towards Daphne’s lower thigh. He was holding her as they were drifting into the depth of those thick pillows stacked up high. Daphne’s right arm was around David’s waist so innocently as they drifted off to sleep, like sweet lovers and best friends.
As soon as the sun rose, David would have to scarper from out of Daphne's room and the girls' dormitory before anyone had caught him, then he had to make his way back to and patiently sit downstairs in the lobby room of the boy's dormitory just so that he could make out he stayed there the night.

Chapter 4

Mon 15th October 2001

The weekend had passed so quickly, and they were back in the academic week, it was still early morning as the gradient of the day was to take place. The night sky drew into a marl grey, with a small hint of glistening reflective light that kept trying to protrude, it was 5:45 am. You could hear the whistling birds, seagulls, pigeons, and the odd few sparrows that often sat on the rooftops from the student's dormitory. Most of the students would have been fast asleep, reminiscing and reflecting on their dreams no doubt from the weekend that they just had, or dreading the academic week ahead as the anxieties drew their attention to what lies ahead of them this week. David was returning to his parent's house and had snuck out of Daphne's dormitory room that morning to work at his parents' pharmacy. Although David's parents were reasonably flexible with David having fun with his university friends, he'd also promised to start working extra hours to pay for the polo team funding. They sometimes took into consideration his welfare and well-being, with all the hard work

and no
play.
David's first thoughts when he woke up from the weekend had left him feeling extremely perplexed. It was like he was in a sudden trance, trying to overcome either the hard academic week or was just dazed by the amazingly outstanding dream he had about the Friday night he'd spent with the most beautiful girl in his academic study classroom. We believe he was left feeling rather perplexed about the two, however romantically, physically, and mentally draining. David was an obedient son who worked well for his parent's appreciation and wanted to pay off the polo team tuition fees he had promised them, and his parents carefully liked to guide David through to his maturity. They knew he needed to spend time bonding with other University students to give him the experience to confidently grasp adulthood and grow as a mature teenager. David was now more awake and very grateful for the day ahead, it was 6:30 as he drew back the curtains in mid-October. Still no bright light outside, weary grey marl with the sun trying to pierce through more and more by the minute. It was still hard to tell by the texture of the sky what the weather might bring, leaving

David feeling baffled about what to wear through the day, he went to his wardrobe and grabbed his trousers, blazer, shirt, woollen cardigan, and matching tie. Towards the end of October, it would usually have left one feeling rather anxious and befuddled about what to wear, even the weatherman was confused. You'd hear him on the live news coverage saying we are having an extremely hot Indian late summer, even though he would be wearing a shirt one morning then the next morning it was supposed to be hot according to his weather report, and you find him wearing a shirt, tie, and blazer. 'The good olde British weather'.

David had a longer day at university today, as he and the boys, Jasper Flynn, William Macintyre, and Darius Silva were all participating in the Oxford University Polo team beginner's training session. With that thought coming to mind, David realised he should also prepare his gymnasium bag, so he could take his training clothes to get changed into after his academic studies. All the boys in their group of friends have been hugely influenced and encouraged by researching and looking at all the triumphant memorabilia that the Uni Polo team brings. With thoughts of the drive, the passion, the composure, the spirit and the adrenalin that this sport must bring, have driven the boys, with lots of enthusiasm to give it their best go and trials.

David's parents had just woken up, with David's mother asking what David had wanted for breakfast "I am making scrambled eggs on toast for me and dad if you would like some David, or something else if you prefer"? : asked Miss Smith,

"Yes please Mother, I'll have the same as you and Dad please" : was David's response.

David was just in the bathroom and about to brush his teeth.

"Ok David come down as soon as you finish in the bathroom, try not to be too long as your dad wanted a quick shower": Miss Smith said.

"No problem, Mother, I won't be much longer anyhow": replied David. The time was nearing 7:00 am. They had an hour before they would need to leave to drop David off at the university, then go and open up their family-run business, the pharmacy. As soon as David had finished brushing his teeth, he shouted through to the bedroom to let his father know the bathroom was free. Then he had headed down the stairs to the kitchen to give a

hand to his mother whilst she was preparing the scrambled eggs and toast. Mrs Smith, David's mother had asked David to go to the fridge freezer, grab the orange and cranberry juices and some clean glasses from the cupboard and place them on the dining table. While David was preparing the table, David’s father was in the bathroom, getting showered and changed into his pharmacy formal wear. No doubt he was having a quick shave to get rid of the stubbly moustache he had left, as some of it had started to outgrow to almost a similarity to whiskers. And they had resembled whisker-like hairs to the left and right outer corners of his chin. As the family-run business was dealing with customers all day, he had thought it was in the best interest and professionalism to remain neat and smart throughout. They had kept it formal attire, neatly shaved and even the ladies had to wear hairnets whilst preparing the medicines.
David’s mum had started to dish up the breakfast. As she was about to dish up David’s dinner, she asked David to tell his father that his breakfast was ready. David walked to the staircase shouting up the stairs, “Breakfast’s ready Dad”: repeatedly shouted David, until he heard his father’s response. “Ok boy, nearly finished in the shower, just getting

in my towel now, I'll get changed and be right down with you": replied, his father.
David could do no more than what was asked of his mother, so he went back into the kitchen area and sat down at the dining table. His mother then asks the most obvious question, "Did you tell your father his breakfast was ready? Or at least almost done?" David moans towards his mother "Yes Mum, of course I did. He said he was just coming". David's mum had toasted three pieces of a nice freshly cut loaf they had brought from the supermarket the previous day. She spread out margarine and dashed the scrambled eggs evenly across two of the slices of toast while leaving one slice buttered and purposefully placed the marmalade on the table to give her son the sweet taste and sugar/energy rush to help him endure the day ahead. By the time David was sitting down at the table, his father had started to stomp down the steps, 'clomp, clomp, clomp, went David's father' as he stepped down the staircase. Great timing! this allowed David's mum to relax and enjoy her breakfast with both her boys before they had to head off to drop David off at university and then head off to work
themselves.

Back at the dormitory, the boys had woken up to their alarm at 7:15 am, Jasper Flynn, William Macintyre, Darius Silva, and Paul Barrera had all gathered in the shared kitchen, to grab some, tea, juice and bread for the toaster. Jasper Flynn had volunteered to make the toast, while Darius Silva and William Macintyre offered to make the drinks. The friendship between the young gentlemen had grown fonder and you could see things working out for them, making it more amicable between the gents. The bread was toasted in the toaster, 'ping' as it rose to the top of the toaster machine. Jasper Flynn had gathered the toasted bread from the toaster and applied butter, Jasper had already prepared jam and marmalade into tiny serving dishes evenly into four pots. These young gentlemen such as Jasper had used all the kitchen utensils adequately in the form to its measure as no surprise as they had become mature with wisdom as their academic studies had progressed, and living amongst themselves they had learned to fend for themselves. As breakfast was dished and good to go, they had ventured into the living room/entertainment quarter, to sit and eat comfortably before they all had gone up to shower. Jasper, William, Darius, and David had their

Oxford University Polo training after their academic studying today, so they would have all needed to prepare their training bags with extra clothing to wear something more comfortable to change into. Paul Barrera and Darius had both preferred marmalade on their toast, while William Macintyre and Jasper Flynn were happy with raspberry jam. Darius Silva and William Macintyre had made a large pot of tea which comfortably served about six cups on average, provided they had filled it to the max with hot water. They had brought along with them a small measuring jug for the milk to be contained in, and the sugar they had just brought the sugar jar over, which contained sugar cubes. Sugar cubes were more convenient than sugar, which you put in with a spoon, as you can't measure it as well as you can one lump or two like you can with the cubes. With a spoon, you can either put in very large heaps of sugar, small heaps of sugar, or medium heaps of sugar with the teaspoon.

The daily text says we need to look after our well-being, welfare, calories, and sugar intake. But depending on one's mood, putting in singular grains of granulated sugar with a teaspoon, you will never quite know how large or small that

teaspoon of sugar will end up.
Jasper Flynn had started to talk about the excitement of today's polo team's practice: "William, Darius I cannot wait until after our pharmacology class today, for our polo training. I have been excited about this since the day we paid our tuition fees."
"Yeah me too" Both replied Darius and William "This is something we can enjoy as a team, and the bit of fun and entertainment what we have been lacking lads, no real zeal" Said William
Jasper Flynn says: " yeah you're right, this will give us some energy and with any luck a triumphant feeling". You could tell how the conversation had lifted the excitement for today, it had brought amusement to their eudemonia, a fun-packed day: from studying with their usual friends in pharmaceutical science class, followed by the lunch break in which they get time to reminisce about the great weekend they just had, then on to do their fun activity later that afternoon.
Daphne, Verity, Eldora, and Samantha Hutchinson had woken up late this morning at 7:45 am, not giving them much time to get ready and have breakfast. So, they needed to rush into the shower room and get ready as soon as possible. That being

said, Daphne had rushed to the girl's shower room first. There were two shower cubicles side by side with separate privacy changing areas as you get in, with partition walls between. Daphne got in the one shower while Samantha rushed into the one adjacent to Daphne's shower. This had left Eldora Jenkins and Verity page waiting in the lobby area until they could use the shower cubicle next.
Verity was left chatting with Eldora, "What a brilliant idea you came up with Eldora to bring us girls closer to the boys" Verity added.
"I thought we would've all appreciated that not only the time together, but the mood, the chick flick, and the romance that the film brought to our friendships," says Eldora "Yeah you're most certainly correct on that note Eldora, as Daphne, you and I have all exchanged numbers with the boys. That for sure was mission accomplished"
Eldora sat smirking happily back at Verity, "yeah you are right, we now have closer relationships with the boys, David, Jasper, and William".
Daphne and Samantha had just finished in the shower room, and were just outside with towels wrapped around them, drying their hair in the large mirror. Samantha shouts down to the other two

girls: “Verity, Eldora the showers are both free”.
“OK, Thank-you Samantha, we are coming right up as it is 8:00 am we haven’t got long” Exclaimed Eldora.
While Samatha and Daphne were getting their hair dried and changed into their uniform for today, Verity and Eldora quickly jumped into the shower.
Back at the boy's dormitory, they were almost dressed and good to go out of the door to meet the girls and then David as usual, who was at the drop-off point. As ‘girls being girls’, they were always twenty to thirty minutes late. Jasper Flynn and William Macintyre were both fully clothed, bags packed for their polo training later this afternoon. They were just about to put their blazers and brown brogues onto their feet, then they would be good and ready. Jasper Flynn had side-combed his ginger slick hair back over to the side, using some hair ointment or gel to give it that shiny slick effect, he was looking extraordinarily suave today. No doubt he had thought it was in the best of his interest, after Eldora Jenkin's performance during the weekend. Giving everyone a weekend of romance at the cinema.
While William Macintyre was sporting the left

comb-over with a right parting in his hair, William had medium short brunette hair which complimented his blue eyes. He had worn a dark black suit with brown brogues whilst sporting a red tie and white shirt. It is rather hard to keep up with these boys as you can imagine they had various suits to wear throughout their academic week inside each of their wardrobes.

Darius Silva and Paul Barrera were both ready as well now and neither had worn a blazer today. Nevertheless, they looked dapper, in trousers, loafers, shirts, and cardigan vests which gave off Victorian tweed vibes. Now the boys were ready, they started to make a slow journey down to the girl's dormitory. Little did they know, only Samantha Hutchinson and Daphne Johnson were ready while Eldora Jenkins and Verity Page had only just this minute got out of the showers and were wrapped in their towels and drying their hair. They had Daphne and Samantha moaning at the pair of them, "Come on hurry up girls, we are running late": pleaded both Daph and Sam.

As the girls asked so passionately, they had asked Daphne and Samantha to grab their clothes from their bedroom so they could speed up the time getting ready. As usual, Verity Page and Eldora

Jenkins had ironed and laid out the clothes they were to wear on their beds before they'd showered. Daphne and Samantha went to their dormitory bedrooms and gathered Verity Pages and Eldora Jenkin's clothes, shoes, and bag for the day to speed the process up and save the girls from being late to meet David by the main entrance.
Daphne was wearing a fleecy baby blue midi dress made from wool, and some baby pink low-heeled shoes. The baby blue midi dress had drawn out her slender figure she had looked immaculate. David was in for a surprise today. Samantha Hutchison wore a black dress with two red highlighted lines that went around the whole outside of the perimeter of the dress, the two red lines had brought definition to her red hair, and she too was looking rather elegant. Verity Page and Eldora had finally dried their hair, rushing to put their clothes on and then makeup. The boys were waiting outside the main entrance from their dormitory. Samantha had to quickly run down to the front door, to let the boys know, Jasper, William, Darius, and Paul that they had to hold on for ten minutes as the two girls were not quite ready yet. David, his mother, and his father had finished their

breakfasts, washed up, and grabbed their bags for work, and University in David's case, then were ready to leave. David was extremely excited for today, being Monday of all days.

Not many students were happy that the weekend had ended to go back to school, university, or work, but after the hard gruelling academic study day they had some entertainment to enjoy and that by chance was the Oxford University Polo training session. The polo sessions should bring some muse, zeal, and team bonding between David and his friends and the energy to give them that phenomenally triumphant feeling. As one could only imagine what it may be like to hit the ball riding on the back of a horse with a long polo stick whilst riding in between two tall metal upright posts. The feeling must be immense, especially knowing how hard it is to try and get a horse to move in a straight line. That alone takes practice, then you need the agility and balance to be able to strike the ball.

The game of polo had taken a lot of determination, endurance, and an awful lot of practice. Lucky the boys at the university had discounted prices for training through their academic year, as you can only but imagine the cost of the horse, the teaching how to ride the horse, the rules of polo, teaching all the tactics, offense, and defence. With so much to learn and an awful amount of time and patience it takes to be taught, the price is a pittance to the time and effort it takes the coaches of the sport. The students at the University were getting a cheap thrill, they could take away for a lifetime. They were getting a sensational amount for their money's worth. This had some Oxford University Polo team players moving on to be World superstars, and many other professional players had come away from the Oxford dedicated team to earn a fair wage. While the boys were waiting for the girls to get ready, they had a lot to focus on and discuss, about the activities after school, they were also still more than likely reminiscing about the Friday evening at the Cinema with the girls. The time was nearing 8:30 am and at long last the girls were ready, just walking out from the entrance of their dormitory.

"Hi boys, we are sorry we took so long, we were waiting for Verity and Eldora," says Samantha.

"Yeah, only because you and Daphne had beat me and Verity to the showers" Grumbled Eldora.

"Anyway, we are here now gents, our apologies" Uttered Daphne. Being gentlemen, they hadn't seemed fazed at all as they were probably used to waiting for their mothers to get ready to go into town with their fathers. So, no doubt they were already equipped with humility and patience when it had come to the expectance of a female's timing in consideration to the perspective of a male getting ready. As the equivalence is far greater than expected. The majority of females take a lot of pride, and joy, in the artistic creativity and passion that they had put into themselves to look glamorous with a touch of female elegance. To be a boy it hadn’t taken them long to notice the exceeding difference it took from waiting for a male friend to a female friend to get ready and in this case, they were impending not one female but four to get ready. The time that it could have consumed could have been inevitable that these girls would’ve been longer than expected. Now they were all dressed, ready to go and meet David by the main entrance of the carpark, and the dropping point for the students who had been dropped in or driven into the University by themselves. Eldora had been reflecting on her academic studies and looking through her written notes from last week’s work throughout the weekend. Like the few dedicated students who may have stayed up late some weekends looking back over some notes or further researching some medical practice for the coming weeks, this enabled the students to become advanced within what they are learning or discover new medicines they had not otherwise known. It highly impressed Professor A. David Smith if his students had made time to gain extra wisdom and knowledge would have shown that they had been prioritizing their time accordingly to learn new things. It made him extremely happy and made him feel that his job was worthwhile. Daphne, Verity, Eldora, Samantha, William, Jasper, and Darius Silva were all waiting at the University's main entrance drop-off point. David's parents had just pulled in through the main gate, and whilst slowly emerging, David's mother had pulled up close by the curb side. David was undoing his seatbelt ready to leave his parents, saying thank you for the lift, and goodbye, David's father had reminded David to grab his backpack from the car boot of the vehicle. "Blimey David you'd lose your head from off your shoulders if it wasn't fastened to your neck": mockingly says David's father. "Shut up Dad, I'll see you and Mother tonight": as David tries to laugh at his mistake and the embarrassment of his father. This had all of David's friends laughing along with David's father. David wasn't highly amused as he appeared to be bashful with red cheeks, it was very unusual for David's father to make fun of David because as a family, as a whole, took life very realistically and seriously. So, for that matter David just had to let that one slide, as he knew it was a one-off from his father's point of view, both his father and mother had always wanted what was in the best interest of David and they had shown that by supporting him with many of the things that he had chosen to do. "Have a good day David, we will pick you up around 4:30 pm". And just like so.... David was safely dropped off at Oxford University by his parents, while happily awaiting his friends by the main entrance. You could see so much zeal throughout the whole friendship of friends after they had spent an amazing weekend at the cinema. Daphne Johnson had an extravagant smirk on her face, almost sustaining the guilty but innocent pleasure that she had hidden underneath her grin, David, having been there that weekend in her dormitory would've known what that grin had meant, he too had a wonderful night with Daphne whilst sleeping next to her in her dorm room.

Fortunately for the two of them, they had to keep it secret for two reasons, one was because they didn't want anyone to know their business, and two, they didn't want to get caught out by the University and then get into some sort of trouble. Daphne Johnson and David Smith were as innocent as two white little turtle doves, that night they had hardly even pecked each other on the beak. Jasper Flynn was happy to be back in Eldora's presence, and likewise with Verity Page and William Macintyre. The whole group of friends had started to pair off nicely, into couples close to relationships while gradually growing closer and closer. Samantha Hutchinson was left feeling rather confused between Darius and Paul Barrera, they were both short but handsome gentlemen. Samantha was a little bit devious. She had always wanted what she had set her eyes on, and from the off, she had liked the look of the Ginger boy, Jasper Flynn, but he was now taken. Knowing Samantha's promiscuous attempts, she would try her utmost hardest to try and persuade Jasper into deep temptation. If Samantha Hutchinson had caused upset to Eldora Jenkins, no doubt the other two girls wouldn't want to be friends with Samantha for doing that. Eldora Jenkin's had put a lot of effort into bringing them all closer together, by looking out for her friends' best interests. It was 8:45 am and they were dawdling along down to their Pharmacology Science block knowing that it would take them roughly fifteen minutes to get to the classroom, and yet another fine day with a slight moisture to the air texture, but clear skies. Although there was a forecast of light spells of rain this afternoon for a short while, then it would blow over, according to the weather reports on BBC Newsround last night in the Oxford Region. Playing polo this afternoon thankfully wouldn't have been affected by rain, even less so slight rain, but possibly a heavy downpour of rain that had caused it to flood would've most certainly affected their days of training, but the boys knew that wasn't going to happen anytime soon. They had hardly had any rain all summer, so with that being said they would've needed an extremely significant amount of rain to cause the playing fields to flood. Besides, playing Polo in the rain was fun. The horses often enjoyed running about in the mud, and boys are built to play in the mud, it had given a chance to separate the 'men from the boys' and an opportunity for those men to impress the young ladies.

With only a few minutes now until A. David Smith would arrive at their pharmaceutical science class, they were all outside confabulating amongst themselves with no real propensity to even want to talk about what may or may not be learned within their Academic class today. Hypothetically, from a speaking point of view, they should've done their homework over the weekend. This led them to divert the conversation to just a nitter-natter between them as it was far less strenuous than talking about something that would bring anxiety before they had even thought about starting the day ahead. Professor A. David Smith had just arrived in the nick of time for the class to be able to start. As he opened the door, "Welcome all, please do come into the classroom and take a seat": mumbled Professor A. David Smith. "Good morning, Sir": Was the answer to many students' responses.

They had carried on waltzing into the classroom with some students rather happier than others, whilst some students had a glum look on their faces. Whether it was the thought of being back at the start of the study week or the fact that they were just welcomed by their teacher or not, goes untold or unknown. They'd be better the devil if we hadn't found out the specific answer to their glum attitude.

Daphne Johnson had chosen to sit between David Smith, Eldora Jenkins, and Jasper Flynn at the back of the classroom, David sat left in the back corner, then Daphne, Eldora, and then Jasper Flynn from left to right in that order. Sitting at the last table to the left-hand side of the back of the classroom facing the front. The group of four were well-mannered, mature, and very dedicated in their study up until now. And after the weekend shenanigans, they had drawn closer which brought the group closer together. Samantha Hutchinson sat between Darius Silva and Paul Barrera on the table in front of them, while William Macintyre and Verity Page had a whole table to themselves opposite David, Eldora, and Jasper Flynn as they were sitting right back at the rear end of the classroom on a spacious table that was supposedly for four, but the two of them had it to themselves.

The students were getting their study accessories out, module books, notepads, pens, rulers, calculators etc.

Professor A. David Smith had wanted his students to quietly reflect on what they had been studying throughout the previous weeks and insisted that if

anyone had any questions they would like to ask before they had gone onto the next medication procedure within the module, to raise a hand and ask any that may have arisen. Professor A. David Smith had allowed them fifteen to twenty minutes to read and reflect on what they had already studied previously before he moved on to the next part of the module and academic reading papers. After they had finished resonating and reflecting on their previous notes and academic modules, Professor A. David Smith had wanted to move on to today's module. Today's pharmaceutical Science papers consisted of: as found in. (Oxford Academic, 2001c)   Today's Objectives:
Through hypoxia-inducible factors (HIF), hypoxic environments facilitate the adaptability and advancement of non-small-cell lung cancer (NSCLC). HIF-1α may control ERβ (oestrogen receptor β) and accelerate NSCLC development. Although its molecular mechanism under hypoxia is unclear, the phytochemical homoharringtonine (HHT) has a substantial inhibitory effect on non-small cell lung cancer.
Techniques:
Cell viability assay, colony formation, flow cytometry, and H460 xenograft models were used

to assess the impact of HHT on NSCLC growth. The underlying mechanisms of HHT-induced growth suppression in NSCLC were investigated using Western blotting, molecular docking, site-directed mutagenesis, immunohistochemistry, and immunofluorescence assays.

Important conclusions
High expression of E2F1 linked to HIF-1α/ERβ signalling promotes tumour development and poor survival. The results in cells with hypoxia, HIF-1α overexpression, ERβ- or E2F1-overexpression, and knockdown cells imply that the HIF-1α/ERβ/E2F1 feedforward loop stimulates the proliferation of NSCLC cells. Through the ubiquitin-proteasome route, HHT inhibits HIF-1α/ERβ/E2F1 signalling, which is reliant on the suppression of HIF-1α and ERβ protein expression. Site-directed mutagenesis and molecular docking demonstrated that HHT binds to the ERβ GLU305 site. In both NSCLC cells and xenograft models, HHT stimulates apoptosis and suppresses colony formation and cell growth.

In conclusion
The HIF-1α/ERβ/E2F1 feedforward loop's development stimulates the growth of NSCLC and

identifies a new molecular mechanism by which HHT causes cell death in NSCLC.

This is their module brochure, which shows an X-ray of a person showing a little growth from NSCLC. The most prevalent kind of lung cancer is non-small cell lung cancer. Your lung tissues are where cancer cells start in this disease. Compared to small cell lung cancer, non-small cell lung cancer grows more slowly, but by the time it is detected, it has frequently migrated to other body parts. In contrast to the opposite side of the skeletal lung chamber, the diagram and visual graphic aren't particularly obvious.
This shows a clear picture of the rib cage with no growth in between it. In contrast, the right side of the rib cage shows a white, cloudy dome-shaped image between the rib cage, which represents the growth from non-small cell lung cancer.

Some of the students by this point may have become overwhelmed by the thought of the importance and privilege of working with medicines and various medical procedures that can decrease or increase cancerous cells throughout the human body, with many other medications that can fight through the core of the membranes and cells

to help fight or protect against various other diseases. To many students, it was a phenomenon! And if it hadn't already made them feel honourable to be learning such academics then we would not be so sure what else could excite their future!
Professor A. David Smith had told his students to revisit this section on the study module material this evening when they got back home or into their dormitory, so the students could reflect on what they have studied throughout the day, as a fair bit of what they have learned from today may come up within their end-of-module examination.
The time now was 11:00 am, Professor A. David Smith's Pharmacology Science Academic study classroom had a two-hour studying session. He was extremely pleased with how his students were progressing week by week, as they seemed to be gaining more knowledge and wisdom: their academic tutor, Professor A. David Smith had walked his students to the front entrance of the classroom and held the main front door open as both a gentleman and lecturer would do, as it had shown the moral principle and utmost respect that he held for his academic students.
The boys were overly excited as they had their polo training session after their lunch break was

over, David, William, Jasper, and Darius, and the rest of the group, Paul, Verity, Eldora, Daphne, and Samantha Hutchinson were going to sit by the sideline to encourage and support the boys. The students were heading to Christchurch for lunch and Daphne, Samantha, Verity, Eldora, William, Jasper, David, Paul, and Darius Silva were all visiting Christchurch together. Christchurch was open all year round for the public, with many functioning rooms available. It holds an Upper library, The Undercroft, The Ante Hall, The Buttery bar, The Cathedral Garden, The masters garden, Tom Quad, and Private dining Mckenna room as cited in.. (Christ Church Oxford University, 2001). The boys who were playing polo this afternoon would've been gasping for a carbohydrate meal if they had any sense of nutrition and the energy absorption that the sport required, even more so as this was their first experience. Horse riding alone was hard work on the legs. You need both agility and stability to be able to ride a horse, it wasn't as easy as it looks, like when you are watching your favourite cowboy movie with Uncle George!
David was going to have a tuna and pasta dish for his lunch with a banana for dessert, William had

spaghetti Bolognese and an apple for dessert, Jasper Flynn had wanted Spaghetti Bolognese after he saw William Macintyre's dish of uniquely designed dressing of Spaghetti Bolognese and Basil on top. Darius Silva wanted pepperoni Pizza and garlic bread, Paul Barrera wanted tomato and basil soup with tiger loaf buttered bread for his lunch, and the gentlemen were fuelling up the correct way for the enduring activity that they were participating in after lunch break. Paul Barrera wasn't participating but no doubt he would be on the sideline supporting the females, Daphne, Verity, Eldora, and Samanatha. At Christchurch College, many students who attended the college were allowed to stay on campus, they received meals daily just for £2.32 and £2.50 as they were all part of the meal plan for those college students who stayed on campus. The students who wanted regular meals had the special benefits of cheaper meals, while the University students had to pay an extra 50 pence charge on top of the bill, but still leaving the cost of a cooked meal relatively cheap. The ladies hadn't yet decided, just as you could imagine, the majority of females were rather indecisive when it came to choosing their lunch or dinner during their break. I strongly believe they were fussing and contemplating about what to eat or what not to eat due to keeping a nice steady figure, while the gentlemen were more like wild boars and gannets. Daphne wanted vegetable soup, and a Granny Smith apple, Samantha Hutchison had grabbed a tuna and cucumber sandwich, Verity wanted Chicken soup, with a bread roll, and Eldora Jenkins had taken a lasagne and a pure orange juice. The girls had all chosen light-calorie snacks, as they knew how to keep their weight down and look slender. It had become all part of the agenda, being a female and it was a clear and stark contrast to the greedy eaters of men. So, if it were a girl they would be counting the calorie intake that they put in their bodies, reading all the ingredients that each food contains. The gentlemen wouldn't be counting the calories but rather they would be counting the amount of food that they can consume in one whole sitting.

All sat down at the Christchurch dining table for lunch together with David sitting opposite Daphne Johnson. Next to David was Jasper Flynn, and opposite Jasper was Eldora Jenkins, next to Jasper was William opposite William was Verity. Then Darius was sitting next to William, next to Darius was Paul, and opposite Darius and Paul was

Samantha. They had adored this place to sit and eat a nice lunch together. Many other students had found it very convenient with the library upstairs, studying, reading with their friends then coming downstairs to eat a meal together. It was the most fascinating place to come and socialize with friends or associates.

Samantha was chatting away with Paul, “You going to come and sit with me on the sideline while we watch the boys at polo training later Mr?”: said Samantha.

Paul replies, “Yes please Samantha, which would make me feel more comfortable as I know you better than the rest of them to be fair”. Bringing Darius into the conversation, Samantha goes on to talk about the excitement of the sport “So, Darius, are you excited and looking forward to your training session this afternoon?”

“Yes Samantha, it is a highly anticipated sport, and this is why I am very anxious but also very excited, both simultaneously,” said Darius.

“Well, me and Paul will be rooting for you on the sideline, we are both happy that the weather is holding out” Exclaimed Samantha.

David is over the table's far side, sitting opposite Daphne. With some deep sensual eye contact and no doubt some flirtatious thoughts drifting through their minds as they gazed back and forth at one another. These two were made head over heels for each other. They have already made strong foundations by spending enumerable time in one another's presence. David was underneath the table with his right foot, rubbing his inner ankle up Daphne's left tibia and fibula. He had Daphne blushing as she sat next to Eldora Jenkins, but as luck would have it, Eldora Jenkins hadn't noticed as she was fixed on her lunch, and so was Jasper Flynn, eating his Spaghetti Bolognese, slurping down the Spaghetti like he was merely flirting by showing off his Spaghetti swirling skills around the fork and the whirling motion of his tongue as he was flirtingly gulping it down towards the muse of Eldora Jenkins. You could see Samantha occasionally eye gazing toward Jasper Flynn, something just hadn't added up. She had the option to two strapping young men, Paul Barrera and Darius Silva. Handsome young men they were, but Samantha Hutchinson had this devious way about her. She was driven by Jasper Flynn's similar hair colour, perhaps with both of them being ginger, and highly intellectual. Before long she would try and get her wicked way with Jasper, given half the chance. I am most certain Eldora Jenkin wouldn't have been happy if she had caught Samantha gazing across the dining hall at Jasper, trying to get his attention. Trying to draw Jasper's attention was little to her promiscuous, convicted, sinful, imaginative muse, you certainly couldn't calculate what Samantha Hutchinson would have planned next to try and leer Jasper Flynn into her trap, and her sensual devious carnal endeavours. You would never know what she could be capable of, but already some of her close relations and friendships had slowly started to grasp her measure.

As Samantha Hutchinson was up to something, like a woman processed. David and William were sitting at the dining table conversing back and forth about the male stigma, why gentlemen feel the need to release their endorphins, and the purpose of males finding a hobby that makes them feel triumphant, the feeling that gives boys/men the buzz, the feel-good factor and a sense of achievement. Both David and William were excited about the anticipated preparation they had while awaiting to start playing the University Polo beginners team, with still so much training to do before they could start playing matches. They were merely starting to learn from scratch and how to ride and control a horse on their first day of training. After they had finished their lunches, they sat for a while conversing back and forth between the group. Like usual they would plan to go gallivanting around the luxurious University Campus Park, to inhale and exhale the open woodland air and endure the pure tranquillity throughout the riverside setting, on a calm spring Sunday afternoon, the River Cherwell flowed through Oxford's Christ Church Meadow. The river for sure will be crowded with passing punts that are rented from Magdalen Bridge a bit later in the year. The tallest of Oxford's medieval towers, the bell tower at Magdalen College, which was started in 1492 and is 144 feet (44 meters) high, can be seen peeking through the trees in the distance. A glasshouse to the University of Oxford Botanic Garden, which is the oldest botanic garden in Great Britain and among the oldest scientific gardens worldwide, is located just below and to the right. One of the main tributaries of the River Thames (or Isis) is the River Cherwell, which is pronounced "Cherwell" in the vicinity of Oxford and "Cherwell" in north Oxfordshire. It originates in Northamptonshire, close to Hellidon, and travels 40 miles (64 km) south through Oxfordshire before joining the Thames (or Isis) at Oxford. Apart from the wonderous views across the waters that flow with the tide or currents of the river, there were acres of woodlands to enjoy. Not forgetting to mention Jimbo's Baguette bar where you would find many other students enjoying their afternoon lunch break or sitting along the riverbed by the pathways on a bench enjoying the fresh breeze, catching up with friends and associates. Many other students just enjoyed the solace place, the views, and the peace that they could find while trying to read a book, it was the perfect place for mindfulness something rather therapeutic about enjoying your favourite novel within the University Park woodland. David, William, Jasper, Paul, Darius, Daphne, Verity, Eldora, and Samatha Hutchinson were enjoying their afternoon casual stroll through the University Park, woodland, down along the winding paths through the trees, up and alongside the river, an idyllic riparian scene. Samantha was acting estranged and out of character holding back on her walk, she was up to something wicked with a mischievous grin, the look on her face. Jasper and David were just ahead of her talking to one another, while she was trying to catch the eye of

Jasper Flynn. She had already located Eldora Jenkins, realizing that she was in deep conversation speaking with Daphne and Verity. Paul Barrera and Darius Silva were on the other side of the girls to the right-hand side chatting away. Samatha Hutchinson had picked up some small pebbles to dash gently at Jasper Flynn to get his attention, she flung a pebble, which had just fallen short from hitting the back of his leg, rolling underneath the small of his right foot. She clenched hold of another pebble and dashed it a little harder than the last throw, this pebble had struck him on his right shoulder, Jasper Flynn had flinched in astonishment but was surprised to see that it was Samantha Hutchinson standing there with a smirk on her face, giggling under her breath. Jasper Flynn knew she was flirting with him, but he also knew that he couldn't entertain Samantha as he was technically spoken for by Eldora Jenkins. Eldora would be devastated if Jasper was to entertain Samantha, it was like Samantha was trying to embark on Eldora's Territory, her property. But the promiscuous girl had no fear of the thought of the upset it could cause. Jasper Flynn smirked back at Samantha, likely leading her to believe she was weakening the young gentleman's knees and indeed turning his head. In reality, Jasper Flynn was trying to remain calm, by shrugging it off so he didn't want to get caught out by any of his friends or draw attention to the situation that was unfolding. After they had finished their lunch break, they were going to catch the bus to Kirtlington as the Oxford University Polo team had their training there during the season and sometimes elsewhere off-season, Kirtlington was around nine miles distance apart from Oxford University, but it was home to the Oxford University polo team. I think Jasper Flynn will be overwhelmed to be out of harm's way from Samantha and to be practising Polo with the boys. If he had spent any more time around Samantha, it wouldn’t have been long until Eldora had been in eye or earshot of her trying to flirt with Jasper, it was in his best interest to be apart only with the company of the boys. Later that afternoon they were all going to Kirtlington by bus, the students had a free local bus pass as it had become part of the university curriculum to support the students, welfare, and well-being. It was governed by Oxford’s local council. All students could apply for the bus pass form which was held in the University's main office. Daphne, Verity, William, and David were enjoying the blissful and peaceful walk on the tranquil terrace alongside the river Cherwell and along the embankment, they walked, side by side, David with Daphne and William with Verity swaying the hands together as they walked two by two holding hands. Eldora Jenkins was walking behind them out of sync, Jasper Flynn was drifting back with Darius and Paul Barrera trying to avoid any miscommunication and any flirtatious behaviour with Samantha Hutchinson- he had needed to keep a wide berth. If Jasper Flynn wasn't such an introvert, he could've kindly told Samantha that he wasn't interested. But knowing Samantha's flirtatious nature it hadn't seemed like much would phase her, knowing already that Eldora Jenkins was enamoured with him. Samantha Hutchinson would go to any measure to try and get her wicked way with Jasper Flynn, it would only take a matter of time before she seductively confronted him when he was at least expecting it, tantalizing and tempting him, perhaps at someone's birthday party or a university awards ceremony. A celebration was always the best time to catch anyone unawares and getting away with acting a little out of character, as it was more likely to go unnoticed when everyone's morale was triumphant, and spirits were high. Daphne, Verity, David, and William were still walking along the riverbank, Daphne noticed two serene white birds swimming amid the river Cherwell. As the graceful creatures had meandered along the river Daphne had reached out for Verity's attention 'Look, look! two large white swans, how cute are they?": declared Daphne. 'Arrrgggh how lovely Daphne they are two beautiful swans': says Verity. Ironic isn't it- the difference between a male and a female, two ladies see a cute animal and it's almost like they purr, how cute is that? Whereas a male would spot two white swans and likely find it interesting but would do more than research and see where the species originated from, rather than just give it the awe factor. To be reasonably honest with you, David and William were both gentlemen who were just content to be in the presence of the two ladies, who were extremely pleasing to the eye, and alluring specimens which were Daphne and Verity, they were stunningly beautiful.

David had found some in-depth Scientific classifications about the species of swans as cited in. (Tikkanen Amy, 2001) it was a cunning idea to bring a conversation about the two swimming swans that the girls had thought were amazingly cute. The swan is the largest species of waterfowl in the Anserinae subfamily of the Anatidae family (order Anseriformes). The genus Cygnus includes the majority of swans. Swans are big-footed, heavy-bodied, graceful birds with long necks that fly with their necks outstretched and slow wingbeats. They swim magnificently. No other waterfowl travels as quickly on the water or in the air as they do, and they migrate at enormous heights in diagonal or V-formation. Swans forage for aquatic plants in shallow waters by dabbling rather than diving. The black (C. atratus) and mute (C. olor) swans frequently tuck one foot over the back when swimming or standing. Swan males, known as cobs, and females, known as pens, have similar appearances. Contrary to popular belief, swans can create a wide range of noises through their windpipe, which in certain species is looped inside their breastbone (as in cranes). Even the mute swan, which is the least talkative of the species, frequently hisses, snores softly, or groans harshly. With the exception of breeding season, swans are gregarious. They are lifelong partners. Mutual bill dipping or head-to-head posture are part of courtship. A half-dozen pale, unmarked eggs are typically incubated in the pen on a pile of vegetation as the cob stands watch; in certain species, he alternates between broodings. Swans, like geese, produce a triumph note after warding off an assailant. The young, known as cygnets, are short-necked and heavily weighted when they hatch. Although they may run and swim a few hours later, they require constant care for several months, and in certain species, they may even ride around on their mother's back. For at least two years, immature birds have brown or grey, mottled plumage. Swans may live for 20 years after maturing in their third or fourth year. Swans are uncommon in the tropics and are typically found in temperate climates. The Northern Hemisphere is home to four (or five) species, whereas Australia is home to one, New Zealand and the Chatham Islands are home to one extinct species, and southern South America is home to one. Tropical Asia, Central America, northern South America, and all of Africa are devoid of them. The mute swan is one species that has been brought to Australia, New Zealand, and North America.

The two white swans that Daphne and Verity spotted from the Botanic Gardens, of Oxford University overlooking the River Cherwell. The

Botanic Garden wasn't just a pleasant place for these University students to visit on a lunch break, it also had many tourists from Primary schools, high schools, visitors, and the general public. They had been decades without spending money on new glasshouses at the Botanic Garden, a Visitor and Learning Centre at the Arboretum, or physical infrastructure. Many people visit the botanic garden to spend the day navigating the plants as they come in extraordinary colours, shapes, and sizes, the more and more we get to know and understand our plants the more we realize how much we need them, our insects thrive and survive off nectar and pollen. We use many plants for medicines, cures and energy sources. A nice outlaid garden can be so refreshing for the mind, the open place, and the smell of the scents from the flora, which gives your mind that feeling of complete tranquillity, a place of solace and healing. And a place free to roam away from anxiety, worry, and distress, and most certainly a wonderous place for students to explore and witness some natural habitat. Eldora Jenkins while she was oblivious to what had been going on, Samantha Hutchinson and her crazy antics. No doubt, Eldora being so innocent, and brought up with morals and respect she wouldn't even have thought someone like Samantha would try to impose onto the gentleman that she was attracted to. That being Jasper Flynn. Eldora had enjoyed her walk throughout the University Park and the Botanic Garden, as she was enjoying the colourful view from the Botanic Garden, she had finally come to her senses to catch up with Jasper Flynn. Like most new friends or couples sometimes, a short time apart makes the heart grow fonder. Why it is lovely to have someone in your presence to take away the boredom? Some friends or couples also like some self-time to recuperate or re-evaluate life's trials and tribulations. While others like time to think about their life goals and aspirations, for this can take some careful thought. We can most certainly get that measure from Eldora Jenkins, she is the most dedicated woman and student that you could ever come across, even more so being autistic. Anyhow, Jasper Flynn was happily in Eldora's presence whilst they were enjoying looking at the variety of plants that the Botanic Garden had to offer. The gardens had awe-inspiring flora and panoramic views that overlooked the River Cherwell. The majestic view of the two swimming swans going up the stream of the river had put the icing on the cake. It was like the two swans had set an example of encouragement for the young couples to flock together. It was rather romantically engaging to watch the two swans swim together like they were Torvill and Dean. David and Daphne sought to find some privacy; they had found a nice picnic bench which was allocated underneath a hornbeam tree.

You could see by the stature of the tree, rather tall an upright with branches that had always seemed to branch out far and wide as its width vert almost the same as its height underneath a camouflage of evergreen leaves. To find a couple sitting underneath a tree, gave off a privacy hideaway. It was almost like it was a notice to other humans, people walking by, or onlookers that they had come here for some peace and privacy, David was holding Daphne's hand, these two were complimentary to each other, they both suited one another, David wasn't punching above his weight, and Daphne as elegant and beautiful as she wasn't punching above her weight and most certainly not punching below either as David Smith was a handsome strapping young gentleman. David had come from a well-kept family, he was fed well and worked hard in his mother and father's family-run business the local pharmacy in Oxford. Daphne Johnson's family and upbringing had many similarities to David Smith's family, as Daphne Johnson's family had worked in the medical field, at the local medical centre in the Royal Borough Kensington and Chelsea. It was evident that these two were made for each other. Like many couples today, would you say it was amicable and reciprocated? Do they share the same hobbies and interests as one another? This was something evolving, an infinite attraction! When you find that one person who shares the same knowledge and interests as you do and then firmly keeps hold of it! It's an ideal marriage mate, business partner, and best friend! You could see by the glimmer betwixt David and Daphne's eyes as they gazed back and forth at one another they had deep feelings of fondness and adoration; they were sitting close together on a wooden Jack 'n' Jill bench. They were growing closer and more amorous from the time before back in Daphne's room in the girl's dormitory. Daphne would kiss David's cheek, and snuggle her face close to David's right shoulder, as they reminisced amid the squealing, and squeaking of the birds. Many other animal species were frolicking around the university grounds such as hares, dears, and stoats, and throughout the University grounds such as the University Park, woodland, and the Botanic gardens. Various bird species have been spotted, such as wetland birds, mallards, coots and moorhens, robins, and bluetits. It was difficult to note what kind of bird was squeaking or whistling as you can imagine without knowing or seeing the bird or recognising the sound. Then magnifying it to its species was an art on its own. As Daphne and David were enjoying the solace place amid the botanic garden on the Jack and Jill bench, listening to the birds' squeak and whisper, while they were both tilting their heads back to look toward the sky to see if they could spot any specific species of birds at all. Daphne was the first to spot a robin from across one of the tree branches that it had just flown off from into the open, the nicely coloured Robin, had an orange/red chest, with a light brown back and white bottom half from the lower abdomen down. You'd often spot a robin in a woodland area or back garden perhaps as they were a quite common bird to see either when you're out walking about or hanging the washing out to dry in your back garden, and many times when you had least expected it. You'd often attach the species of a robin to romance; you buy a

Valentine's card or a Christmas card to your loved one and quite often you would find an illustration of a robin. It where quite significant that David and Daphne had spotted a robin in the middle of some romance and sat there like two love birds themselves. Any moment that the two students could find some alone time would be some moments to cherish while at university around study time, being with other academic friends and associates it was hard time find the time. So, they'd best enjoy the opportunity when they could. David, William, Jasper, and Darius Silva all had Polo training shortly after they had enjoyed their brisk walk around the University Park and the Botanic Garden. They were then heading to the bus stop to catch a bus a few miles down the road. For some bizarre reason, the gentlemen had forgotten to ask when they paid the Polo receptionist the fees to train. And to whether Oxford University had enabled their own sports minibus down up to Kirtlington which was around nine miles in distance away from Oxford University. For now, they were going to have to catch the public transport bus into Kirtlington and ask the Oxford team Polo coaches if they ran a university private service, which we can only assume they would, as it would remain beneficial for the team to have their own transport. The time

was getting closer to 2:30 pm, they had to catch the bus at 2:45 pm as the Polo team training had started at 4 pm. With a few bus stops along the way from Oxford University, and it being 9 miles in distance and several stops, the bus took 35 minutes stopping at bus 24, Oxford Court, departing from Keble Road- St Margarets Rd East-Lathubury Road East- Summertown Shops (Stop A)- Squitchey Lane east- Harefields- Five Mile Drive- Jordan Hill- Oxford Parkway Railway Station (Stop E)
Bicester Road (N-bound) – Bramley Close- Oxford Road (NW-bound)- The Bell- Hampton Gay Turn=Lenthal-Blacks Head Inn-Gossway Fields, The Mount- Oxford Arms.
Daphne and David had noticed the time, so they went to meet up with Jasper, Eldora, William, Verity, Samantha Hutchinson, Darius Silva, and Paul Barrera who as luck had it hadn't gone too far ahead within the botanic gardens and were roaming around aimlessly, not finding what they were looking for. In such a beautiful garden with plenty of sights to enjoy and great company, no doubt they had already had just what they needed, good company, and a great solace place to enjoy the fresh, green, and clean air. Daphne and David had spotted the group of others, David spotted William at a distance, and as they got closer, they

analysed the time and thought it was best to start to head towards the front entrance bus stop. The Polo team training would be starting at 4 pm with the bus arriving at 2:45 pm and the bus ride taking 35 minutes to get there in Kirtlington which would make it 3:20 pm when they arrived, they were cutting it fine but at least they'd arrive just in the nick of time. It is far better to arrive on time than not at all.

The bus was slowly emerging towards the bus stop, you could hear that the bus driver had enabled his air brakes as the noise had ousted from underneath the carriageway of the bus making a whirling sound. The bus got closer and closer as it pulled up closely to the curb side. The driver spotted Jasper Flynn and William Mcintyre's rather extraordinarily over-extended hand signal, which looked extremely peculiar as they waved the bus driver down. The bus driver always knows his day-to-day bus route, and which stop he has on the route, so to the driver it was very evident that he would take note of each bus stop, and then scan across to see if any people were sitting or waiting either in the seated area or even with their backs to the road. Bus drivers are supposed to stop as they have to take on passengers although this is not always the case. It looked an overwhelming sight for the bus driver to see two rather eager students

with outstretched arms, you could tell they were either excited or in a rush to get out of town.
David, William, Jasper, and Darius were extremely excited to start their hobby this afternoon.
The bus driver opened the sliding doors to let his passengers on-board his bus. The bus driver was sitting behind a plexiglass screen, to protect himself from theft, violence, and to some extent to protect himself from any viruses the passengers may have brought onto the bus. Throughout the course of the day, there would've been many, if not hundreds of passengers getting on board the bus whether they were heading into Oxford City or just the next bus stop. The driver was picking people up from each location.
They had all entered the bus, Daphne, Verity, Samantha, Eldora Jenkins, William, Jasper, Paul, Darius Silva, and David Smith in that precise order, they gave their university student bus passes to the driver, pressing them over the touch screen. That was the nine of them on the bus with four more other passengers, one old lady, and two middle-aged people who appeared to be a mother and father to their little daughter who was in a pushchair. It had come to the driver's attention that he could've lowered his ramps to let the pushchair on, but already with great ease, the father had lifted it himself onto the ledge of the bus. To be honest

with you not knowing the mother and father's circumstances, their baby daughter had only looked around two years of age, either of them could have prepared to enter the bus by taking her out of the pushchair. They may or may not have been running late for the bus so we cannot assume they should've already been prepared. The bus driver was patient.

To be a bus driver, you need compassion, empathy, humility, and a lot of patience in dealing with customers daily.

Everyone is now aboard the bus. The old lady sitting on the driver's side, the right-hand side, third row from the front. The mother and father sat right at the front to the left of the bus, which had an open space for wheelchairs and pushchair access.

The new polo team players took the back seat from left to right. David, Jasper, William, and Darius Silva were seated next to one another at the back, in front of them was Paul Barrera and Samantha Hutchinson seated to the right-hand side, Daphne, and Eldora were seated to the right-hand side, in front of them two rows in front from the back of the right-hand side was Verity Page by herself. Well, she wasn't left by herself, as everyone was seated relatively close to each other, in earshot. She wasn't out of sight, or about to be left out of an interesting conversation either. The bus had taken around thirty-five minutes to travel the nine miles from Oxford University, stopping for at least ten stops along the way.

David, William, Jasper, and Darius Silva's first objective, when they reached the other side, was to ask the receptionist or the polo team coach if they had provided or allocated a team transport minibus for picking up the players from the University itself. They had needed to speak to either the receptionist- Hector or the Oxford team coach- Cameron Walton Master about this query. Still on the bus journey, with four more stops still to go. The girls had made their very own entertainment and were singing along to a smash hit from 2000, (Santana Carlos, 2001) Samantha Hutchinson, Eldora Jenkins, Verity Page, and Daphne Johnson, the beautiful girls hitting all the high notes along the way on the bus journey, a vibrant nuance had bellowed from the girl's vocal chords, oh, Maria, Maria, she reminds me of a west side story. Growing up in Spanish Harlem, she's living just like a movie star. Maria, Maria (Maria), she, fell in love in East L.A.

The song was written by Wyclef Jean, Jerry Wonda, and Carlos Santana, and released on, September 14, 1999. It had brought a sudden muse to their eudemonia; and had even brought a smile of joy to the boys' faces whilst they listened to the girl's beautiful, elegant singing voices as they sang along. The bus driver was just getting ready to make a manoeuvre, as the driver of a large red bus full of passengers, he had some careful, patient skills. Not just having the ability to be able to drive the vehicle but also have a lot of love and empathy for carrying customers all day long on your 9-5 with travels from drop-to-drop, pulling up at each bus stop slowly, slowly as the bus driver edges in closely to the kerbside pulling on the air brakes to gradually slow his big red bus down. As the bus came to a halt, he would slide his big red buses sliding doors open at the bus stop to let his customers off.

They arrive safely at the Kirtlington bus stop, Daphne, Verity, Eldora and Samantha get off the bus first, then David, Darius, Paul Barrera, Jasper Flynn, and William Macintyre get off the bus second, as they get off the bus David & Jasper Flynn say to the driver of the big red bus "Cheers driver, have a good day".

As per the bus rota, they had arrived in Kirtlington at 3:20 pm, or as near as dammit. This had given them ten minutes to get to the Kirtlington Polo playing field. The Oxford University Polo team training wouldn't start until 3:30 pm and no doubt the receptionist Hector and coach Cameron Walton

Master would be expecting them to turn up at some point anyway. The walk from the bus stop to the Kirtlington playing field was about five minutes. En route to the polo team training ground, you could see the energetic, gracious smile that the boys had on their faces, they were so pleased to be partaking in such a privileged sport that was formally known to have been played by Kings of the Country!
The boys turn up to the Kirtlington Polo playing field and walk right into the main entrance from the recreational ground, "Hi chaps, you ready for today's session?" the voice from the receptionist Hector... David's response: "Yes, we spoke with you a while ago about today's first-day training session for complete novices"
"OOOOh right yes, I think I remember you young men, go down to the bottom right-hand side of the hall and get changed into your training clothes. Then your coach Cameron Walton Master, will be in to see you." Said Hector the receptionist.
"That's superb, thank you Hector, we will all head down there now, mmm actually Hector where can the girls, Daphne, Verity, Eldora, Samantha, and Paul go, can they come and support us as they wanted to come for encouragement?" Exclaimed David.

"Yes, of course, they can go out through the back sliding doors onto the field, they will see the spectating area and see you as you come out of the changing room. They can get refreshments from either inside our cafeteria or at the tea & coffee bar outside." Explains Hector. "Thanks again Hector," said David. David, William, Darius, and Jasper Flynn Walk down the corridor to the changing rooms, while Daphne, Verity, Paul Barrera, Samantha, and Eldora Jenkins Walk out through the sliding doors and onto the recreational grounds. The temperature is gradually getting a very mild chill within the air, it was about 14 degrees C which isn't bad at all, but enough to notice that the winter wasn't far in the future. Cameron Walton Master had caught up with the boys in the changing room while they were getting into some comfortable training attire to wear throughout their polo training session. Contained in Cameron Master's hand were some red and yellow team bibs, two red and two yellow bibs. He had wanted the group of four boys to start working in a small separate group.
It would help them all to work in small teams, to analyse the performance of each player, and see who worked better with the other player and vice versa. It would then give Cameron a chance to alternate the players to see the strengths and

weaknesses of each player and who worked better with whom. Coach Cameron Master was planning the teams of two red and two yellow, David and William in red bibs while Darius Silva and Jaspe Flynn in yellow, the coach was saying that they were merely riding the horse today, as the main goal was to get to know your horse before you can start to run. He then went on to say about some of the drills that they will discover today, holding the reins of the horse, walking by the side of it gently around the field.

This gives each rider the chance to know their horse, and how the horse reacts with each rider, by walking around the field in both directions.

By the end of the session, they would've taken a little stroll on the back of the saddle, but as beginners, today they'd only be learning to walk. As the weeks progress, they would then learn to be able to trot, canter, and gallop as they grow in confidence with the horse. Getting to know your horse was a fine thing, but another thing was growing in confidence. Last, but not least was having the agility, ability, and balance to be able to start swinging a mallet and hitting a ball with it whilst on the back of the horse, another fine thing. To fully master the skill, it would take a lot of practice to develop competence within the sport, these boys were rather adamant about getting the training underway. Coach Cameron Masters took the boys with him to the horse's stables to go collect their horses. He wanted them to work in groups of two so he could easily keep an eye on them. First, he wanted the red bibs, David and William to go up with him to collect the two medium-sized thoroughbred horses, that they had to use for polo, as they have the agility and speed over all the other horse breeds. Already these horses would've been fine-tuned horses, very tame and well-trained in and around many other riders mounting them in previous months, and over the years.

The very first step was getting to know your horse, and after they had got to know the horse, the next step would be choosing the right riding gear to wear. A helmet, boots, gloves, and a pair of close-fitting trousers. This was so the trousers would not catch onto the horse or cause friction burns on your legs while riding. Coach Cameron Master had called the red bibs; David Smith and William Macintyre to collect their horse by the reins and then start to walk around the Kirtlington polo field clockwise, all the while walking in front and pulling the reins slightly in front, outstretched to the right as they gently pulled on the rien and ensuring that they hadn't tugged at it. From sitting on the saddle to walking, you applied different motions of action. While walking with the horse you would only apply pressure by pulling the reins, whereas sitting on the horse you could pull the reins and apply pressure with your legs to move a lazy horse. David and William had started moving with their thoroughbred horse, by the reins as they had started to walk clockwise around the perimeter of the polo field. You could hear William speaking with his horse, “c’mon boy that’s a good boy” he was merely signalling to his horse with human gratitude. You may or may not have wondered if a horse could even understand human language, or if not, what language was it they understood? It was hard to tell the horse's emotions from his long face and extra-long elongated jawline if the horse was even happily smiling or not. One thing for certain is that the horse is happy to be out from its stable and able to move about from a small, contained space into the open.

They were told by the coach to walk five laps around the field and then switch over with the yellow bibs, which were Darius Silva and Jaser Flynn. It was important to note that Coach Cameron Master had the best interest of the horse and the trainee's welfare and well-being at heart, taking his time to teach them step by step in a safe and timely manner.

One thing was getting to know your horse, the next thing was sitting and riding on a saddle.
Most of today's session was getting to know their horse, and how it feels moving in each direction. Coach Cameron Master was also telling his students to visualize sitting on the horse if you wanted to move your horse to the right you would shorten the right side of the rein to pull his head toward that direction and slowly kick both feet together inwards if needed. After doing five laps each, the red and yellow bibs clockwise, they then alternated back to the red bibs. They were to walk the thoroughbred horses by the reins to the left side around the perimeter of the polo field, anticlockwise. While walking out in front of the horse slightly to the left with the reins pulled. Engaging with vibrant animal talk had been the norm in trying to encourage his horse like you would a young son or daughter. As the horse moved, you would be encouraging the horse by saying, c'mon boy or girl, or 'well done' in an awe-inspiring tone of voice. It had sounded far better to be vibrantly happy with your horse than become angered by your horse, as this wouldn't be acceptable to the welfare and wellbeing of yourself or your horse.
After David and William, both red bibs had walked anticlockwise with their horse, Cameron

Master, the Coach had told them to walk the horse back to the stables, then come back to support and encourage Darius and Jasper Flynn as they had their turn to walk anticlockwise with the horse in their yellow bibs.   En route Jasper Flynn, with his dark brown thoroughbred horse, was walking anticlockwise. You could hear him speaking to his horse gently, "Here boy, walk this way", it was important to be gentle and friendly with your horse, this gives a kind signal to the horse but also lets the animal know that you, as a human friend were friendly and gentle. At the end of this session of getting to know their horse and how to make the horse change direction, Coach Cameron Master was going to help them choose the right saddle to fit each rider and horse comfortably. This was a highly important part of the equipment.   They had to make sure the saddle would sit comfortably within side their inner thighs without chafing too much otherwise this could cause friction burns. Coach Cameron Masters offered each of the rider's saddles onto one of the horses, he held the reins of the horse, so it stabilized as they each climbed onto the horse inside the stables, this was to make sure they had hand-picked the correct saddle that suited them best. The coach best advised the boys to get some horse-riding boots and told them that they

had some spare in the lost property if they hadn't been able to afford new ones.
After they had tried the horse saddles on, they had to measure the horse for a saddle and place the saddle over each horse they had wanted to ride. By placing the saddle over the horse's withers and then sliding it back until it was in its natural position. They then measure the horse's body at a specific point behind the saddle's pommel.
After they had fitted the saddles, the boys had finished for the day, so then David, William, Jasper, and Darius Silva headed towards the changing rooms, to get showered and changed. They were all overwhelmed with all they had learned today; and had commended their coach Cameron Masters for his excellence in training advice and guidance.
Into the locker room, the boys were all hyped up with the joy that polo training had given them. David was getting undressed, polo shirt off, riding trousers off, boots off, socks off, and all of a sudden was left feeling rather perturbed. A squeeze to the left buttock's cheek. As he looked behind him, the ginger smiley face of Jasper Flynn appeared, being extraordinarily courageous.
"What was that for?" : squeamishly says David
"Well David, I had the perfect opportunity to squeeze your tight buttocks, and I thought we were

close friends so, we could have fun couldn't we? : Replied Jasper Flynn
"That makes you a pan-sexual in my book Jasper, I thought you liked girls, Eldora Jenkins, ring any bells?" : outrageously said,
David.
"Well, I guess that does make me pans, doesn't it? But there is no need to get shirty with me, sounding all angry with me." Exclaims Jasper
"Sorry mate, I guess I am just into Daphne Johnson and that is my gender of affection I am afraid" Explains David.
Onlookers Darius and William hadn't seen the bum squeeze, but they had now overheard all the commotion, which had led William to go on and say: "This has just got weird in here boys, please sort out your differences and get back to normal".
Darius says: "Yeah imagine what the girls would say, Eldora and Daphne, don't be so weird"
"It's certainly not me lads, it's him, Jasper": replies David.
"Yeah, big deal it was me, I messed up, not such a great joke huh?" Said Jasper.
"Just shake hands and forget about its boys, get changed, and let us move on," says Darius and William. That was certainly not a great feeling for David's mental health and well-being when a friend of the same sex gropes you so unexpectedly.

No wonder David was left feeling perturbed, disorientated at the grope that it appeared Jasper was eagerly awaiting to give him.
Whether he was pansexual or not, it wasn't at all fair or relevant behaviour. Looking at the time it was 4:50 pm, and the next bus was coming in at around 5:25 pm. All the boys were changed and ready to leave, walking back through the corridor to the main entrance was the reception area where Hector the receptionist stood. William had asked him for a future training session, and about transport to and from the University to Kirtlington's training ground. Hector said "Of course, I must have forgotten to tell you before, that we have a couple of minibuses running from here to the University"
"That's awesome, thankyou Hector, please book us four in for next week": Said William,
"Of course, I'll put you in for pick up in our diary, see you next week chaps and take care": Exclaimed Hector.
"Brilliant see you next week, bye Hector,": Said William.
David, Jasper, and Darius had already walked out the main entrance door to meet the others out the front, Daphne, Eldora, Verity, Samantha, and Paul Barrera had seemed fairly impressed by supporting the boys on their first day's training

session.
It is always encouraging to have some friends around to support you while you are playing your new hobby or interest, as it gives moral support and encouragement.
Daphne, Eldora, Verity, and Samantha congratulated the boys as they walked out from the front entrance: "Well done boys." Paul Barrera smiled and patted the boys on the back to congratulate them. Paul Barrera hadn't felt left out by not playing polo with the other boys as he wasn't remotely interested. He was happy to be sitting amongst the girls showing his moral support. I mean who wouldn't in their right mind want to be sitting amid these beautiful ladies?
William had just walked out of the main entrance front door and from speaking to the receptionist, Hector. With some insightful news for them for next week's training session, with no more public transport. William has just pre-booked them in for the private Oxford University team polo minibus, to pick them up from Oxford University, and then down to the Kirtlington recreational ground. The time was 5:10 pm and they had only had fifteen minutes to walk to the bus stop, David noticed the time and told them they had better start walking to the bus stop so they wouldn't miss the bus back to

the University campus. David's parents were picking him up this evening at the University by 6:15 pm as they knew he had a polo team training session that evening.
I think David was eager to get home this evening after feeling rather disturbed by his supposedly good friend Jasper Flynn and his strange antics of grabbing his bare buttocks. I mean, in this instant how can you gauge the immoral sense of it potentially being a sexual insult, from a man's perspective of fancying or liking what he sees and grabbing hold of it? I mean being the man who had his buttocks grabbed, David. Who could he turn to without being extremely embarrassed? After all, it was his close friend Jasper Flynn and as awkward as it had been, he surely should have just shrugged it off and in time forgot about it rather than escalate the matter into something dramatic. Needless to say, not that I believe all sexual matters shouldn't be reported, but in this case, it may be worth speaking to an elder such as your parents if it leaves you feeling extremely inadequate. But as it is your close friend you should be able to settle it, between you before it turns into such a fracas when it may have not been necessary. Sometimes it is best to settle your differences with close acquaintances in the first instance, after all, Jasper Flynn and David Smith

were like two best friends. It was 5:24 and in the mist in the distance by the bus stop you could see a blurry red bus incoming, and just in time, as the temperature had started to drop into the early autumnal evening. The bitterness in the cold had started to crawl up their arms and legs, and their hairs had started to electrify on end and heighten their senses of numbness even further. The red Bus was nearing closer and closer, signposted across the front of it, 'The Kirtlington bus, Via Oxford University'.

The bus driver had scanned across the bus stop and had noticed pedestrians sitting and waiting for his bus service, he then switched on his left indicator to indicate to the vehicle driving behind that he was about to turn inward towards the kerbside at the bus stop, to drop off and pick up passengers from his bus route. He gradually came to a halt, pressing gently on the air brakes. Four passengers got off from the stop at Kirtlington before David, William, Paul, Darius, Jasper, Verity, Eldora, Samantha, and Daphne could get onto the bus. After the four other passengers had left the bus, the friends had got on, scanning the bus passes over the scanner, one by one as they entered the bus headed to Oxford University. David was eager to sit next to Daphne and away from the others, as I think he may still have been left feeling a little fragile. Disturbed by what had happened in the boys' changing room, the immoral behaviour of Jasper had affected him. I even think Jasper Flynn was slightly confused, it's his best mate and he was truly involved with Eldora Jenkins. Sometimes a chemical imbalance or confusion can mask the happiness from within thinking the same sex and opposite sex can at times become attractive, hence why they had now adopted this sexual agenda as a pansexual. Nevertheless, Jasper Flynn wouldn't have wanted to lose his best mate and in time would strongly apologize and make it up to David for his frantic actions earlier today. David had it his way with Daphne and she came and sat in the middle of the right-hand side of the bus, just them two. He snuggled in close with her like he was still scared, shocked, or just trying to shrug it all off. Daphne was happy with the attention, and just gathered David was exhausted from a long day and hard training session perhaps. Jasper Flynn sat near the back with Eldora Jenkins, William, and Verity. Samantha Hutchinson sat between Paul Barrera and Darius Silva right in the back row from the main entrance of the bus. Sometimes Jasper Flynn's excitement and emotions make him a little overwhelmed at times with him having ADHD and he sometimes just goes and does things out of the ordinary, right out of the blue. Jasper Flynn was happily conversing back and forth with Eldora Jenkins; he hadn't seemed at all fazed by what happened earlier and seemed very happy to be in the presence of Eldora's company. These two were chatting to each other, more than likely about their study week and what they had planned for the weekend. Paul Barrera and Darius Silva had the pleasure of being in Samantha Hutchinson's company who was acting extremely flirtatiously with the two gentlemen and speaking of romance with both boys, asking them who was their last romantic kiss. Was it a kiss on the lips, the cheek, or with tongues? She pulled her shoulders back, so they became broad. Her blouse was undone from the top button, which spread wide her breasts. Samantha then grabbed hold of Darius Silva's left hand as he was sitting to the right of Samantha, "give me your hand Darius, close your eyes and open the palm of your hand": teasingly said Samantha, with that enticing comment Samantha, Darius open his hand. "Okay then," said Darius. Samantha then drew his hand close to her chest and firmly pressed Darius's hand on her breast. "How does that feel"? erotically breathes Samantha. "Nice and soft": was Darius' response. "OK Darius, open your eyes," said Samantha. Darius opened his eyes to not a great deal left to his imagination. He thought what he had felt was right when he had his eyes closed, but to his amazement, Samantha pulled him in by the back of his neck for a snog on the back of the bus, in full view of Paul Barrera who was just sitting opposite. Paul was more than likely mischievously getting aroused as an onlooker watching his close mate getting some boy-to-girl action. The redhead truly was a promiscuous girl. One moment she had leapt for Jasper Flynn, trying to snatch him from underneath Eldora Jenkins' own eyes, now it was Darius.

We could see from the first day, when the redhead entered the pharmaceutical science classroom, that this girl (Samantha) would bring torture and torment to the boys. She had an indecisive act that she had tended to play very well for attention, and this time, this moment it was Darius Silva in for a treat. We can only believe it was moments like these that Darius was longing for.

Darius was a young half-Brazilian undergraduate student who had spent days/months/years with his eyes solely focused on the purpose of academia, and very little time for fun this kiss had just come to his excitement, of course, he was overwhelmed with joy. It had become a hopelessly good distraction for Samantha to draw her attention to either Darius Silva or Paul Barrera. For the time being, at least. Darius Silva and Paul Barrera were both single, but Jasper Flynn wasn't, why she's bothering either of the two boys? She is leaving the other boys alone because they were spoken for either by Daphne Johnson, Eldora Jenkins, or Verity Page. But, like a lot of people, they hate to settle for what is easy and convenient and usually want what they cannot have. Even though, as we have witnessed previously, If Samantha is eager and willing, not much will get in the way of the promiscuous redhead.

On the other side of the bus were William Macintyre and Verity Page. William had his hands spread up the back of Verity Page's cranium stroking her long soft blonde hair. William was a gentleman; Verity Page adored her young man William, and she had her hand on his lap. Verity was conversing with William "Do you know what William? I cannot wait to get some alone time with just me and you": whispered Verity gently.

"Yeah me too sweetheart, a nice romantic walk perhaps along the Cherwell riverside just me and you" agreeing spoke William,

"Yes that would be a fine thing, William, let us do it together one lunch break out the way of everyone, just me and you" : Said Verity

"Yeah, that could work, or even after a Uni class, there might be fewer students hanging about also," said William.
"Lovely idea, William, let's plan it this week to give us something to look forward to," joyfully says Verity.
Both David and Daphne had realised they were nearing their stop, coming down Oxford University's main road. David signalled the red stop button on the upright pole that is located at the end of each bus seat. The red button sends a stop signal to the bus driver; then, the bus driver hears a bell. With the sound of the bell, the bus driver would then be ready to stop his bus at the nearest bus stop. The bus driver steps on his air brakes. The students, David, Jasper, William, Darius, Paul, and the girls, Daphne, Verity, Eldora, and Samantha, start to collect their belongings as they make their way to the front entrance of the big red bus, with the bus coming in at the bus stop at 5:25 pm in Kirtlington then taking thirty-five minutes to get back to the Oxford's University the time drew nearer to 6 O'clock, 5:55 pm to be precise.
The Autumn evening chill was in the air as they stepped off the big red bus, "Thanks, driver," murmured a few of the students, David, William, and Jasper, as they got off.
Verity's arms came up with goosebumps, as she

took her foot off the bus and onto the main road footpath, a sudden gush of traffic wind blasted across the street. As with many main roads, traffic can build up, causing a whirl of wind as the motion of cars builds up. This brings a feeling of decreased temperature throughout the air, having 10 degrees Celsius feel more like 6' Celsius.
William offers Verity his suit blazer and wraps it around her shoulders to cover her arms, with that, he wraps his arms tenaciously around her to keep her enclosed with warmth. These young adults/late teenagers have so much inspiring adoration for each other in how they show so much empathy and compassion towards one another. It brings deep respect to the different generations that walk into Oxford University to know that they are setting an example and can show how having such decorum will influence a deep sense of tenacity and loyal love for each other. This is a perfect example of William offering Verity his jacket/blazer as she was cold and William, being a gentleman, had improvised.
William improvised the factor that he was a man/boy; he realised it was getting a little colder, although he was wearing trousers, a shirt, and a tie. He sat and thought momentarily and realised that Verity had accompanied him while sitting with the other girls and Paul, supporting him and the other

three lads. Jasper Flynn, David Smith, and Darius Silva while they were training for polo. To his notice, she was his delicate, elegant girlfriend, and at that moment it hadn't taken a lot of convincing to wrap her up in his warm blazer and then put his arm around her to keep Verity enclosed and warm. David and Daphne were hand-in-hand as they were walking close to the main entrance of Oxford University. Darius, Paul, and Samantha were walking and talking side by side. Darius was still more than likely in exotic shock from the moment Samantha had tormented him as she drew his manly hands over her firm breasts. That was enough to send any man's thoughts into an arousal of oblivion! Jasper Flynn appeared to be carrying his school/gym bag along with Eldora Jenkins's girl's holdall bag that was most likely full of textbooks and study notebooks full of references to pharmaceutical Sciences academic study notes, different definitions of medicines, comparing and contrasting empirical knowledge, and most likely some makeup, a hair brush and usual women's essentials. These young gentlemen surely acknowledged their ladies and took care of them, and it clearly showed that the boys appreciate the girl's moral support in physical activities just as the males support the females with tenderness in return. After leaving David at the main

entrance to be picked up by his parents, Daphne hugged and kissed him on the cheek goodbye, they then carried on towards the girl's dormitory as the gentlemen; Jasper, William, Darius, and Paul took the lead to walk the young ladies back to the main entrance of the girl's dormitory. William had held the girl's front door open at the entrance of the girl's dormitory, "Enjoy your evening, ladies," said William. "Good night, boys", said the girls, Samantha, Verity, Daphne, and Eldora Jenkins. Verity kisses William on the lips, a little cheeky peck' (smooch), and the sound of both William's and Verity's soft lips as they touch.
All the girls walk into the main sitting area to wind down for the evening before they head up to their dorm rooms. Daphne, Verity, and Samantha sat around the living room dining table and, all of a sudden decided to play Connect Four. It was a game of choosing red or yellow, then you either had to connect four of the same colours, red or yellow, in a line either vertical, horizontal or diagonal. The opposite player had to try and stop the other from completing his connect four by misplacing a red, or yellow with the opposite colour to distract them from winning the game. Eldora just sat in the armchair, reading an old Charles Dickens tale, 'a Christmas Carol', it was a fictional story and a very well-articulated

manuscript by Mr Dickens, it was a story of 'Ebeneezer Scrooge' and his best mate Marley. They were both debt collectors, but his best friend Marley had died and came back as a ghost to haunt Scrooge. The tale was set around Christmas time, and Scrooge hated Christmas time, a time when friends and family surrounded people, and of course, his friend Marley was now dead. Throughout the constituency of London, and around London, many of the townhouses, due to the Government of Westminster, were facing public austerity, which made it a horrendous time for families across London. You could see the poor families in their three-story, old Victorian townhouses across London, with barely any presents under their Christmas trees and hardly any Christmas meals out on the dining tables. Ebenezer Scrooge dislikes Christmas and refuses a dinner invitation from his nephew Fred. He turns away two men seeking a donation to provide food and heating for the poor and only grudgingly allows his overworked, underpaid clerk, Bob Cratchit, Christmas day off with pay to conform to the social custom. Eldora Jenkin's analysis and thought processes were phenomenal in how she could conclude as ethically and carefully to summarise it as this. Nothing was surprising about Eldora as she was a genius. Let's be honest:

Charles Dickens was a fabulous author during his time. Understanding Eldora Jenkins's power of thought in the way she would resonate and then analyse a story was such a phenomenon.
Back to the Connect Four game at the dining table in the girls' dormitory, Samantha was screeching out "four" with joy and so much excitement as she had connected four yellows diagonally up from the built-up red counters and mixed with yellows, the red counters belonged to Verity, She had lost this game, so the winner stayed on, which was Samantha in this case and was against Daphne. The fun, laughter and joy that such a simple game had brought to the girls' amusement was almost effortless.
Back at the boy's dormitory, they were in the entertainment room, William, Jasper, Darius Silva, and Paul Barrera had played table tennis in the two groups. William and Jasper were 3-1 up, with Paul Barrera hitting the net on Williams' last backhanded shot, he had hit the ball from his standing position to the right side of the table, hitting just before the next with a high-speed top spin on the ping-pong ball which then had caused the ball to ricochet the net, and had caused the net to ripple up the line of the next. This caused a propelling ripping sound as the ping-pong struck the net at high speed but did not slow down the

ping-pong ball; it crept over the net swiftly and then hit the back square across the other side of the left-hand side of the table. This had caught Paul Barrera off guard, and he just managed to strike the ping-pong ball with his open hand, ping-pong racket the ping-pong ball was travelling with top spin at quite some speed this had caught Paul unaware he only just managed to hit the ball in an untimely manner, which caused him to hit the net. They stayed up for an hour playing ping-pong before they decided to call it an evening.
While they were playing ping-pong, Jasper Flynn had a giant-sized pepperoni pizza in the oven, and at the halfway point of their playing, with the first to reach 6 points, Jasper Flynn was going to stick some macaroni cheese on the hob for a further ten to fifteen mins and then dish macaroni cheese and pepperoni pizza out between himself and friends.
The first game had ended Jasper Flynn and William 6-4 against Paul Barrera and Darius Silva with the first game, and the score marginally abutting each other's ability which made this an exciting game to watch. By the halfway point, you could smell the masculinity, the endorphins that had become porous from the sweat and their bodies' aromas. The boys were happy to refuel at the dining table with the giant-sized pizza that Jasper Flynn had been preparing with macaroni

cheese that he was heating on the hob in a saucepan; they had four pieces of pepperoni pizza each, cut in reasonable size triangles, equalling to a total of 16 triangle pieces which were cut evenly to share between the four of them.

They all sat at the dining table, ate and drank orange squash until they were either full or satisfied.

William had volunteered to wash up all the cutlery and cooking utensils etc, after they had sat for a little while before commencing back to the game of table tennis. Taking a few moments to get their breath back, digest their food, a few bloated farts from Darius and Jasper, and burps from William Macintyre,

with William saying, “It would’ve been a lot better out than kept inside, as it is far better to burp then become congested”.

This had Jasper laughing, and then he went on to say,

“Haha, a bit like mine, it had popped up from down below, it had popped back up to say hello”.

Darius was laughing.

But Paul Barrera wasn’t remotely amused, which led him to say, “I am so glad the girls weren’t in earshot of your hideous behaviour as its appalling as young gentlemen to act in such a manner”.

"Alright, Paul, calm down! at the end of the day, the girls aren't here, and we are men. Keep your blouse on," remarks William.
It was evident no matter what social class a gentleman was, they had no boundaries regarding the thought of congestion and stomach aches, as young men, they wouldn't allow themselves to be ashamed to let go of their wind. After they sat and let their dinner go down for a short while, they carried on playing their last game of ping-pong. The last game had ended 6-5 to Paul Barrera and Darius Silva but not forgetting that Jasper Flyn and Wiliam Macintyre had won the first game 6-4, meaning that overall, Jasper Flynn and William had a total of twelve games to Paul Barrera and Darius Silva's nine games.
After the game, the boys headed upstairs to grab their bedtime clothes, then into the bathroom to wash, and then head to bed. Such a remarkable evening spent amid the friends on both sides of the gentlemen's dormitory playing ping-pong in the entertainment room.
Meanwhile, in the girl's dormitory, Eldora was reading her magical book of Charles Dickens, and Samantha, Verity and Daphne where busy playing Connect Four. The girls had cooked and eaten a vegetable pasta bake with cheese for dinner that Eldora had prepared the day before. The girls had

not long before the gentlemen headed up to the bathroom to get showered, changed and ready for bed.
Daphne was in her dormitory room, door number thirteen when she lay at rest tucked in her bed. She had sent an SMS to David, "Hi, David, I wished you were here with me on Campus, but goodnight, my Luv". David was back at his parents' house and was slouched upright on his bed, reading his study notes for pharmacology. Then his phone bleeped, and to his notice, a notification flashed across his mobile device: a message received from Daphne. David had now acknowledged the message from Daphne, so he replied to her, "Hi Daphne, I miss you too, sweetheart, but not long now and we can spend the summer break together, and when I am not working, we can see more of each other at the weekends".
Daphne was feeling a little lonely as the other girls, Eldora, Samantha, and Verity, had the other boys just staying across the road in the boy's dormitory. This had made Daphne feel dejected, which you could sense by the emotions of sudden sadness and of her then reaching out to David, trying to plead with him. David's response may not have been what Daphne was searching for, but David had other priorities, such as keeping his parents happy.

His parents had kept a close eye on David's progress throughout his academic study, so he soon could take over from the family-run Pharmacy within Oxford City Centre. Daphne had remained compassionate and flexible with David as she knew he was a gentleman who would support his family and remain loyal to her. Daphne had sent one last SMS back to David before she went to sleep, "Yes, David, you are so right, and I look forward to spending more quality time with you, as I adore you. Goodnight, handsome man".

David grins at Daphne's response, and his heart rejoices; "Daphne, I cannot wait to spend all summer with you, sweetheart. When we graduate from University, I intend to spend my life with you, darling. Goodnight, beautiful girl!"

These two were always smitten with each other, like Tom and Jerry, Cat and mouse chase, one after the other. As soon as one of them gave up for a break, the other would pounce on the other. Daphne and David were accustomed to being together; it was as if it were written in the starlight from the first time they met at the beginning of their open day at the Oxford University Pharmacology classroom with Professor A. David Smith. The way they both acted in each other's presence, the sneaking into Daphne's dormitory was unfolding rather tenaciously, with both David and Daphne having flair, integrity and intellect, they already had much in common. Daphne had also shown her supporting David in his dream hobby, and that alone had shown a great deal of sustenance. And being a man, his prerogative was to impress his audience with his performance, and that being Daphne!

The other girls had decided to get into bed now. Eldora was now tucked into bed, and she had pulled out her cell phone to message Jasper Flynn. “Hi Jasper, I feel like we hadn’t connected so much today, I hope we can start spending some much-needed time together soon! Goodnight, my handsome boy”. The SMS message was received by Jasper Flynn as he was laid up in bed, a face of concern: “Hi Eldora, rather strangely I had felt the same way, we need to spend more quality time together. Like a date night, perhaps? Good night, my darling”. “Replied Jasper Flynn.

Often when Eldora was lying in bed to comfort herself to sleep, she would sometimes reach for the kaleidoscope that she left on her bedside cabinet. This kaleidoscope had various reflective colours and shapes, to Eldora’s notion this had put her thoughts into a trance, as if she were looking into the depths of the stars. Eldora had found the use of

her Kaleidoscope had often helped to ease her into a peaceful, dreamy sleep.
People often try various sleeping methods and techniques, such as listening to mindfulness background melodies and possibly reading story books. Samantha went to her room and got undressed and into her pyjama set, silk shorts and a frilly blouse; it was purple. She sat on the edge of her bedside using her makeup mirror to remove her makeup with some makeup wipes. She then started to brush her hair to untangle any knots that may have occurred throughout the day. Like most girls, Samantha, too, had become cautious in how her hair looked, with the temperature dropping, and as they were just out of summer. Giving yourself some TLC was an important part of the day, and after Samantha had brushed her hair, and taken her makeup off she would then apply some facial moisturiser to soften her skin for when she woke up the next morning. Verity Page was just climbing into her bed now. She had gotten into bed with grey tracksuit bottoms and a white blouse and had already washed her makeup off from her face with Johnson baby wipes. They were not your original makeup remover Johnson baby wipes, but they were pretty much good at cleaning everything. And besides, they had left the skin feeling refreshed, very smooth and soft.

Like most girls, she would have probably been left feeling rather inadequate when they thought of purchasing Johnson baby wipes, and they hadn't even had a baby of their own, or it may have generally been that they hadn't known that baby wipes could do the equivalent job as makeup remover. While Verity was lying in bed, she sent an 'SMS message to her William, saying, "Hi William, it was lovely watching you training for the Polo team today, I know it's very early days in your training. Just know that you will always have my encouragement and loyal support, you gorgeous boy. Good night, Willy". William was just out of his bed at the time his phone was bleeping on his bedside. He had opened the curtains to look out up to the sky, and Jupiter and Saturn had become visible in the Southern evening sky, which had appeared bright and nearly stationary to the naked eye. William was fixated on the planets until his phone bleeped, and then he rushed to his phone only to realise it was Verity, with her sweet and kind message to William, he then responded. "Thank you, Verity, you are so adorable; I cherish having you in my life. With your loyal, moral and encouraging support which doesn't go unnoticed, I feel as if I am the luckiest man alive to have you in my life. Good night darling, sweet dreams,"

Glorified William. The doublets that have evolved among these six students have become a tenacious dalliance, which being Daphne Johnson and David Smith, Eldora Jenkins and Jasper Flynn, Verity Page, and William Macintyre. It was like they were tandem sexting most evenings around the same sort of time.

Had it become the process of being a psychic, the fact that they had all managed to text one another at the same time, or was it just a coincidence and the feeling of being lonesome at nighttime? Could we speculate and point a finger, or just call it a social norm to be texting the opposite sex in the nighttime before you go to bed?

After William had finished his last message to Verity Page, he went over to the curtains for one last look as he stood by the dark window staring into the depth of the western horizon. By the time William had finished the task of talking to Verity, the night was fully present. It had felt like the whole world was in his reach, and he had tilted his head back to investigate the depths of the darkness- and had seen stars, the stars that had been springing to life.

William could see the stars through the twigs and branches of the trees, above the other buildings of Oxford University, high above the rooftops, stars that shone so bright. Not so much as a cloud in

sight, and it had happened all at night with so much delight.
As you can see, William had so much fascination with the stars; maybe it was his touch with the infinite and many things that could be said, it was the planets that were above his head. Without any scientific knowledge, you'd probably at least have to have some Astronomy insights that were possibly gained from college.
Now we wonder how?
With William studying pharmaceutical science, how have we come to this compliance? "I ought to broaden my horizon", William did say. You may have thought that he was from a different planet by looking into the stars that were bright and xanthic, But to my distress, I had often sat and wondered, if we were to look up into the skies more often, we might be able to clear our heads from the anxieties and distractions from the day behind us or what the day ahead may bring or have brought, so no need to feel distraught. Looking into the night sky with luminous colour coming from the planets and stars should ease one's mind into a whole new level and let loose from great oppression by letting your thoughts unwind and transpire. This night sky should be all that you require, to put your mind at rest, and to declare your last prayer while you hold your hands entwined in the air. Now your tension

has left, do take care as you lie back to encumber. And it was late at night (Mon 5th) was its number. The heavenly body's iridescence grounded one's presence. It had almost given a rebirth to understand your presence here on earth, in William's life for all it was worth. Just like so the day was done…. William was the last one to recline into his slumber.

Chapter 5 Mon 4th July 2002

It was the students' last academic year at Oxford University, and last year; they had gained so much insight and knowledge. But not with just knowledge, integrity, and wisdom, the boys had gained agility, confidence, self-control, strong communication skills, teamwork, leadership skills and many other physical benefits from playing their new favourite hobby, Polo for Oxford University. And now with much-needed experience, they had begun to play games at an intermediate level, requiring weeks, months and nearly a whole year of consistent training.
It was the crack of dawn, as the day breaks, and the sun had started to rise through the brow of the

few clouds that were amid the purely blue sky. With the time at approximately 6:15 and only a few clouds in sight. Ironically enough, clouds that were in sight would have indicated no doubt to have a short downpour of rain. Rather extravagant, I know, and on days like this, you wouldn't usually take a blind bit of notice of what the weatherman had said 'if he were to predict a shower of rain amid the purely blue sky. You'd often take one look out your bedroom window and prepare yourself for the beach or with that kind of attire; this weather was extra peculiar and unpredictable. I very much doubt the short downpour would last much longer with hardly a cloud in sight.
As usual, the birds, pigeons, and seagulls were up and awake with the sunrise, scavenging for food as they perched on the rooftops of the Dormitory and University Academic buildings to prey on left-over food. You could hear their talons/claws, which had sounded like a herd of thudding to patting, like tap-dancers--------
David Smith had just awoken from his bed at his parent's house, and he had his alarm clock on his bedside going off at 6:20 am. The Alarming sound wouldn't go off by itself, either you had to hit the snooze button or turn it off completely by the off switch. David would sometimes just hit the snooze button to get a bit more of a lay-in, but this time,

he needed an urgent toilet. With that, David got his pyjama trousers back on before he walked out across the hall from his bedroom to the bathroom to give himself some common decency as his parents may have seen him in his underwear if he had walked out from his bedroom without pyjama trousers on. As you first wake up and go to the toilet for a number one, you are usually in a slightly somnambulist state, just about finding your feet as you step out of bed. But enough to notice the emergence of going to the toilet first rather than the opposite of wetting the bed.

As David walked across the landing to the toilet almost as if he was in a drunken state, but realistically still in a trance, he managed to stumble across the landing to the bathroom, just about holding himself up onto the wall behind the toilet, and just about managing to lift the toilet seat as he went. As David was in great delight, a sudden relief had become empty from his bladder. David noticed a burst of zealous happiness had started to awaken him, now his anxious bladder had become empty.

He refreshed himself with fresh water by the sink by turning on the cold taps, soaking a navy flannel, and then holding it over his face. The cold water had cascaded down his face through the pores of the membrane of his skin, and the shock from the water had brought his awareness to alert. David was more awake and to his notice, so he had started to brush his teeth.

David had an eventful day ahead of him, his last academic year at Oxford University. David had a great start to his second-year study of Pharmaceutical Science, however, his grade gradually weakened toward the middle of last year. Now in his third year, it was going to be a test for him, and he'd be lucky to get a 40-50% grade as it were. That was a third-class 40-50 per cent pass rate, whereas top marks were first-class 70% and above, with 50-60% being second-class for honours degree pass rate in Pharmaceutical Sciences. This had David left feeling extraordinarily perplexed between the thoughts of academic studies, Daphne Johnson, and playing Polo for Oxford University. As any young man would, he loved all three: his future, his love life and his hobby. These are the essentials to life; no man can want for more. He either would carry on as he were, or he'd need to make changes if he wanted to get his pass rate higher. There was no way he could fall behind. Which one would you choose in this situation if you were David, give up his beloved girlfriend 'Daphne Johnson' or give up his hobby? I mean it wasn't like he could spend less time with his girlfriend as they were both in the same classroom. But he could choose to spend more time in the library, perhaps, and study more in the evenings just so that he didn't fall behind. Anyhow, David was more excited about his day ahead when coming around to the motion to realise that he and his friends. David, William, Jasper Flynn and Darius Silva, was playing this afternoon in the semi-final against Cambridge University with the Intermediate polo team. The boys had come a long way with their training sessions since last year, as they were barely just about riding the horse. With days and weeks of training, the boys have come a long way. After David had finished brushing his teeth in the bathroom, he went back to his bedroom to get his Uni bag ready. His parents wouldn't have been asleep much longer as they would usually be awake by now and making breakfast and preparing for their day ahead at their family-run pharmacy in the town centre.

Now, back at Oxford University and the girl's dormitory, Eldora Jenkins and Samantha Hutchinson were awake first. Eldora went straight to the kitchen as she had an awfully dry mouth and was gasping for a drink. Samantha was already in the kitchen area with the kettle on and had noticed she could hear Eldora's footsteps walking through into the kitchen area from the main hallway. "Hi

Eldora, do you fancy a cuppa tea darling?": says Samantha. "You could read my mind, Samantha, you're a psychic, Thanks so much, tea two sugars": was Eldora's reply.
"No problem, Hunny, make yourself comfortable, and I'll bring it right over to you, darling: was Samantha's response.
Eldora sat down in the living room with her baby blue dressing gown and teddy bear thick black socks that had rubber spots/grips placed sporadically all over the bottom of each sock. A rather unique design, they were like a slipper sock, comfortable and warm to the feet.
While Samantha and Eldora Jenkins were about to have their morning cup of tea. Both Daphne and Verity Page had also just woken up, walking out from their dormitory bedroom onto the upstairs landing, and both had noted that Samantha and Eldora were downstairs talking in the living room area. So, with that Daphne had suggested to Verity Page that it was best if the two of them would get showered and ready for university, so then they could alternate with Samantha and Eldora in the kitchen area, as that would become feasible, more convenient, rather than the four of them getting in each other's way in the bathroom area.
'It most certainly made more sense to narrow the margin amid the bathroom sector rather than to

cause a congestion of four people, as it was most definitely more sensible to squeeze in two at a time instead as the girls Daphne and Verity had already suggested'.

Daphne Johnson had just covered herself with her towel as she had finished in the shower. She had managed to fasten a knot to the top of her towel around her bosom just so the towel would clench closely to her slender figure. She had a smaller towel strangled to her head, which was wrapped around like a cornetto would recapture ice cream, but this instance draining out the wetness in her beautiful brunette hair.

As soon as she had covered herself and climbed out of the shower, she walked to the main mirrored area and unravelled her hair towel by untying the top knot from the towel and withdrew it from her head, she out-flicked her soft wet brunette hair to release and free her hair. She had already had her hair dryer prepared by the bathroom sink and mirror, so she could get ready, dry her hair, and with the hairbrush she had brought along with her, straighten her hair from any knots or tangles.

Verity Page had also just come out from the shower and was walking out into the mirrored area where Daphne Johnson was getting herself prepared for the day. Verity had her hair up in an ice cream cone, and a towel wrapped around her bosom. Both girls looked slender as their towels had wrapped them, snugly around their firm bodies. You could see it was evident with their womanly slender fine figures that they had masked with towels. From any eyeshot of a man, it would've been jaw-dropping, wolf-whistling, and complete arousal to have witnessed if they were so lucky. Both Verity and Daphne were by the mirror drying their hair, then were going to do their make-up, get changed and go downstairs.

"That shower was lush Daphne, wasn't it? And warm": Said Verity. "Yes, exactly what I had thought myself, a shower certainly wakes you up fresh in the morning": Exclaimed Daphne.

"You know what Daphne; two elegant minds think alike": Jokingly says Verity.

"Elegant, mmm that's a rather interesting way to have put it, I guess we are both unique and stylish females that think and dress ourselves very similarly,": Said Daphne Johnson.

Both Daphne and Verity had dried, straightened, and brushed their hair. They were both about to apply facial moisturizer, foundation, make-up, lipstick, and eyeliner. Then it would've been just about throwing on some clothes and getting their university essentials and bags ready.

Both Eldora Jenkins and Samantha Hutchinson went to the shower room to get showered and dressed themselves.
Over at the gentlemen's dormitory, William Macintyre had drawn back his bedroom curtains to see what the day was like ahead of him, and just like earlier that morning, hardly a cloud in sight, the odd glistening spot here and there from the sight downpour earlier in the morning. But clear blue skies, more or less, and not a wind that had blown the trees.
It was a summer’s day, about 18 degrees Celsius, which is the same as 64.4 degrees Fahrenheit. William wasn't going to dress himself in a full suit but rather in trousers, a shirt, a tie and the matching suit vest that goes underneath the blazer instead. This had given him the option to be able to take it off if the sun had started to beam down on the students throughout the day ahead. 18 degrees was a fair and mild day, considering it was the start of the summer months, but nothing unusual for British weather.
Jasper Flynn and Darius Silva were downstairs in the kitchen area, making some marmalade on toast and a cup of Earl Grey tea. They had thought it best to stock up their stomach with carbohydrates with the long day ahead and the great match game, Oxford University ‘vs Cambridge University Polo

team. Paul Barrera was in his dormitory room getting himself set and ready for the day ahead, packing his university holdall bag with his academic study books, notepads and studying accessories. He would then casually grab hold of the furniture polish and get a cloth to rub down his black leather brogues to make them look shiny. Most people would generally buy black shoe polish to scrub their shoes clean, but as it happened, it had seemed more convenient and cheaper for Paul.

While the students were awake, getting up, showered, changed, or even getting their study essentials together, David Smith was back at his parent's house, now sitting around the breakfast table with his father, and his mother was making them some scrambled eggs on toast. David's father, Mr Smith, had been up and showered for a while now, and was now sitting with David, and his lovely wife/David's mother was cooking them a well-needed breakfast to help them endure the day ahead.

David had a challenging day ahead of him; he still needed to keep focused on his academic studies, as well as look forward to his after-school hobby which this evening would be, playing in the tournament against the Cambridge polo team. Like most parents, they are proud and happy that their

son David is enjoying himself and doing well for the University Polo team. They were concerned about his academic study grades sitting below average and kept prompting him to seek further assistance or focus more on study.
David's mother was just dishing the plate of scrambled egg on two pieces of toast with butter; she had already prepared the cutlery on the table, with fresh orange juice and three plastic beakers. Mrs Smith was an exceedingly good role model as a mother and wife to her husband and son, making sure most mornings that she would take the lead in looking after her boy's wellbeing by taking care within the kitchen. Mr Smith would often take the lead within the kitchen area if Mrs Smith had either wanted to take a break from this or she had felt under the weather. The whole family relationship between them was amicable and reciprocated, with David also putting his effort into the family-run business. David and his father were conversing at the table, David was talking to his father about his concern regarding his academic study. So, Mr Smith, David's father, was saying to David, "Why do you think that your study grade is falling behind David? Could it be you're spending too much time with Daphne? Or do you think it could be you're spending too much effort on this new hobby of yours? It does seem like you might

not be spending too much time on your academic studies because surely you wouldn't be falling behind otherwise," remarks Mr Smith.

"You know what, Dad, you are probably right, I have taken note, and I probably need to find some more spare time to take up extra revision. Like getting my academic module books out more often in my bedroom at nighttime rather than watching television or sending SMS to Daphne, maybe I could go to the library more often".

"Listen, son, me and your mum are only going to advise you what to do for the best. Both me and your mum were in the same predicament as you are now. Our life hadn't all been so perfect as it might appear now, I mean since you came along, the family business. You're a smart man, and I know you will choose what's right to do," explains David's father.

"Thanks for the wise counsel; it has helped me open my eyes. I know in my mind and heart what I need and should do. It is just a matter of processing it and putting it all into practice," says David.

"Here you go boys, eat up", David's mum brings the scrambled egg on toast to David and his father. Although reflecting on David's possible outcome to his grading with his father, David may have realised that his procrastination could cost him

dearly. His final EMA assignments were happening today. The conversation between David and his father is inadequate and unpunctual, a little too late.
Considering David's grade is low and not quite the pass rate he had been expecting, he felt that he had to look at the brighter side of life, as he is still getting work experience and learning the practice of a variety of medicines at his family pharmacy. But by no means should David give up trying to pass his undergraduate University degree in Pharmaceutical Science, just because his family had his future secured for him in the family business. His degree could help him become more flexible in the future if all else fails in his family business, he then could rely on his degree to open more avenues to a variety of different businesses. After David, his father and his mother had eaten their breakfast, they started to get their stuff together for work. David got his stuff together for his day at university, not forgetting to mention his polo kit for the cup game this afternoon, Oxford Uni vs Cambridge Uni.
Now back at the boy's dormitory at the University block, William was waiting for Jasper Flynn, Darius and Paul Barrera to hurry up and get dressed. Jasper Flynn was in his room leering through his bedroom window, trying to get an idea

about the day ahead, just as William Macintyre had noted earlier, hardly a cloud in sight, with clear blue skies with its heights of the heat about 18 degrees at the moment and throughout the day with rising to 24 degrees, we can say 'possibly' as not one weatherman is usually correct.
Jasper Flynn, looking through his window couldn't tell the temperature unless he was to look at a thermometer or check the weather forecast. So, it was more of an observational estimate. Knowing Jasper, he would take precautions and bring his blazer, trousers, vest, shirt and tie as he had never liked taking much risk with it being typical sporadic British weather. Jasper had drawn out his navy blue and white chequered tweed three-piece suit, white shirt, and chequered tie, with white patches, navy blue patches, and baby blue patches; his tie was ultimately captivating, the whole suit, including the tie, had brought out his blue eyes. Jasper Flynn, today, was looking like a suave gentleman. Without any doubt, Eldora Jenkins and Samantha Hutchinson would end up squabbling over Jasper Flynn with his appearance today. And just like so. William Macintyre, Paul Barrera, Darius Silva and Jasper Flynn were ready to go, clothes on, bags packed and ready to meet the girls. William was wearing his grey suit trousers with grey vest, white shirt, black tie and brown

brogues; he looked smart with his brunette hair combed over to the side, Darius Silva was wearing his navy blue trousers, suit vest, white shirt, red tie and white trainer pumps on, casual footwear but more to the point he was being sensible looking after his feet rather than sweltering in the heat. The boys were just about to leave their dormitory to go meet the girls outside their dormitory, then walk to the main entrance to meet David, who was being dropped off as per usual by his parents en route to their Pharmacy within the Town centre. The boys had arrived at the girls' dormitory, and Samantha Hutchinson had walked out first wearing a long two-piece velvet grey knitted bodycon dress and cardigan, she looked fabulous, her red hair was straightened, baby blue eye shadow on black eyeliner, midi high heel suit shoes on. After Samantha had walked out, Daphne Johnson walked out wearing a wool, midi two-piece baby blue dress and white sandals. Both girls looked immaculate, Eldora Jenkins and Verity were just collecting their Uni accessories to put into their bags, and then they, too would be coming along to go and meet David. When Samantha had walked out from the girl's dormitory, she had brushed past Jasper Flynn, trying to taunt him by flaunting her stuff toward him as she walked up close past him, brushing herself against his arm. Jasper Flynn was

trying his utmost hardest to ignore her; his rosy cheeks had shown signs that she was getting into his head. Knowing Samantha's cunning ways, it was right into the trap she had wanted him.
Daphne spoke to William, “Verity is just coming, William. She and Eldora were just collecting their stuff from their room,” exclaimed Daphne. “Thank you, Daphne, for letting me know, your hair and outfit look nice, by the way, Daph”,: Says William as he eagerly awaits Verity.
All the boys were extremely geared up for today: Jasper Flynn, William Macintyre, and Darius Silva as the excitement awaits this afternoon’s cup game, Oxford Uni vs Cambridge. You could see the zealous energy coming from the emotions on the faces of the boys.
Eldora Jenkins and Verity Page Walk out from the dormitory, with Eldora closing the door last behind them as they wander down to meet David, who was being dropped off at the main entrance by his parents. As they were heading down to the main entrance, Eldora clutched onto Jasper Flynn’s hand as they walked side by side. William Macintyre had his right arm around the back of Verity’s neck, and his right hand would be dangled over her right shoulder as the two were walking by the side of one another. This had left Samantha walking between Darius Silva and Paul Barrera, as we have

already witnessed, Samantha wasn't overly fussy about which boy she would be teasing next, as she had teased Darius previously on the big red bus back to Oxford University. They arrived at the main entrance and waited for David's arrival. The time was 8:40 am, and David's parents were usually around this sort of time, dropping him at the University between 8:40 and 8:50. The boys were all hyped up and excited for tonight's Polo match at Kirtlington, and the girls Daphne, Verity, Eldora and Samantha were trying to discuss between them away from earshot of the boys a surprise evening, a celebration of how far they had all come, with University studies, and how proud they are of the boys representing Oxford University polo team, as that alone is some big ambitions to have. To be able to represent the Oxford Uni polo team is inspirational to the youth of today and leads by example for the generations to come. So, with that thought, they were trying to decide between themselves whether to have some adult amusement at the well-known Varsity Club or at 'Plush' Oxford, this is a place where they can unwind, relax, celebrate, enjoy, dance and drink the night away like the young adults they were. The boys, William, Jasper, Darius and Paul were deep in thought about the whole day ahead. Paul was thinking about his academic study day ahead

and supporting David, Darius, Jasper and William at the Oxford Polo Cup game later this afternoon. The other boys were just zealous and hyped up for the game ahead of the day.
David's parents had just pulled up to the main gate of the entrance, pulling closely to the curb side. David gets out of the rear door, "Thanks Mum, Dad for the lift, I'll just grab my bag," says David. David walks to the rear trunk of the car to collect his belongings from the car boot. "Have a good day David, we will let you contact us after the Polo match tonight to let us know if you want to be picked up or not?" exclaimed David's parents. "Yes of course, bye for now and speak to you later," David says, as he walks off with his friends. Daphne had overcome a sudden deluge of feelings at the first sight of David as he had walked onto the path toward them, butterflies perhaps. The feelings between them had become tenacious the more time, days/weeks/months/ and years spent together, they had both loved being in each other presence. William Macintyre and Jasper Flynn were happy to be in David's company too, ahead of today's Polo game and tonight's shenanigans. The gentlemen hadn't known what type of celebration the girls had planned for them yet, but one thing was certain: they all knew they deserved to be celebrating after tonight's cup game.

They all carried on walking to the pharmacology science block as they had only 5 minutes left before the class began and the time was 8:55 am. On the way to the classroom, the girls had decided among themselves to pre-book the Varsity club. They were going to have to ring up the Varsity club in their morning break or lunchtime to book VIP service for the nine of them this evening, hoping that it wouldn't be too late a notice. Many places would normally take up to last-minute bookings because quite frankly they are a business that thrives on customers.

David, William, Jasper Flynn, Darius, Paul, Samantha, Daphne, Verity and Eldora arrive at their pharmaceutical science class, with Professor A. David Smith who welcomes them at the doorway "Good morning troops": Professor Smith says in great delight. "Good morning, Sir": say his students.

"Please do come in and take a seat, then will discuss your final examination papers": said Professor A. David Smith.

Professor A, David Smith, was giving his students an example of how he wanted them to approach the EMA assignment, which had to be written by hand. In the header at the top of the page, they have to write their University Identification number, their name, the name of the University that they attend, the title EMA, and today's date: Many students were anxious, but some were happy they had come this far in their academic studies. If some students had failed this year, they could either take a year out, then resit their final year, or they could resit the whole last year again straight away. Some of the students began by looking at the EMA Module study sheet, as cited in (Ramanathan-Girish and Boroujerdi, 2001) while looking through, they were to look at the strengths and weaknesses of the medical procedure and try to learn what they were reading in a simple readable text for the average reader to be able to understand and acknowledge what their talking about. Doxorubicin and epirubicin share a similar molecular structure and anti-tumor activity, but the incidence of their cardiotoxicity varies at different cumulative dose concentrations. This study aimed to determine the most relevant samples among total blood, plasma, or blood cells for pharmacokinetic analysis by examining the in-vitro interactions of these two drugs with various blood components, namely intact erythrocytes, erythrocyte ghosts, haemoglobin, and plasma proteins, as well as evaluating plasma protein binding. The methodology involved incubating each blood component—the intact erythrocytes, erythrocytes, haemoglobin, and plasma proteins—at physiological pH and temperature with varying concentrations of each drug, followed by measurement by HPLC and fluorometry at excitation and emission wavelengths of 480 and 580 nm, respectively. Doxorubicin and epirubicin bound to plasma proteins, erythrocyte ghosts, and whole erythrocytes in essentially the same way, according to the results. Nonetheless, both substances' binding to intact erythrocytes differed markedly from that of erythrocyte ghosts, suggesting that haemoglobin is crucial for both binding and erythrocyte absorption. The maximal binding of doxorubicin was around 0.42 μg mg−1 haemoglobin, according to the isotherms of binding to haemoglobin; this value was ten times higher for epirubicin than for doxorubicin. There were two different binding sites for each drug in the Scatchard plot of the two medicines' binding to haemoglobin. For epirubicin, the constant of association between high affinity and low-capacity binding sites was noticeably higher, while the constant of connection between low It was calculated that there were 0.072 high affinity binding sites for doxorubcin and 0.030 for epirubicin per milligramme of haemoglobin. Compared to doxorubicin (0.305), epirubicin (1.963) had a considerably higher number of low-affinity binding sites. Because epirubicin had more binding sites overall than doxorubicin and erythrocytes absorbed both medications equally, it was determined that because epirubicin is a more lipophilic substance, it might diffuse into cells more readily. Because of its self-association feature, doxorubicin stays more adsorbed on the cell surface, whereas it binds more to haemoglobin. It was determined that although the two medications' interactions with erythrocytes seem identical, they differ greatly because of the way haemoglobin interacts. It is anticipated that variations in

this interaction will affect how both medications behave in vivo.
Jasper Flynn had taken a deep sigh with his hands fully stretched in the air, with his writing pen in his right hand and like many students would've been anxious about the last examination. The result also generated their future. Eldora Jenkins had looked fully pleased, focused and ready to start her assignment. There wasn't a day that had passed us by that Eldora was unhappy about studying academia, as she had adored her reading, understanding and acknowledgement of every tiny thing, it was purely evident that Eldora wouldn't struggle with her assignment today. Professor A. David Smith had called for pure silence as they were in examination conditions. They had from 9:30 am until 12.30 pm this afternoon until they could finish their two-thousand-word assignment drawing on the information from the module examination paper that was referenced. They had three hours to finish this assignment. Some students may have had difficulty with academia, so they may

have filled in a special circumstances form, which would have allowed them extra time and possibly some extra support depending on the disability or difficulty they had. David Smith looked slightly baffled by the literature they had received for the assignment and was scratching away at his scalp with worry. Darius Silva had seemed to be grading just over average this year, he had been managing his hobby and academic work nicely. Some study statistics say that doing a hobby, or a form of exercise is good for keeping healthy, active and motivated which you'd automatically then think would help you succeed towards academic study. The look on the girls' faces as they didn't seem to show as much emotion as the males did, or did they hide it better than the boys? Was it the fact that they were female and had managed to fully engage with their academic study better than the men had? The Study of Pharmaceutical Science was more convenient for girls or for boys to study, it all depended on the purpose of the study in the first place, and who wanted it more than the other person. I don't believe sex came into the equation, and the same goes for any other academic work. As they say with mathematics, boys are supposed to be more interested in it than girls and that's all irrespective of the actual purpose of the study, if a person needs or wants it. That person, boy or girl would try their utmost best to be in their interest to go grab hold of it. Some people may find it not within their DNA, or it becomes too mundane for them to achieve.

Professor A. David Smith said they could stop halfway through and step outside for a fifteen-minute break then return to study. So, eleven would've been one hour and a half gone from 9:30-11:00, as 12:30 had made it three hours which was the allocated time for all the curriculum of university students. It wasn't mandatory that they had to take a break, but it was beneficial and seen as fair for the welfare of the students being offered the opportunity if necessary to take a break. William had put his hand up during his assignment to go to the bathroom, "Yes William" Professor A. David Smith responded to William, "Can I rush to the toilet please, sir" was William's response. "Of course, William, just come back quietly," said Professor A. David Smith. The look on Eldora's face was focused like academia was a comprehensive element she needed in her life. What any students today would be lacking, Eldora hadn't seemed to have lacked anything.

Daphne, Verity and Samantha had their heads down analysing the assignment they had been given. David looked slightly perturbed, although now he had started to draft up his assignment and was finding it hard to acknowledge some of the key aspects of breaking down the medicines in layman's terms which was the key part of this assignment to make it easier to understand for the reader, as the assignment is supposed to be like a magazine article. The students met the halfway point so were able go outside if they felt they needed to grab some fresh air, a drink or a quick bite to eat. Daphne, Samantha and David had waited in the classroom so they could carry on with their academic assignment. The others, Verity, Eldora, William, Jasper, Paul and Darius left their seat to go grab a drink and some fresh air. As soon as they stepped into the corridor Verity was like:' "William, my goodness, how are you finding this EMA assignment?"

"Verity, it's strenuous, I seem to be over halfway with 1235 words so far, but I need to reflect on what I have written, but it is hard. Let's be honest we have all come this far": Anxiously says William.

"You're a damn sight further than me William I have written about 968 words so far, so just under halfway point" says Verity.

"Yeah, Verity but most girls like yourself write with precision so I wouldn't stress too much" explains William.

Eldora said, "Let's get a drink before we run out of time". Verity, Eldora, Jasper, William, Paul and Darius, walk to the water fountain down the corridor then step outside for five minutes before heading back into the classroom for the last part of the day. Darius gasped for water and quickly stuck his head underneath the fountain. It was a chrome basin with a curved chrome pipe which worked like a tap at the very front of

the basin. There was a silver button which worked like a compression button, when it was pressed it would release the pressure of H2O from the Chrome curved tap. Darius had soon quenched his thirst, then William gulped down at least four great mouthfuls of water, Paul, Jasper, Verity then Eldora in that order had taken it in turn in taking some well-needed water. Being hydrated during any activity, whether studying or exercising, is extremely important to help you stay focused on the task you want to achieve. After they had rehydrated, they headed back to the Pharmacology classroom for the last part of their end-of-module assignment with just under an hour and a half left, then they could relax and look forward to this evening's shenanigans to begin. They had walked back in with the group, and William wished them all luck just before they walked back in to take a seat for the second part of the EMA "Good luck you lot, all we can do is concentrate and try our utmost best": Encouraged
William.
"Thank you, William, that's very nice of

you to give us motivation and encouragement as we all generally need it from time to time": Politely, said Eldora. Walking ever so quietly as they had crept back into Professor A. David Smith Classroom. Jasper Flynn was first to take his seat, straight back in with his head down elbows sprawled out across his examination papers, with full-on concentration upon his face, analysing from where they had left off. Same with Eldora, Darius, Paul, Verity, and William gaining focus from when they just stopped for a short break.

David, Daphne, and Samantha hadn't stopped for a break as they were happily just carrying on with their assignment trying to get it done. David had struggled the last couple of years just managing to get a bare minimum grading, with the hope to pull the EMA 'out of the bag' with a high pass rate. If he hadn't, he may have to re-sit the whole year three of his academics again. Knowing David, he would've been adamant with the thought of knowing his future was already with his mother and father's family-run pharmacy, but maybe his being so complacent had left him to let his education slack a little, which may have resulted in him having to re-sit another year. Verity was way over halfway finished and was reflecting on what she had already written to check the clarity and grammar of her assignment before writing the last bit she had left to do, with just over four hundred words remaining. Samantha had already had the time to look over her work. While they were on the short break, she had remained seated to get herself ahead of schedule with just two hundred-odd words mainly which would've been analysing and concluding her overall assignment, and if she was then happy she could put down pens and examination paper, then either walk out of the classroom for a fresh-air break until the others had caught up, or remain seated until everyone had finished together. Within examination conditions, they only had the use of 'Martindale. The complete drug reference' to help them to reference the various pharmaceutical sciences medicines which could be time-consuming if they weren't focused. Finding the mechanism of the medicines, and the definitions, was as important as understanding the end-of-module assignment and how to channel a better understanding for the reader of the assignment. Which would've shown competence to the lecturers when marking the assignments. Coming to the last part of the assignment, and with fifteen minutes to go Jasper Flynn seemed like he had finished, as he had downed his accessories, pens, module books, and Reference book. Reclined to the point on his upright chair, that it was almost impossible to recline on those stiff steel and plastic fabricated chairs. But as you could imagine looking at Jasper Flynn, both hands to the back of his head, elbows stretched apart leaning back with his buttocks to the front of the chair, whether he was just causally stretching, posing or feeling exuberated. Professor A. David Smith had noticed Jasper Flynn looking extra comfortable in his seat, so he quietly walked over to his chair; to speak to Jasper Flynn in silence so he wouldn't disturb the other pupils.

"Jasper, I can see that you have finished, but

why don’t you proofread what you have written in your assignment”?
In response “Yeah you're right, let me just have a quick stretch then I will proofread and make any changes that are needed to be done if any grammatical mistakes are made”: Says Jasper
Flynn.
“That’s perfect Jasper, you are a fine example! Always better to analyse your written statement to make sure of any errors”. Just like so…. Jasper put his head down for the last part of the exam and was reading back through his work and prepared to change any grammatical mistakes or other errors he had noticed.
Eldora Jenkins and Verity Page both seemed like they had finished as they both had their pens down to the side of their academic papers, but like Jasper, they had looked like they were carefully reading through what they have written so far, and most likely word counting to make sure they had written enough words for their assignments. At the start of the EMA David had seemed very overwhelmed, but I think he had most likely

come to terms with the fact, if all else fails. He still could rely on his parents Mr & Mrs Smith, as his father had already suggested that when he and his mother retired from the Pharmacy, they would be handing it down to David anyhow. The worst-case scenario for David would just have to re-sit another year if he didn't make the grade for an overall pass rate. These students would be glad when the last ten minutes had finished after an exuberating few hours of assignment under examination conditions with only a few of them left to finish their assignment now.

Jasper, Eldora, Verity and Samantha had finished proofreading their assignments a short while ago and were double-checking for any grammar or spelling mistakes. David was finishing his last paragraph, with not much time left to proofread his assignment so he would have to hold onto hope with the thought that he hadn't made many mistakes as he could lose points from his grading, for any bad grammar or spelling mistakes.

Samantha Hutchinson was the first student to leave her desk to hand her assignment to

Professor David Smith at his desk, she placed it neatly on Mr Smith's desk and quietly walked out of the classroom, Professor A. David Smith kindly walked her to the classroom's door. As he opened the door for Samantha, he took a step outside of the classroom to discuss what happened next with her end-of-module results. "So, Samantha, firstly I would like to congratulate you for getting this far. Now all you must do is wait a couple of weeks for the marked end-of-module result which will be collected by all students, and I will send it to your email addresses and by post, don't stress or worry too much, as you will receive a copy by both email and post. Please enjoy the rest of your summer term. Take care, Samantha".

Eldora, Verity, Jasper and William were finished too, grabbing their academic study accessories together and placing them neatly in their rucksacks. Taking their finished assignment to Professor A. David Smith, as all the students place their assignments with their name, personal identifier number,

academic module code, The Place of
University

Eldora Jenkins

EMA

PI:K25174A

The Oxford University

Mon 4th July 2002

BsC Pharmaceutical Science

Doxorubicin and epirubicin are both drugs to treat cancer. They share a similar molecular structure and anti-tumor activity, but the incidence of a negative impact on the heart varies at different cumulative dose concentrations. This study aimed to determine the most relevant samples among total blood, plasma, or blood cells for analysis of how an organism affects the drugs by examining the interactions of these two drugs with various blood components in a test tube environment, namely intact erythrocytes, erythrocyte ghosts, haemoglobin, and plasma proteins, as well as evaluating plasma protein binding. The methodology involved incubating each blood component—the intact erythrocytes, erythrocytes, haemoglobin, and plasma proteins—at physiological pH and temperature with varying concentrations of each drug, followed by measurement by high-performance liquid chromatography (HPLC) and fluorometry (which measures florescence) at excitation and emission wavelengths of 480 and 580 nm, respectively. Doxorubicin and epirubicin bound to plasma proteins, erythrocyte ghosts, and whole erythrocytes in essentially the same way, according to the results. Nonetheless, both substances' binding to intact erythrocytes differed markedly from that of erythrocyte ghosts, suggesting that haemoglobin is crucial for both binding and erythrocyte absorption. The maximal binding of doxorubicin was around 0.42 μg mg−1 haemoglobin, according to the isotherms of binding to haemoglobin; this value was ten times higher for epirubicin than for doxorubicin. There were two different binding sites for each drug in the Scatchard plot of the two medicines' binding to haemoglobin. For epirubicin, the constant of association between high affinity and low-capacity binding sites was noticeably higher, while the constant of connection between low It was calculated that there were 0.072 high affinity binding sites for doxorubcin and 0.030 for epirubicin per milligramme of haemoglobin. Compared to doxorubicin (0.305), epirubicin

(1.963) had a considerably higher number of low-affinity binding sites. Because epirubicin had more binding sites overall than doxorubicin and erythrocytes absorbed both medications equally, it was determined that because epirubicin is a more lipophilic substance (has the ability to dissolve into fats, oils, lipids, etc), it might diffuse into cells more readily. Because of its self-association feature, doxorubicin stays more adsorbed on the cell surface, whereas it binds more to haemoglobin. It was determined that although the two medications' interactions with erythrocytes seem identical, they differ greatly because of the way haemoglobin interacts. It is anticipated that variations in this interaction will affect how both medications behave in vivo.

“Well done students, let me quietly walk you to the front entrance”. Eldora, Verity, Jasper and William were overwhelmed to be walking out from the last module into the adult world, little did they know they weren’t free at last. They were merely entering into the adult world, conforming, to better prospects and a broader occupational list. Graduated, educated bright Students, were now fresh intellectual adults in the new world of business. “You will be receiving your EMA assignment result by email and post, so please do not panic as I will be marking them and sending them back within the time frame of two weeks. Congratulations and enjoy the rest of your summer” Paul, Darius, David and Daphne were just bringing their assignments to Professor A. David Smith’s front desk too, and just like so….. They too walked to the front entrance after placing their EMA on the Professor’s Desk, Verity, Samantha, William, Jasper and Eldora were all huddled out in the corridor waiting for the others to finish, they were happy they were now finished. “Well done, Paul, Darius, David and Daphne, as I was telling the others, you will be receiving your EMA results by email and by post, enjoy the rest of your summer break”. And just like that “Schools Out for Summer”, wasn’t specifically their graduation day as they hadn’t received their assignment results yet,

but it was most certainly a worthwhile time to be celebrating.
That afternoon, the girls, Samantha, Verity, Eldora, and Daphne planned on booking a private function room during their break to surprise the boys after their cup game for the Oxford Polo team. Oxford Uni Polo team Vs Cambridge Uni Polo team, semi-final. The boys, Jasper Flynn, William, David, and Darius Silva were going to run back to their dormitory and grab their training bags before coming back to meet, Paul, Verity, Samantha, Daphne, Verity and Eldora. They were heading towards the University Park and Jimbo's Baguette place, then most notably their luxurious stroll up and along the river Cherwell. En route, the girls were telling Paul to keep a top secret as they were about to make a phone call, Samantha was the one to dial the phone number to pre-book a VIP table at the Varsity Club, which was a plush cocktail bar at 9A High Street. The manager answered the telephone, "This is the manager at Varsity Club, taking bookings for this evening, would you like to make an enquiry or book a reservation?" :

Exclaimed the manager
"Hello, yes we'd like to enquire first before we book anything, there are nine of us, and we would like a VIP Table. With the booking price, can we take the shampers on ice with our first two cocktail drinks free?" Asked Samantha. "Yes of course, that is certainly something we can do, but of course there will be a fee to pay. Let me just calculate the overall cost for the VIP, the first two cocktail drinks, free for nine of you, and champagne on ice. There would be a one-time fee, and let me tell you a special offer for you this evening, £175, you can either pre-book now, pay in total now over the phone or pay in total when you arrive"? Explains the Bar Manager.
Samantha was happy to pay £50 from her own money to pre-book the evening, the rest of the payment would have to be shared equally between the rest when they arrived later that evening. "Thank you, see you later this evening. Put our table under Samantha Hutchinson, goodbye now": says Samantha. Well, that was their celebration evening sorted, a student end-of-academic-year night

out at the Varsity club. The cocktail bar, what could go wrong or right in their group of nine friends, David, Daphne, Samantha, Paul Barrera, Darius Silva, Verity, William, Jasper Flynn, and Eldora Jenkins, how would the night end? Could the only possibility be a happy ending with some in-between mischief, or could the nine of them all end up back at one dormitory either back at the boy's dormitory or all of them back at the girl's dormitory? Something extra extravagant was bound to happen with all the students in high spirits as they had just passed out the end-of-year module and their last hopeful assignment, hoping they got the pass rate they had intended for, otherwise, they'd have to re-sit a whole year again.

On the way down to Jimbo's baguette bar, Paul, Verity, Daphne, and Eldora were heading out for some food.

Jasper Flynn, William, David and Darius Silva had got back from collecting their gym kit for the Polo Match from back at the boy's dormitory and had just caught up with the others as they approached the back of the queue at the baguette bar. They had to line up for a short while before being served, there were six other students in front of them at Jimbo's baguette bar. You would often see teachers, and professors of all sorts within the queue trying to get some lunchtime food during the afternoon break period. As you might be aware by now, the Baguette bar wasn't a far walk to and from the River Cherwell and the University Park had acres of open space, which was enthralling. A spacious woodland, riverside, with both flora and fauna it was a solace place to open your mind and heart. To let free from all those anxious or depressed feelings. Free from the study, and the thoughts of marking assignments for the lecturer's purposes. It was such a wonderous ground for all aspects: students, teachers, lecturers, professors and all Oxford University staff in general, whether kitchen staff, Librarians, cleaners etc, it was an exceptional place for all to enjoy.

The nine of them had grabbed their lunch from Jimbo's baguettes bar and had started to walk up toward the woodland walkthrough to find a bench to sit and enjoy their food. Along the walkway, through the woodland parkway they found their benches to sit and eat their lunches just before the River Cherwell. They had thought it best to take a pew, with five of them who had taken a seat on the long wooden bench with the upright wooden back and the other four of them had sat on Daphne's blanket, David, Eldora and Jasper Flynn had all huddled together on the blanket that she had kept within her bag. William, Verity, Samantha, Darius and Paul all sat on the wooden bench with the upright wooden back, it was nice to be on a wooden bench, but the ground on a blanket on the grass would've been more comfortable than a solid wooden bench. Samantha had thought it best to explain to all the boys that hadn't known about the surprise this evening

"Right then boy's, we have some explaining to do. This evening after your Polo Match in the semi-final against Cambridge Uni, we have decided as a pass out, on graduation day. That we should celebrate, so the girls and I have booked the Varsity & cocktail

club": Cheerfully explained, Samantha.
"That's just superb": Said, David.
"What a way to end the year,": Shouted William
"Just amazing,": exclaimed Darius.

As you are aware by now everyone was looking forward to the shenanigans of this evening, it was a phenomenon, a triumphant ending to the last of the third year at Oxford University, Pharmaceutical Sciences end of Module assignment. They as Students were heading to the plush Varsity Club, it is such a superb way to end a hard year of academic studies and a perfect way to put all those memories of waking up together each day and walking down the same corridors into the same academic classrooms for three whole years. It was time to celebrate adulthood, it was time to reminisce about the friendships, relationships, memorable laughs, jokes, kisses, and cuddles the whole three years they had spent to bond, reflect and enjoy one last dance before they all head back home into the real world.
After they had eaten their lunches, they would usually just swander around the university park for a while, to let their food go down and enjoy the awe-inspiring view throughout the topography and

within the Oxford University landscape and woodland area, it was a commendable feature of the oldest recorded University in the United Kingdom, which included the botanic gardens, the woodland, Greenland area that had the overview of the river Cherwell. It was a phenomenal setting. Quite often you would see students taking a stroll, jogging, laughing, joking, reading, eating their packed lunch, listening to their favourite music track, playing an instrument, singing, playing card games, board games, being creative, artwork, painting, drawing, or just plainly sightseeing. As you can imagine the Oxford University landscape was extremely overarching for all the various walks of everyday life to explore and enjoy and most of all find themselves at complete solace and peace.

David, Jasper, William, and Darius Silva were over-excited for the game this afternoon with a build-up of anxiety, happiness and joy, with local Universities against the other causing a rift amid the two rivals, the Oxford Polo team and the Cambridge Polo team. Both teams would be roaring to please the crowd and cause upset to the other team. Their ultimate aim was to make the Monthly Uni pamphlet/magazine headlines, as one team would

become triumphant over the other, it would most notably hit the mainstream journalist articles within the local and national newspapers, as a cup game is highly anticipated, as the two main rivals within University Polo history. This has the making of inspirational headlines leading generation after generation.
Many of the youth of today end up turning to crime or becoming involved in other unwanted circumstances. It is moments like this that can help uplift the spirits of the youth of today throughout Cambridge and Oxford and help them drive the youth of today to become inspired by success.
Daphne, David, William, Verity, Jasper Flynn, Eldora, Paul, Samantha and Darius had continued their walk through the University Park through the woodland amid the Oak trees, squirrels, and rabbits. All within the extraordinary view as the group of students loved to ponder and gaze with amazement at the existence of the natural habitat and throughout the grounds. Their last view was of the River Cherwell as the girls watched two swans that had paddled along the river, it was visions such as these that had brought a completely tranquil sense to the environment and the wellbeing of the students. The girls, Daphne,

Verity and Eldora had often taken some monkey nuts during their lunch break to feed the little squirrels, often the little rodents would come up close by to take the monkey nuts from the girls' hands, and many times they would scamper off anxiously. The tiny little creatures were many people's best friends from young and old, but the girls loved the tiny rodents. This time Verity had some monkey nuts stashed in her bag. She crept down to one knee as she spotted a few squirrels in the woodland area they were passing through. A small rodent had jumped down from the wooden fence that separated the walkway and the River Cherwell, and the squirrel had smelt or spotted the monkey nuts that Verity had in her outstretched hand whilst crouched down on one knee to entice the rodent to come and collect the feed of nuts. It was times like the present when you begin to realise that wildlife's best friend is humanity when they take pride in their surroundings. After a short while of enjoying the walk, the surroundings, and the feeding of the little rodents, they had thought it best to start heading towards the front entrance of Oxford University to catch the polo team Minibus to Kirtlington.

Since their first session training for Oxford's polo

team, the receptionist, Hector had told them that they didn't need to catch the bus anymore as they had their minibus service which picked up the students who wanted to represent the Oxford Uni polo team.
The time was 2:45 pm the Polo match was about to begin at 3:30 pm early evening. The polo match was played for a duration of around one and a half to two hours which was then divided into periods called "chukkas", with each lasting 7 and a half minutes; most matches would consist of four to six chukkas, with half-time break between.
The aim of the game is when a polo player directs his pony to the side of an opponent's pony to move the opposing player offline with the ball, formally known as the bump, or ride-off which is similar to a body check in ice hockey. The field is around 300 yards long by 160 yards wide, roughly the same as ten football fields. The game begins when the umpire throws the ball in at the opening of the first chukka. After a goal is scored, the umpire will resume play with another "bowl in" at the centre of the field.
To score a goal: The aim was to whack the ball using a mallet while riding the horse and to hit the ball between the goalposts. The ball has to reach

over the goal line. Depending on who scored, home or away team, it would count as either a goal or an own goal. They would use the wide part of the mallet, the wide face to strike the ball with. Today's match was an extremely significant game, with hundreds of spectators in attendance. They had the top intermediate players from the Oxford University Polo Club, Cambridge Uni Polo Club, Harvard Polo Club, and Yale Polo Club that would be competing in the Atlantic Cup which was an annual competition among the four most prestigious institutions in the World. But today was the semi-final with Oxford University Polo Club vs Cambridge University Polo Club with the final match being played at the end of October. The mini-bus had arrived at the main entrance, and the four boys who were playing got aboard. David, William, Jasper and Darius boarded the Minibus which had seven seats in the back leaving two spare seats in the front, Daphne Verity and Eldora jumped in the back of the minibus with the boys, while Samantha and Paul Barrera sat in the front two seats. Their coach Cameron Walter Master was the driver of the 1999 Toyota Hiace GL 4WD Cargo minibus, which sported a decal of the Oxford University Polo Team and logo across the side of the bus. The young gentlemen who were representing the Oxford Polo Club had no idea how many spectators were turning up today, that is without the local press. If adrenalin hadn't already kicked in with the thought of how serious this rival match was against Cambridge, they would soon start to realise when they heard the roar and the applauding from the spectators as they arrived at Kirtlington recreational grounds. Usually, they would catch a bus that stopped around ten times from Oxford Uni into Kirtlington and would take approximately thirty-five minutes, Cameron Walter Master would take about ten minutes with his seven-seater minibus with a straight-through drive to the destination. Samantha and Paul Barrera buckled in their seat belt at the front two seats, Cameron Walter Master had reminded those sitting in the back seats, Verity Page, Daphne Johnson, Eldora Jenkins, Jasper Flynn, William Macintyre and Darius Silva to fasten their seat belts also. Of course, everyone was as excited as they were and obedient to their Coach's command.

As Cameron Walter Master gathered on their journey, the other nine of them were zealous and extraordinarily excited as this was their first Semi-

Final cup game to be attending or playing in. Whatever the outcome, it would be good to look back and reflect on how far they had come since they had first started training for the sport of polo at the start of last year. Everyone was also excited for the end-of-year celebrations to start this evening at the Varsity Cocktail bar, and couldn't wait for this evening's shenanigans to start. Let's just say a well-earned celebration will take place tonight, it is not something that is just taking place for the sake of a student get-together. It is taking place because of all the hard work and sheer determination going through academic research papers, modules, assignments and sometimes having to settle differences with your dormitory best friend, it has been ultimately a gruelling three hard years of academic study.

On the way to Kirtlington David was engaging in conversation with his best friend Jasper ahead of their semi-final cup game, David was encouraging Jasper Flynn to play a defensive role and try to body-check anyone who tried to attack from the opposing team, Cambridge Polo team players.

The four boys were geared up with anxiety and adrenalin running through their veins. As soon as the umpire threw the ball across the centre half they knew that the game was on. The crowd too would also be roaring for their team to win with many supporters coming along to support the away side, Cambridge University. Fans, Family, friends and students would all come along to support their team.

In past Polo Cup games, they had averaged anything between 500 to 5000 spectators, and anticipating a semi-final cup game would be something significant to attract a high number of both home and away supporters as it were two rivalries facing each other. This wasn't just a game of 4-6 rounds of Chukka's and who scores the most, this was a battle of integrity, sheer determination, strength, stability, and brutality, this was two rival Universities that had been trying to outscore one another.

Who had the better educational curriculum and by proving a point today would get their university mentioned as triumphant over the other in tomorrow's newspaper articles? When most parents look at placing their teenagers or young adults into any University placement, they would generally look at many statistics to see why their son or daughter would best be suitable to attend any option that they went for. So, a win for either

University Polo Team today could put them ahead in the newspaper headlines tomorrow, triumph and success were always the keys to proving the credibility of the dedication that the teachers would put in for their students.
For the Sport Polo you needed, strength, stamina, agility, hand and eye coordination, team building skills and leadership skills, these were all significant skills that you can take away and use within any business opportunity.
Just as Cameron Walter Masters was pulling up to the Kirtlington recreational ground, the away team Cambridge University Polo team were just pulling up as well. Already piles of cars and minibuses were there, full of eager spectators. The time was just gone at 3.10 pm and the match was due to start at 3.30 pm.
Both teams arrive with about twenty minutes to get into the changing rooms and then onto their thoroughbred ponies for the start of the match, Oxford University's starting line-up was David, Jasper, William and Darius Silva, who would be wearing Navy Blue polo shirts, Cambridge University starting line-up Tarquin, Tristan, Raffe and Elizabeth, their kit was pale blue. The majority of university polo teams would have a mixture of

both genders, male and female players depending on the ability and quality of the player. This year at Oxford University there weren't many girls who wanted to participate in playing for the university Polo club.

Both teams, Cambridge and Oxford Uni would have a general game plan and a strategy, with the Oxford team having Jasper Flynn and William playing a key role in hanging around a defence, while David and Darius Silva would be looking at a more attacking role. The Oxford team wasn't very aware of what strategy or game plan to expect from Cambridge, other than what their coach Cameron Walton Master had noted from their previous fixture and results, with Tarquin and Elizabeth being in the headlines on the scorecards often. This likely means they were offensive players and that would leave Tristan and Raffe as defensive players. With some small observational skills understanding and signposting Coach Cameron had given everyone some insight into who to mark, and who to look out for as key players.

Each player would get changed into white jockey riding trousers, and riding boots.

The Oxford University players would place on

their navy-blue Jerseys, each with numbers on the back from 1-4, David being the attacker wore number 1. Darius Silva mid attack wore number 2, William defence mid wore number 3 and Jasper complete defence wore number 4, they pulled on their riding helmets and reached into the locker for their striking mallets.

Tarquin wore the number 1 jersey for Cambridge as the attacker then Elizabeth wore the number 2 jersey as attack mid, then number 3 was Tristan mid-defensive and Raffe 4 was the main defensive player for Cambridge who wore a pale blue Jersey, they threw on their jersey, riding/jockey trousers that where tight white's, they then slid into their riding boots and grabbed their striking mallets from their locker room, then they were off out on to the playing field. There was a huge crowd, and the audience was roaring, chanting for their favourite team. You could hear the crowd, 'Oxford, Oxford, Oxford!'. 'Cambridge, Cambridge, Cambridge!'.

From both sides of the fence, friends' family, loved ones, and relatives, along with some national and local journalists getting ready for some footage and anticipating headlines for tomorrow's press release.

Today's Match's University Umpire had worn a black and white striped jersey, with a black helmet and white stripe around the bottom of his helmet, white trousers and black riding boots, he also rode a pony. He would come to the centre of the pitch/field and blow his whistle. To get the teams ready for tee-off.

As he threw the ball into the centre field, both teams, navy jersey and light blue jersey would have a game of, whoever gets the ball first and ultimately has the ball would be the attacker.

The game was underway, Darius was the first to collect the ball, he chased with it up to the far right of the field breaking out into a trot, and turning into a gallop upfield until he got body-checked by Tristan, knocking Darius slightly off the line but he manages to strike the ball across the pitch to David as he quickens to a gallop up field on the left flank flying past Raffe, the last man standing at the backfield, to head on to goal which so far is left wide open with a hundred and twenty yards to go. So many Oxford University spectators are screaming at David, "Go get it, David". David was pressing on towards the goalpost, the Cambridge defence was on him, and chasing him back with

Elizabeth, number 2 closing David down. With 5 minutes twenty seconds played in the game so far of the first chukka, Elizabeth has managed to close the gap, body-checking the behind legs of David's Thoroughbred pony and causing David to topple off his mounted horseback. There was a sudden boo from the crowd, some girls screaming at the sight of the pain David could've landed in.
As he hit the floor, he dropped his mallet but rolled straight up onto his feet and quickly mounted onto his pony, fastened into his saddle, back to business. Elizabeth, now the attacker, with limited time left until the first chukka was finished, knocked the ball up the front, trying to find Tristan by the far-left flank midfield. The ball went out of play.
The Umpire throws the ball back into play, while both teams line up, side-by-side five yards back from the ball, a throw-in by the left flank. This had drawn William to collect the ball amid the opposition and then over to knock the ball back into play with under one minute left of play. Striking the ball with his mallet into the centre of the field and back to their number 4 - Jasper Flynn as he rose from the centre-back line with a trot up with the ball, holding onto the ball as he awaited

his option to open play.
Not a great deal of movement between his players and the opposition. He carries on moving forward to the halfway mark. The Umpire had blown the first whistle. That was the first chukka finished.
During the first interval, David Smith came off the pitch flustered and went and had a word with the umpire for not scoring that knockdown as a foul. It is down to the umpire to look after both the well-being of the rider and the horse on this occasion David and even the crowd booed the foul play that had occurred just minutes before, he blew the first whistle to the end of the first chukka. David was hinting to the umpire that he should've had a free hit when the foul was committed, but the umpire responded that he couldn't see everything, although he would continue to try his best.
That was the first seven minutes thirty seconds over with. They were to change horses between the interval with a three-minute interception before they could resume play.
It was a key three minutes to reevaluate, unwind, and overlook any changes that each team had needed to amend or adjust, to better their opportunity of winning the next chukka. After both teams had refreshed, and had a cold drink, they

went to change their horses. It was a vital part of playing polo that each player cared for the well-being of each horse by alternating with a new horse between each chukka.
The Umpire rides out to the centre of the pitch and blows his whistle calling the other players from both sides to attend their positions so they can get the second quarter/chukka underway. The Umpire in his white and black stripy jersey and his pure white riding jockey trousers gets ready on his horse to trot away from the centre of the pitch as he knocks the ball into the centre of the pitch, leaving Oxfords Attack mid-Darius Silva and Elizabeth of Cambridge attacking mid polo players both galloping toward the ball with the mallet in their strongest hand. This time Darius Silva with the much-calculated trick, that he's trained for through months and weeks of training, hits the ball with his mallet, down to the far left of the field, knowing full well that David, their star attacker would be out on top with his gallop aggressively attacking the by line. David has caught up with the ball with 80-90 yards of make-up ahead of any defending player from the Cambridge side, this had given David time to collect the ball with his mallet and adapt direction

with his horse facing goalward to the goal posts which were 7.3 metres inside width with the goal posts 3.05 metres high.
Tarquin, the Cambridge defender was caught by surprise coming out of the second chukka as he was away from his goal line and had realised slightly too late as David galloped towards the goal faster, and faster, Tarquin was tailing David's horse now 50 yards behind. David was already goal-bound with the Oxford spectators on the sidelines screaming and roaring at David as they anxiously awaited David to strike the ball with his mallet. David lifts his nose as he closes the gap between himself, his horse and the goal. As he moves in closer with a nod motion of his head, he looks up goalward, aims, then swings his right shoulder parallel with his wrists swings the mallet with an open hand and smacks the ball about half a metre from the inside left flank of the goal post. David has scored, what a phenomenon, David had a dream come true! It was 1- 0 up and David was Oxford's University goal scorer, a game of Kings and the home side was winning. The home side was swinging their mallets on horseback in the air as they celebrated David's first goal on their hopeful way to victory.

One Minute forty-two seconds into the second Chukka and already Oxford were out on top. After the first goal, the Umpire collects the ball to the centre field again and knocks the ball into the centre of the field. That first goal taught both teams a lesson to hold their positions a bit better, with the defence holding back a lot more and keeping the attackers near the halfway mark. Tarquin and David chased toward the ball as soon as the Umpire let go of the ball, with a bit of a tussle amid both riders swinging their mallets at the ball, it seemed as though Tarquin had knocked the ball through David's horses' legs. As Tarquin managed to follow up, moving into a trotting pace from about 90 yards in from the centre way mark, Darius Silva started closing in on the Cambridge side. Tarquin, having no option other than hitting the ball to the right flank with high hopes that the Cambridge number 2 jersey would collect the ball, that being Elizabeth.

Elizabeth Opened up the gap, galloping past William - the mid-defender of Oxford's Jersey number three. Collecting the ball as she galloped further goalward, William now trailing behind her by forty-something yards as she picked up speed. It was only Jasper Flynn - Oxford's number 4 defender who was left to try and stop her in play. Jasper Flynn had quickly become aware that he was the last man standing, and Elizabeth was a smooth and competitive rider. Jasper knew he had his work cut out to try and stop Elizabeth. Knowing what she was capable of, he tried to toy with her to change direction, but Jasper now had no choice but to run her down as she moved into a trot which led to a gallop and catching up with Elizabeth about 50 yards from the goal. By not giving her enough chance to even have the thought of striking the ball, Jasper swings his mallet towards the ball as he tries to body check Elizabeth on her horse. Jasper manages to intercept her course of action.

Without any anticipation, Jasper Flynn then whacks the ball to the byline and out of play to get his team back in position. One nil up and just over a minute to go until the halfway point. They played a total of 6 minutes and thirty-eight seconds and as mentioned earlier each chukka was seven minutes and thirty seconds long.

With the ball out of play by Jasper Flynn near the halfway point and down the left flank. The Players from both sides line up as the Umpire rolls the ball back into play as they stand five yards back. The ball is back in play as Elizabeth knocks the ball backward towards Tristan who trots to the right of Elizabeth 90 odd yards behind her and to her right. Collecting the ball with little time to go and being chased down by Darius and William wasn't leaving much choice or hope for Tristan, making him quickly anticipate his next motion. Tristan feeling inadequate as he aimlessly whacks the ball up field without much precision and hoping that Elizabeth or Tarquin would chase after it. Tarquin being the closest to the ball, was being tailgated and marched down already by Jasper Flynn and Wiliam from the home side. It was a tight margin just before the halfway mark, the half-time break was a five-minute break this time. Jasper Flynn had outplayed the attacking side, by clearing up his spot, knocking the ball forward aggressively toward the attacker Darius Silva.

Now, the Umpire brings the game to a close of the second chukka and with a five-minute break, a few more minutes to rekindle, re-fresh, recuperate, and plenty more time to change over to new fresh horses and ready to begin the second half of the last two remaining chukkas.

Before both teams go back out to start the second half of the game, the spectators are encouraged to walk across the whole field to stomp down the divots within the grounds, through any lumps or bumps that the horse hooves have churned as they gallop, trot or canter side to side of the polo playing field. The umpire is pleased with everyone's efforts in stomping down the divots as best as they possibly can and rides his pony to the centre of the field and blows his whistle to get the second half of the game underway.

We are coming into the third chukka, and the Oxford University polo club are 1-0 up so far with David scoring the first home goal between the upright stakes. Oxford already had an encouraging start; you could only imagine the halftime talk. Keep applying pressure, don't lose your heads or you can let the game slip and then start to lose the lead. Whereas Cambridge University's half-time preparation talk would've been gung-ho if they wanted to make up the difference in the second half.

Both teams back out on the field, the Umpire releases the ball to the centre field as he gallops off the side of the field with his pony. From afar the Umpire looks like a running zebra with his black and white umpire's jersey on, you could only but imagine within the distance amid the mist.

Game's underway and Elizabeth attacks the ball, pelting the ball backward to her teammates. Tristan collects the ball in the second half of the field, and as he looks up and glances across the field, he notices Tarquin making a move upward towards the right flank. Tristan knocks the ball with his mallet to generate top spin forward and to the right side of the goal, as he had seen Tarquin make a swift move goalward. The only thing left between Tarquin was the goalpost and Jasper Flynn, Oxford's defender. Tarquin collects the ball as it whizzes past him and looks goalward where he sees Jasper Flynn defending the goal. He strikes the ball with a lot of hope across the goal to the left flank, and Jasper Flynn with an outstretched arm just manages to stop the ball with the mallet. Jasper Flynn anxiously whacks the ball out to the centre field, "if in doubt whack it out" goes the old saying for any defender needing to clear out to safety. The away side had managed to collect the ball up again, and Raffe; just behind the halfway point shot the ball forward again and into the path of Cambridge's number 2, the smooth rider Elizabeth. As she gallops forward, she slickly goes through Darius and William, which leaves just Jasper Flynn, the defender to try and clean up this attack once again. With 300 yards to go for Elizabeth to the goal line, she continues to close the gap. Jasper Flynn must surely be feeling a little overwhelmed with all these sudden attacks getting through. It must have felt like his defence had been letting him down today which had put him in an emotional state. Elizabeth had let rip a swift swing with her mallet striking the ball to the inside leg of Jasper Flynn's pony, tucking the ball away in such a position Jasper Flynn couldn't stop with his mallet. Elizabeth had scored, and the score was 1-1 five minutes and 30 seconds in. There were two minutes remaining, and just as coach Cameron Walton Master had noted at halftime 'don't let the defence slip'.

Oxford University Polo Club were going to have to apply pressure come the second half if they wanted to win this grudge match against their rivals. The Umpire had brought the ball back into play at the centre field. Darius collected the ball and played it to his left flank.

William collected the ball, pacing amid a trot from a canter, with not a great deal of options opening up for him as yet, waiting for David to open up space in the attack position which was being closed down tightly by the opposition, Tristan.

William too was being marched down by Elizabeth; Cambridge's number 2 closes in on William. Her Pony barges into the side of William's horse, knocking the ball out of play with just under a minute remaining. With the Umpire's last byline throw-in' it was important to note that if the Umpire was unsure who had knocked the ball out, he would take the throw in himself as this occasion was hard to determine who the ball touched last before it went out of play.

It was a highly anticipated semi-final, and both teams would've preferred just to get on with the game rather than argue the toss whose ball it was anyway. The last touch of the third quarter with forty-five seconds now remaining, the Umpire hits the ball into the field as both teams tussle for the ball between Raffe, Tarquin, David and Jasper, all four players, two from each of the esteemed University Polo Clubs, Oxford and Cambridge scurrying after the ball in the final seconds.

The Umpire may have blown his whistle, and not unless one player on a mounted pony had taken one miraculous swipe at the ball with his mallet and hit a guided missile past two goalposts. With

the chances being improbable, and just like so...
The Umpire blew his third and final whistle until the end of the last quarter.
The last quarter is still to be played, and the scorecards were Cambridge University Polo Club 1, with Elizabeth on the scorecard vs Oxford University Polo Club 1, with David on the scorecard.
It was one apiece as we enter the last chukka.
So, far what a game! For friends, loved ones, family, and the University itself, it was an awe-inspiring grudge match to be a part of and to witness. After the last interval, they change horses one last time to bring fresh legs and give the horses time to rest. The last and final chukka of the semi-final, who was going to win or was it going to go to extra time as a draw? Both teams Cambridge and Oxford University polo clubs have refreshed and replenished just before they come out to the last and final whistle.
Both sides came out with enthusiasm, and encouragement from their coaches looking to grab the decider in the last chukka, to come away the winner of this much-anticipated rival Atlantic Cup game. With high hopes to reach the final against either Havard University Polo Club or Yale

University Polo Club depending on who won their match-up.
The Umpire comes to the centre of the Kirtlington recreational playing field to blow the whistle for the final chukka and both teams come out to their positions on the playing field. The Umpire knocks the ball into the centre half with both teams chasing the ball down hammer and tongs galloping after the ball. Tarquin is out front and after the ball from the Cambridge side and David is out front chasing the ball from Oxford University Club. Tarquin shudders up against David's Horse, taking the ball away with his mallet and skilfully does it. William tries his utmost best to close the margin on Tarquin from getting onto goal sight, having a tussle for the ball as William takes a swing with his mallet to get the ball away from Tarquin. Tarquin is serious about his handling of the ball as he rides through William. William was left bedazzled by the phenomenal horsemanship of Tarquin as he knocks the ball past William and marches forward with a gallop goalward. This time as he approaches the goal, we have an upright and focused Jasper Flynn mounted on his horse and sat guard with his mallet at the ready. Tarquin wallops the ball towards the

right upright goal stake, Jasper Flynn; Oxford University's Number 4 top-grade goalkeeper outstretches his arm, mallet in hand and stops the ball. Jasper quickly hits the ball to the left flank as he sees Tarquin trying to close the gap to chase the rebound. Jasper Flynn clears goal bound. Darius Silva collects the ball by the far-left flank and wanders into a trot as he notices Tristan, the Cambridge University Club player coming towards him. Darius, as anxious as he was after Cambridge was just on the attack, still had the hope David or William would make up some space so he could release the ball. Tristan closed the gap more and more, which forced Darius to hit the ball forward without any finesse. Of course, not into the path of any of the Oxford University players, the ball had ended back with the defensive side of Cambridge. Raffe had the ball and was playing it straight back to Tristan. Tristan took on the ball for a while, galloping past Darius. This had opened the gap, and he saw Elizabeth moving into the space on his right flank forward. Tristan released the ball to his right flank. Elizabeth collected the ball, moving forward, being chased down by Oxford's number 3 William.

William bumps Elizabeth and takes away the ball

with a tremendous body check to stop Elizabeth in her tracks.
Now with the ball, William comes through with strength and agility on the last defence, making swift progress as he moves up the field trotting forward into the space just before the halfway mark, with 2 minutes 36 seconds remaining. He looks over his left shoulder down the left flank and sees 150 odd yards in front awaits Darius Silva with his number 2 jersey. William lets off a spectacular pass as he swipes his mallet right onto the path of Darius Silva. Darius collects the ball with ease as he stops the ball dead still in its motion with the mallet and smoothly changes the direction of the ball moving forward to put oppression on the defensive side.
With Tarquin holding up the goal upright stakes, standing amid the two. Darius Silva knows his only chance is to gallop forward for this last opportunity by himself. He is being chased down by Tristan.
Darius Silva's eyes were focused goal-bound with tunnel vision as he galloped forward goal-bound. He wasn't at all bothered by what was behind or to the side of him chasing him down, he was hungry for this opportunity moving forward. In his eyes, it

was just himself and Raffe, the goal-stopper that could spoil his motion. He carried on aggressively galloping forwards, his horse churning up the turf as he marched forward, with spits of mud flying from underneath the horse's hooves as he went. Darius Silva was about 50 yards out from the goal side, Tristan was getting close, and Darius knew his only hope was to hold on to faith as he took a mighty swing at the ball. As he swung, he looked up to the left flank of the goal and noticed that Raffe was just off the centre of the goal stakes to the right flank, a couple of yards in. Hitting the ball with his mallet clean, which hit the left stake, thinking he had hit the post, and the ball had come back out of play. But no, the ball had ricocheted in and off the post. Darius had put Oxford University Polo Club back in front, 2-1.

The umpire looks at his watch and notices only forty-five seconds left ticking on the clock. With the final whistle drawing closer than close it is almost impossible for a comeback for the away side. The Umpire plays the ball back to the centre of the field one last time, Elizabeth and Tristan galloping forward with their final chance and closing down for Oxford's side was William, with a tussle between himself and Tristan for one last

chance. William had managed to hit the ball to the far-left flank and out of play with only moments left on the clock, with the ball out of play.
The Umpire gives the throw clean to the away side, Cambridge. Tristan takes the throw. As he knocks the ball back into play and onto Elizabeth, the final whistle concludes the end of the game with a 2-1 victory for Oxford's University Blues'
The crowd roar at the result.
Hoisting their mallets in the air with victorious joy, the proud champions today gather around for a team photo.
Paul Barrera, Samantha Hutchinson, Verity Page, Daphne Johnson and Eldora Jenkins had huddled around their champions, proud as punch. Flicking the caps to their water bottle lids as they smothered their team, their boys with H2o like true champions with a memorizing 2-1 victory. A win in such a prodigious and formidable style that would live on to inspire generation after generation hitting the hall of fame, as they now enter the final. The four boys go back in superior fashion into the changing rooms, get cleared up, showered and dressed. Coach Cameron Walton Master must have been overjoyed that all his excellent coaching had

paid off, and the victory had become the witness within the outcome. The boys flung their jerseys and riding trousers into the kit bag, then to the showers they went, Jasper Flynn winding up his towel as he fiercely whips it against David behind. Whipping his buttocks again. Jasper was rather assertive in how he had kept on hitting and flirting with David. It was becoming a bit ironic. David was getting annoyed with how Jasper was behaving. “Stop it, Jasper, stop acting out of character:” in anger said David.
“Calm down David, was just a bit of fun:” said Jasper. “No, you have got to stop, otherwise everyone will be talking. I am not gay my friend:” concerns David.
After the boys had all showered, got their bags and ventured out of the main entrance to meet back up with Daphne, Samantha, Verity, Eldora and Paul Barrera.
Coach Cameron Walton Master was out front waiting in the minibus to drive them all back to the Oxford University. Coach was overwhelmed by how his side played today, all nine of them had got on the bus, and fastened their seat belts.
With the fifteen-minute drive back to the University, the students looked forward to this

evening's well-earned commemoration with one last dance at the Varsity cocktail bar. Three gruelling years of studying pharmaceutical science were extremely mind consuming, tonight was a chance to unwind, celebrate those memories and look into the future with positivity in their moving forward. Cameron Walton Master had commended his four stars for how well they played on the journey back to the Uni from Kirtlington recreational ground. The praise from the coach had uplifted the boy's spirits even further.
The Oxford University Polo Club were bound to be in the press tomorrow as the semi-final winners after the amount of paparazzi present during and after the game, they were sure to hit the news headlines in tomorrow's local and national newspaper articles.
Cameron Walton Master had pulled up the minibus outside the main entrance to drop them back just outside the Main entrance of Oxford University.
"Superb result on the rival match today chaps, I will update you in the week and let you know who was playing in the final, which will be scheduled to be played in a couple of weeks": Explained Cameron
"Thanks Coach, we are grateful for your coaching

and look forward to hearing from you": Both David and Jasper, mentioned together.
"The rest of you, enjoy your adulthood now that you have finished your academic journey and hope to see you at the final to cheer the home side on again": Exclaimed Cameron.
"Thanks, Coach, see you again soon": Said Eldora and Paul Barrera. The time was closing in, David had noticed as he pulled the scruff of his sleeve up his forearm to look at the time. It was 6:15 pm Monday 4th July in the early evening. Their end-of-module assignments had been handed in, and the school was quite literally out for the summer.
Most of the Students would be planning on going back in a few weeks as they had until the end of July to be out of their dormitories, and not forgetting the final polo match would be played between Oxford University Polo Club, and either Yale or Havard University polo club depending on who won the semi-final. The boys were heading back to their dormitory.
Jasper had suggested just placing a pizza in the oven as they had a couple left in the freezer to share. David, William, Darius and Paul had thought that was the wisest option as the pizza was

simple, quick and convenient giving them more time to get changed and have a couple of cans of beer while waiting for the girls to get ready. Jasper had gone straight to the kitchen area within the boy dorm, while the other chaps went to their room to unpack their bags, search through their wardrobes to find some smart attire to wear, have a shower and prepare themselves for this evening.
Daphne, Eldora, Samantha, and Verity had all gone to their single dormitory bedrooms to unpack their academic accessories and module textbooks and find something trendy or glamorous to wear this evening. Samantha and Verity were the first two ladies to find a fashionable outfit and shoes to wear, Verity had a three-quarter white silk dress to wear, with white flat shoes and a silver handbag, and Samantha had a red flowery embroidered silky cloth linen midi dress, with red midi heel shoes to wear. While Verity and Samantha were in the showers, Eldora had wanted to make a pasta bake, with mince and Bolognese sauce, chopped tomato, onions and mushrooms. She would bring the pasta to a boil, then place all the ingredients in a large pasta bake tray and place it in the oven for a further 35 minutes. In the time it was cooking, she would

have enough time to get in the shower and enhance herself by applying some cosmetics to bring out the finishing touches to the woman.
Both Samantha and Verity were wrapped up in their bathroom robes, in front of the mirror, and were blow-drying their hair before straightening it and applying cosmetics to beautify their appearance. Both Daphne and Eldora had come to the shower room.
Eldora asked Verity to keep an eye on the oven when went to take a shower. “Of course, Eldora, how long are you expecting it to cook for?”: says Verity
“Thank you, Verity, it will take another 30 minutes from now”: Explained Eldora.
The girls were in and out of the shower like clockwork, two went in first, Samantha and Verity, then Eldora and Daphne Johnson got in the showers last. As soon as Verity and Samantha had finished pampering themselves, they would head to the kitchen and serve up the pasta bake. Samantha had a bottle of mulled wine left in her dormitory which she had just remembered. Hearing this had brought excitement to Verity’s ears. After the girls got dolled up, Samantha went to her room to grab the mulled

wine and Verity headed towards the kitchen, to take out the pasta bake, grab four wine glasses and start to pour out the mulled wine.
Over at the boys' dormitory, the boys were all showered, suited and booted, they had eaten their pizza already. It had taken the boys half the time to get washed and changed than it had the girls.
For a girl to look elegantly fashionable takes a lot of preparation, compared to a man to look half presentable. They hadn't felt the need to apply cosmetics, and most males would just grab some smart attire, brush or comb their hair, maybe apply some hair products to keep that wet look, then do a 360 in the mirror a few times, then the man was good and ready.
David Smith was wearing his brown suede Chelsea boots with a grey suit and blue tie looking rather suave. Jasper Flynn had his navy-blue suit on, brown loafers and red tie with his hair combed to the side. William, Darius, and Paul were in the entertainment room playing a few games of pool while drinking cans of fosters larger. William was wearing a black fitted suit with a black Dicky bow and black brogues; he was looking casual and smart with his colour-coordinated attire.
Darius and Paul were playing winner stays on with

Darius having two reds remaining on the table while Paul had four yellows left until he was on the black. Jasper Flynn and David were standing in the kitchen area talking about Daphne and Eldora Jenkins, both chaps were looking at making a good impression this evening. With a few drinks and everyone merry, would the boys end up back at the girl’s dormitory or would the girls end up back at the boy’s dormitory?

With all the gents dressed, and ready to go, back at the girl's dormitory Daphne and Eldora Jenkins had finished getting ready and had come to the living room to sit and eat the pasta Bolognese that Eldora had prepared before they both got in the showers, which they had thoroughly enjoyed along with the flavoursome mulled wine. Verity and Samantha had eaten their food already and were pouring the last residue left at the bottom of the mulled wine bottle between them, with only 750ml to the bottle and averaging around 5 wine glasses, they already had one glass each between the four of them, so that left half a glass each between Verity and Samantha.

Darius had beaten Paul while playing pool and was left with two yellows. Darius potted the black in the centre left pocket winning the game.

The boys were just about to leave the dormitory to meet the girls, “this is going to be a blast lads!” Said William,

“You’re not wrong there Will, let the shenanigans begin!”: Exclaimed David. All the boys arrive at the girl's dormitory, Jasper goes up to the door and gives a knock. Verity Page answers the door. “Hi Jasper, hold on outside for five minutes, Eldora and Daphne are just finishing up their food”. “No problem Verity, we will just hang about outside.”

The boys had thought it was better to walk than catch the bus into the town centre as it had just seemed too much of a palaver to jump on a bus and stop several times before it arrived at the destination, the complete annoyance of it all was drama. So, they had thought it best and just to walk up fifteen minutes outside to the main entrance of the Varsity club. The girls had started to walk out of the dormitory, looking as stunningly remarkable as ever. Most notably Samantha had highlighted this evening by wearing the red flowery embroidered silky cloth linen midi dress, with the red midi heel shoes to match, she and Daphne Johnson had shone out, Daphne was wearing her baby blue maxi dress with her pink fur, half over jacket which covered her arms, shoulder and came up to the small of her back. The four girls had looked Pulchritudinous as usual, and the boys were hyped up to be spending their last celebration with these extraordinary looking females. They carried their walk from the main road to the varsity club which was around 400-odd metres away from Oxford University.

With the temperature at heights of 14 degrees Celsius at the start of July on a Monday evening, whether wearing high heels or uncomfortable brogues the walking distance hadn't seemed such a horrendous idea. The ladies had clung onto their gentlemen and were arm in arm as they tandem strode step by step between man and female, David with Daphne, Verity with William, Jasper with Eldora, Darius and Paul with Samantha Hutchinson as they went! Although it was still relatively young in the evening the sun had started to withdraw gradually into the depths of the sky, and colour the slate blue and dark grey. The night was upon us, the time was 7:15 pm.

They had arrived at the Varsity Club, which inside featured uniquely a multi-level interior with a pristine design, including a Moroccan-inspired lounge setting within the top floor, a bustling bar area, the rooftops featured an awe-inspiring panoramic view of the city's insightful reflected transcended dreams, with a relaxing and comfortable seating area with a dedicated bar. As they arrived Samantha walked over to the main reception area. It was downstairs, and at the front desk before you walked to the first bar. The receptionist asked Samantha, "How can I help you?"

"Hiya yes we have booked a VIP table for nine of us, which I had already paid £50 towards the total amount of £175" Said Samantha.

"Oh, I see, let me check. Can I first ask the booking name you used to book the VIP table under please?" Asks the receptionist.

"Yes of course, its Samantha Hutchinson" "Please wait a moment while I check that out for you….. ohhh here you are, £50 paid for nine of you, that comes with the first two cocktails free and a bottle of champagne on ice. That is £125 left to pay please" says the receptionist.

Samantha had already paid £50 from here own pocket so she would let the eight of them divide the rest between them, with just over fifteen pound each among them wasn't asking for much. Samantha collected the rest from Daphne, Verity,

Eldora, David, William, Jasper, Paul and Darius.
“Right, here you are” exclaimed Samantha to the receptionist with the exact amount in her hand.
“Your VIP lounge table is up the stairs to the rooftop terrace, but before you go upstairs, please place these wrist bands on so you can collect your VIP deals at the bar”: explains the receptionist.
“That’s awesome thankyou so much” remarked Samantha. To the top terrace they wander, laughing and giggling as they take the staircase to the top floor, trying to wrap and stick their wrist bands around their forearms as they went. As they got to the top of the stairs Samantha and Jasper went to the bathroom, while the others sat round at the VIP lounge table which had been reserved under the name Samantha Hutchinson. There was a comfy sofa chair which could seat four people, David, William, Daphne and Verity had sat. There were two single seats where Paul and Darius had sat, and a bench the other side of the table, which could probably hold four people. Eldora sat on the bench while she waited for Samantha and Jasper Flynn to get back from the cubicle.
While they were waiting, they looked at the drink

menu for the choices of cocktail drinks that they could choose from. David and William wanted a Daiquiri, which was sweet flavours of rum, sugar and lime. Daphne and Verity found the dry Martini, which was made with dry gin, dry vermouth and orange bitters with a lemon twist. Paul and Darius had chosen the Mojito, which originally appeared when sloppy joes was a famed bar in Havana, Cuba. Eldora chose a bloody Mary, which was made with vodka, tomato juice, black pepper, celery salt, and lemon juice.

The barmaid came and took their order. Her name was Sarah, and she was around mid-twenties. She was petite with brunette hair, Caucasian and wearing a waitress pinny with the logo of the Varsity Cocktail bar on the front left pocket.

Jasper Flynn was just walking out from the men's cubicle as he had to take a wee. As he walked by the girl's toilets he had collided with the ginger promiscuous girl, Samantha. The feisty red-haired girl was eager to attack Jasper Flynn as soon as he was out of the way of any eyewitnesses.

Samantha drew him in close by pulling Jasper Flynn around his hips, with a firm grope to his buttocks. At that point Jasper was frolicking in toward her, anxiously, but he wasn't trying to pull away, Samantha had her best aroma, perfume that lingered which had an erotic potent smell that drew on anyone's attention, as you would imagine a hot looking lass, wearing a nice red dress with red hair.

The dress had smouldered on her curvaceous skin. Samantha had cupped her hand and placed her hand to Jasper's private region to mask his full attention. "What are your thoughts now Jasper?" Was Samantha's response. "Well Samantha, you had caught me by a surprise, but at this moment you can sense my thoughts" Was Jasper's reply. Samantha moved in to kiss Jasper, they ended up colliding into a passionate kiss.

"Wait, wait, we must stop before someone catches us" Jasper had melted. "Okay Jasper, fine we can leave that there for now". They both walk back to the table to join the others like nothing has happened.

Both Jasper and Samantha take a seat next to Eldora Jenkins on the bench one either side. They notice everyone sat with their cocktails at the table, and had waived Sarah, the petite brunette-haired waitress over to take their order. "What can I get you both?" says Sarah the waitress. Jasper asks for the Mojito, same as Darius and Paul just had, as that seemed rather presentable with the mint leaf floating amid the glass with ice, which looked evidently refreshing and a cocktail of choice. Samatha asked the waiter for a cocktail famously known as the Clover club, with tastes of raspberry gin, and includes egg white. A fine evening to be celebrating on the rooftop at nightfall for end of the academic year's celebrations. Surrounded by graduated like-minded students resonating and conversing back and forth. With the night still being relatively young, David, Daphne, William and Verity get up to dance. The UK'S top 3 in the charts favourite has come on through the bass speakers by the DJ stand, to the dance floor. Dancing to (*Will Smith – Miami*,) a song from early 1999, David bopping his shoulders in towards Daphne, as she was swaying her hips reluctantly from side to side, enticing to David as she allured him towards her with her slender figure and cute outfit. William was sporting a two-step and rolling the arms amid the dance floor flaunting his stuff with Verity Page, as she looked like she was clicking her thumb and index finger, turning her hips from side to side. The sudden zeal had brought movement throughout the students to lift their spirits. The others were still adrift in

conversation at the table and onlooking while drinking, smirking and conversing between themselves. It wouldn't be much longer before they had wanted in amongst the action.
Eldora Jenkins had just finished her cocktail; the bloody Mary had gone down a treat and by this time they have all had a couple drinks. The girls have all had a glass of wine each before they came out as well as their first cocktail and the boys had enjoyed a couple of cans of beer and their first cocktail too, they were all joyful and lightheaded, not long now and they'd be merrily tipsy.
Eldora and Jasper Flynn had joined them on the dance floor. Jasper had remained close to Eldora after that frantic spell when he got cornered by Samantha Hutchinson outside the cubicle. Jasper grabbed Eldora around her waist as they danced to this song together. Samantha may have lost her attempt to endeavour some mischievous behaviour with Jasper Flynn as he was now happily back dancing with Eldora. She was sat down gobsmacked next to Darius and Paul Barrera.
After the Miami, the Will Smith song had finished, they called out to the waiter for the same order as previous and sat back down for a short while. They had their last cocktails to order, then the

champagne on ice.
After that Cocktails were half price until the bar closed. David was now seated with Daphne, William with Verity and Eldora again with Jasper on the bench. William was enjoying what looked like a sensational kiss amid the tender red lipstick lips of Verity, as she ran the open palm of her hand around the back of William's neck, the tips of her finger gently quenched his scalp without clawing away at his flesh with her newly painted nails. A gentleman likes to be man handled by his lady when she is being dominant for some attention. David and Daphne were deep in thought, and love. Having already spent one evening in the same bed, with no doubt their plans would end up the same this evening. With everyone drinking, which brings out Dutch courage, a personal stigma some may say is foolish when others will describe it as confidence. Personally, I strongly believe that depends what extent you drink, get drunk, and remember in the morning. Was it good or bad, and ended up with the person you wanted to either enjoy the moment with or get the right things off your chest perhaps. What did you need the Dutch courage for? With a group of nine graduated students, who had spent the last three years

together. What could possibly go wrong? End up back at the wrong place/bed at the wrong time? Be sick over your date? Slip, trip or fall over on your way home? Everything and anything were possible.
Indulging in deep conversation, enjoying the smoothness of the cocktails in their pairs, a romantic RNB song by Joe (*Joe – I Wanna Know Lyrics | Genius Lyrics*,) A hit released in 2000. Had them all up grooving slowly in their couples, but Samantha had danced amid Paul and Darius, grinding gently around both boys bringing them much delight. David danced smoothly with Daphne, William and Verity were getting intense on the dance floor caressing each other with Jasper Flynn and Eldora Jenkins smooching on the dance floor before they turn the kiss into a foxtrot with an uneven rhythm, the movement of both slow and fast paced footsteps back and forth.
The night was moving on and spending some much-needed adult bonding time together to express the relief they now had away from academia. They now feel free from having to keep their composure, free from being speculated, regulated and under surveillance twenty-four seven under dual restrictions of Oxford University rules,

teachers, lecturers and so on.
Tonight, at the Varsity Cocktail bar it was time to make some admirable moments to resonate for the impeccable behaviour that they have just achieved within the past three years of Oxford University study, time to relax,
enjoy.
The song had finished so they all came and took a seat back down, ready for the next order from the waitress Sarah. Paul had held his hand up to get Sarah's attention.
As she came over, "Could we please have our bottle of champagne on ice, with nine glasses please" says Paul.
"Yes of course no problem, champagne and nine glasses coming right up". Explained Sarah the waitress. Paul had an observant and fascinated look in his glazed eyes and was stunned by the petite brunette waitress. His eyes would wander behind the bar as she walked to collect their drinks. Like a hawk preying over its feast. Paul Barrera had become slightly tipsy, and as Sarah the waitress came back over to the table with their champagne bottle, and nine glasses, Paul lent over the table. "Excuse me miss" "yes what is it I can help you with" replied Sarah. "I was just thinking,

could I have your contact details, maybe we could go on a date?": slurring as he spoke, Paul. "I am afraid I will have to say no on this occasion, as it is not my role as a waitress at a bar," said Sarah. Paul sighed; he was stood up. You could see Sarah had thoroughly enjoyed her waitress job, which helped pay her bills, holidays and brought satisfaction to her day rather than be bored and unemployed sat at home twiddling her fingers. They had poured out the Taittinger champagne into the long neck wine glasses, the champagne was a notably vintage by using 100% Grand Cru vineyard grapes to construct its delicious taste. Daphne and Verity had found this as an exemplary gift for the hard efforts from the past three years and were conversing back and forth about what the future might hold for them when they return home. Verity was looking forward to returning home to support her parents at the Wappley riding School, within the periphery of Bristol. She was saying that once she was settled, she would like to meet up with William to see where their future lies. Daphne hadn't had far to return home, but her main interest was to set her sights on her future with David and his parents' pharmacy. Both the two girls were upright and rather astute, they would be more than capable of finding their way on most charted courses that they may endeavour to take. Besides, they both experienced fabulous upbringings.

After everyone had sat talking, catching up and drinking amid the gang. After a short while the girls favourite song from the hits of 1999 charts came on through the bass speakers, which had them up swiftly to the dance floor, quoted in. (Shania Twain,) That don't impress me much. The girls would purposefully entice the gentlemen by winding their hips back and forth and dipping their knees whilst sliding their upper raised hand down their man's chest, then onto their feet, just before the words are sung, 'that don't impress me much', as the girls would then pirouette then push the boys back. Eldora had done with Jasper Flynn as she enticed him inwards, Then Daphne with David, Samantha with Darius and Paul, and last but not least Verity Page with William. It was like the girls had planned to toy with the boys in sync, was like it were rehearsed before the song came on.

After the pirouette Daphne held her arms around Davids's neck and brought him in closely for a smooch on the lips. They adored each other's company and you could see the adulation had become transparent between the pair. Their love had enthralled and that was evident within their motions. The time was 9:45 pm with only a couple hours before the bar would close. Without a doubt some of the boys and girls would disperse in one another's dormitory bedrooms later that evening. The words from the Shania Twain song had lingered, 'That don't impress me much, so you got the brains, but have you got the touch? Now, don't get me wrong-yeah, I think you're alright but that won't keep me warm in the middle of the night, that don't impress me much, uh-huh, yeah, yeah'! The words depicted had reminded the gentlemen the actual valuable lesson about the empowerment of women, as a sociologist would've put it. Giving the men a direct lesson to the importance of women and that we should value them. Samantha and Darius walk hand in hand to the edge of the Varsity Club rooftop terrace to admire the views at nighttime, with lampposts that lit the way down Oxford street. You could see an overview of the tall castle-like building that made up the scene of the Oxford University buildings and colleges. They had log burners to keep them warm through the evening, although temperatures weren't

horrendous with lows of 12 degrees Celsius.
The promiscuous girl was always in the company of a male's attention whether that be Darius, Paul or Jasper. It hadn't seemed to faze her that Jasper was taken by Eldora, which was morally unacceptable.
After they had finished their two cocktail drinks, and the last of the Taittinger champagne they had all become mildly inebriated, the odd one of them staggering occasionally.
Eldora had started to slur with her words when she was engaging conversation with Jasper. Both girls Daphne and Verity were overly tipsy as they had opened their hearts about their future aspirations.
They were all intending to order another cocktail from the waiter, "waiter can we order the same cocktails as before, two Daiquiris, two dry martini, two mojito, one bloody Mary, and two sex on the beach cocktails": ordered David.
"Yes, no problem": had noted Sarah.
The two Daiquiris were for David and William the two dry martinis were for Daphne and Verity, the two mojitos were for Paul and Darius, while Eldora had a bloody Mary, and Samantha Hutchinson and Jasper Flynn both had sex on the beach cocktails.

The nine students having a fantastic time, could one more drink possibly send them over the edge? Anyway, give them some slack, who were counting anyway? It wasn't the usual occurrence of substance misuse, and in this case it was more of a case of substance well used for the right reason, amid a well earnt celebration.
Sarah, the pleasing to the eye waitress had held elevated in the air what appeared to be a waiter's tray full of cocktails for the boys and girls, which she bought over as they sat around the table awaiting their drinks. Paul's face was a sight for sore eyes as he couldn't keep a glance away from the focus of the brunette petite waitress as she approached their table leaning outreached across the table they were sat around. Like a pervert possessed and drooling as he looked on. Even Sarah had said, "do you mind please picking your jaw up from the floor?" As Paul had carried on gawping at her until she had caught his attention. "ooooh I am ever so sorry, I was rude for admiring the view": said Paul. "Well please don't, I had already told you I have work to commit to": explains Sarah.
The group of them are sipping their last drinks, enjoying and reminiscing as they reflect on the

past years spent together. Conversing amongst each other and dancing the night away frolicking amid the nine of them! One last dance before they had even thought about making their way back to their dormitories back at Oxford University. A song by Eminem as quoted in, (*Eminem - Stan (2000 Music Video) | #4 Song*,) another superb song for the evening's extravaganza. It wasn't so much the lyrics that made this song, it was more the tone of voice which 'Stan' had been sung in, and the backing and musical within the background that made this song. 'My tea's gone cold, I'm wondering why I can't get out of bed at all, the morning rain clouds up my window (window) and I can't see at all" as you can see the words weren't exactly inspiring or encouraging but it was the perfect slow song to dance to along with a partner. For the last dance, and for the walk home. There was a peculiarly sentimental means to this song that could quite proudly signify the end of a night, and that was truly yours Stan.
After the song, they had all gathered their belongings, clutch bags, handbags and overcoats or blazer jackets. Holding on to the railings as they walked down the steps back down to the first floor. The waitresses and cleaners would be cleaning up

the tables, glasses, bottles and spilt drinks that had been knocked over at the bar and tables within the sitting area of the cocktail club. Back out on the main street as they stumbled up the road, Samantha had nearly 'stacked it' just outside the front door as she clipped her heel taking a stride down the pathway. Darius had held her up to get her back on balance. It had taken them fifteen minutes from Oxford University to walk to the Varsity club earlier, but to walk back from Varsity club with a skinful of alcohol inside your system, back to Oxford University was another question. 500 metres hadn't seemed so far of a distance, but laughing, giggling and balancing a stable mate as you went was a fine thing, but it certainly may take a little while longer than when they arrived earlier!

They were up against stupidity and barely legal lights that shone the little way ahead, and very dimly. Daphne was supporting a drunk David, as the athlete Polo player that he was, wasn't used to a few alcoholic beverages. Daphne was letting David basically lean on her, as she had his left arm wrapped around her shoulder on the way.

William was planning on having Verity back at his dormitory room this evening and he was just suggesting the idea on their walk back. David was going to end up back at Daphne's room, and Jasper Flynn was going back to Eldora's room. While Samantha Hutchinson was happy to go back with Darius and Paul. As they arrive at the Oxford University just after 11:00 am at the main entrance, it was seemingly dark as you can imagine, it was only an hour away from mid-night with very few lights, lamppost that had lit the footpaths around the periphery of the carpark main entrance, and with some wall mounted lights that surrounded the perimeter of the Universities walls. These were beneficial for those students coming back late so to avoid any nighttime slips, trips or falls. William was happy to be bringing Verity back to his bedroom as they hadn't had much privacy, this would give them time to grow and plan a foreseeable future together.

As they arrived back at the boy's dormitory William had held the door for Verity, Samantha Hutchinson, Paul Barrera and Darius Silva. Samantha, Paul and Darius had waited downstairs for a while having a few drinks that the boys had left over from before they left, as they had a few cans of fosters in the fridge still. They had stayed up for a while and played on the pool table. The

boys were happy just to have a beautiful red head present and Samantha was a wild girl. William had gone up to his room with Verity, both of them got undressed. Verity got unchanged into her underwear and stole one of Williams t-shirts and wore it like a night dress. While William was just in his briefs, they both got under the duvet cover. William was overexerting himself with enticing words to try and allure Verity in deep thought, "Verity if me and you carry on being amicable and reciprocated, there is no reason why we shouldn't have a long future together" "Exactly William, you are all that I want as I love you. The more and more time we spend together the more tenacious we have become": utters Verity. William pulls Verity into him, as she mounts her leg across his waist, a soft French kiss as they cascade their tender lips passionately between them.
William was from Liverpool, and Verity was from Bristol. She was planning on going back to her family business with high hopes that William would support her. As they were both trained in pharmaceuticals it could be a perfect match if William was serious and inclined to want to support animals as well as his future wife.
Eldora Jenkins had gone back with Jasper Flynn to

the girl's dormitory, Daphne and David were already back at her room. Jasper Flynn was in awe as he had wandered in Eldora's room, it was just as he had imagined. Like a library, full of academic studying books and notebooks. "You know what Eldora, you are one of the most dedicated people I know," Said Jasper. "What made you say that, Jasper?" Says Eldora. "Your room is just as I imagined, full of academia. You are a dedicated Scientist" explains Jasper Flynn. Jasper and Eldora get unchanged in to bed, and under the duvet. Eldora places her side lamp one. Jasper Flynn still half tipsy, has Dutch Courage and not his formal self but rather confident. He places his right hand over Eldora's right breast as he reaches over from the left of her. Eldora groans "mmmm Jasper" entices him more. Jasper Flynn kisses Eldora, then mounts on top of her. Eldora fights Japer Flynn off, with an affectionate manner, as she wants to become the dominant one. She rolls him over onto his back with her strong thigh muscles, holding his arms back behind his head. She releases one hand, as she reaches down towards his groin area and fondles around his privacy region. Teasing Jasper Flynn, she is basically edging him to an almost climax sensation

as she tussled back and forth around near his scrotum and shaft. Jasper Flynn couldn't hold out much more, and asked Eldora to stop as he hadn't wanted to take the advantage of her. He respected the moral principle of them both being intoxicated and wanted to wait till they meet after they get back home away from university. Jasper Flynn can be wayward at times, but his heart was always in the right place as he always cared about the welfare of the other person. "Yeah, you're right Jasper, we should take our time. When we get back home, we can plan our future" says Eldora.
"Exactly Eldora, I deeply respect you, and I certainly don't want to rush and ruin something good. Why ruin a short future when we can plan a long future together. Let us expand our chemistry and look forward to meeting up when we get home" Exclaimed Japer Flynn.
"Now that makes perfect sense, come here Jasper. I am sorry I rushed things. Let's just snuggle and forget it all happened" states Eldora. "Jasper kisses Eldora on the forehead, then snuggles in as they lay to sleep". Back at Daphne's room they're already in bed and under the duvet, her and David, both drowsy. David is very intoxicated from this evening's shenanigans.

Daphne wasn't too phased by David enjoying himself as it wasn't his usual activity of choice. Just a celebration drink gone a little to far. And for all the students it was a well-deserved end of the academic year treat. David and Daphne had already planned a long-lived future together. With Daphne eventually working at David's family run business at the Pharmacy of Mr and Mrs Smith, David's parents.

We won't go in to how the promiscuous girl Samantha Hutchinson evening had ended, that can be left only to your imagination, a feisty red head girl, playing pool with two young strapping gentlemen. Not only have they had three cocktails, a glass of champagne they had carried on the night drinking within the boy's entertainment room, cans of larger. Let us reflect on David's dream. He attended Oxford University, reading a three-year Pharmaceutical Science degree which focuses on the study of drug discovery, development, formulation and manufacturing, encompassing various disciplines like chemistry, biology, and pharmacology, to prepare graduates for careers in the pharmaceutical industry. But despite this, David may fail his last assignment with his lack of focus the past year, as he fell in love not only with

a girl, called Daphne, he had also fallen in love with the Sport polo and represented Oxford University Polo Club.
David, Darius, Jasper and William have got the Oxford Polo club to the final. For David, that was a dream come true. With his ultimate dream partner Daphne Johnson, they were tenaciously involved with each other and were looking at a bright future together.
Remembering when we were late teenagers, wondering where our life could lead. If we had chosen the wrong aspirations, the wrong life partner. Throughout life, it's all about building dreams and encouraging one another. Start by building your foundations from the ground up, by making it palatial, fit enough for your version of King and Queen to endure, enjoy and live happy ever after.

References:
© Wapley Stables Ltd and Wapley Riding School Ltd (2001) 'Wapley Stables', *Riding lessons. #Horses, Prices* [. Available at: https://www.wapleystables.co.uk/.

Christ Church Oxford Univeristy (2001) 'Christ Church Lunches', *University of Oxford* . Available at:
https://www.chch.ox.ac.uk/college/undergraduate/meals.

Deborah Loeb Brice (2001) 'Department of Medical Sciences: Pharmacology, University of Oxford', *Art UK* . Available at:
https://artuk.org/visit/venues/department-of-medical-sciences-pharmacology-university-of-oxford-7495.

Eminem - Stan (2000 Music Video) | #4 Song (no date) *Playback.fm*. Available at:
https://playback.fm/charts/top-100-songs/video/2000/Eminem-Stan (Accessed: 12 March 2025).

Google (2001) 'Famous fix', *Mobile phones introduced in 2001* [Preprint]. Available at:
https://www.famousfix.com/list/mobile-phones-introduced-in-2001.

Herd (2001) 'The Ultimate Picture Palace', *Oxford's home of independent cinema* . Available at: https://uppcinema.com/.

Horse & Hound (2001) 'Varsity and Commonwealth Polo Day Report', *Horse &*

Hound . Available at: https://www.horseandhound.co.uk/news/varsity-and-commonwealth-polo-day-report-39115.

J Howard Rytting (2001) 'Novel approach to improve permeation of ondansetron across shed snake skin as a model membrane', *Volume 53, issue 6 June 2001* . Available at: https://academic.oup.com/jpp/article-abstract/53/6/789/6149851?redirectedFrom=fulltext.

Jamie Spencer (2001) '1973- The very first Mobile device', *The first invented Mobile phone device* . Available at: https://www.practicallynetworked.com/history-of-the-cell-phone/#:~:text=Motorola%20developed%20the%20first%20portable%20cell.

Joe – I Wanna Know Lyrics | Genius Lyrics . Available at: https://genius.com/Joe-i-wanna-know-lyrics (Accessed: 11 March 2025).

Mr Kentucky (2001) 'Fast Food takeaway Resturant/ Oxford Cornmarket Street', *Kentucy Fried Chicken (KFC)* . Available at: https://www.kfc.co.uk/kfc-near-me/Oxford-Cornmarket-Street.

Oxford Academic (2001a) 'Pharmacy and Pharmacology, Volume 53, Issue 6, June 2001', *Royal Pharamaceutical Society* . Available at: https://academic.oup.com/jpp/article-abstract/53/6/779/6149802?redirectedFrom=fulltext.

Oxford Academic (2001b) 'Pharmacy and Pharmacology, Volume 53, Issue 9, September 2001', *Royal Pharamaceutical Society* . Available at: https://academic.oup.com/jpp/article-abstract/53/9/1207/6149846?redirectedFrom=fulltext.

Oxford Academic (2001c) 'Yanmin Zhang Journal of Pharmacy and Pharmacology, Volume 76, Issue 12, December', *Royal Pharamaceutical Society*. Available at: https://academic.oup.com/jpp/article-abstract/76/12/1647/7754977?redirectedFrom=fulltext.

Oxford Mosaic (2001) 'University Parks', *Univeristy of Oxford* . Available at: https://www.parks.ox.ac.uk/.

Ramanathan-Girish, S. and Boroujerdi, M. (2001) 'Contradistinction between doxorubicin and epirubicin: in-vitro interaction with blood components', *Journal of Pharmacy and*

Pharmacology, 53(6). Available at: https://doi.org/10.1211/0022357011776162.

Santana Carlos (2001) 'Maria, Maria', *Genius* . Available at: https://www.bing.com/search?q=Maria+Maria&form=ANNTH1&refig=7BC3A1AD945942CDB2A8A9FB1D528948&pc=HCTS.

Shania Twain (no date) *Shania Twain – That Don't Impress Me Much*. Available at: https://genius.com/Shania-twain-that-dont-impress-me-much-lyrics (Accessed: 12 March 2025).

The Univeristy ofOxford (2001) 'Oxford University Polo Club', *Oxford Polo since 1874* . Available at: https://www.sport.ox.ac.uk/polo.

Tikkanen Amy (2001) 'Where do swans Originate from?', *Britiannica/Animal/waterflow-bird* . Available at: https://www.britannica.com/animal/waterfowl-bird.

Trending on RT (2001) ''There's something about Mary!..', *Rotten Tomatoes* . Available at: https://www.rottentomatoes.com/m/theres_something_about_mary.

www.jjohnsonauthor.com

Website by, Passenger (2001) ‘U5 Bus Brokes Buses’, *Oxford Bus company* . Available at: https://www.oxfordbus.co.uk/brookesbus.

Wikipedia (2001) ‘Bodleian Library’, *Wikipedia.org* . Available at: https://en.m.wikipedia.org/wiki/Bodleian_Library.

Will Smith – Miami . Available at: https://genius.com/Will-smith-miami-lyrics (Accessed: 11 March 2025).

Bibliography:

In the very early stages of my writing career around three years ago, I started writing short Novels with daily struggles that I faced both physically and mentally, my first two books that I wrote were called, The Mind I and The Mind Matters II, which I were a significant candidate to be able to talk about the various aspects of anxiety and depression and how that can affect you on a day to day basis, in and around work, making friends. The books themselves are very engaging and give direction to different supporting networks. Some things that I have tried to maintain my Mental Health and well-being, besides looking after my vitality to the best of my ability, but without giving up hope I had wanted to give others direction. Do not panic about making life-changing circumstances as it is not a sprint it's a marathon; I have found a love for writing which has become therapeutic and if you can at least engage in reading then you have half a chance to switch off from this mad world we are living amongst. Finding many hobbies and interests that you find therapeutic can better your Mental Health and many things can help you endure such trials to switch off.

I had then begun my academic integrity of Arts and Humanities which is History and Politics a PHD, I am a disabled Student at The Open

University of Milton Keynes,
Admittedly I have had some guidance and support, but thankfully that has helped me grow as a writer, being able to understand referencing and

researching for Historians and others that want to find factual evidence within your writing. This was something that I had struggled to get to grips with as you can only imagine a young man with dementia, I had to write down every single step of how to input citations and references, at first had caused me a lot of stress and anxiety, but in the end with some moral support with good friends around I had managed to achieve it with ease within the end. Down to sheer determination to keep wanting to improve as an author.

Here are some of my latest books:

Daniel, The book, The life, and the Story!
Daniel, The book, The story, The journey.

Looking through a scope throughout Daniel's childhood, seeing his daily struggles. Walking along his journey, noticing the many cognitive altercations he had suffered from on a day-to-day basis. Seeing how he had interacted with his small circle of friends that he had made between his school life and activities that he had loved to engage with. Soaring through his family life with binoculars, the entertainment, the love, and compassion throughout the family household. The adventures they all had and enjoyed together inside the family household, the drive down to the village school through the countryside. The Saint Micheal's church is where the whole community from the village had rejoiced. The fun-filled tenacious compelling story of Daniel, the historical journey through the magical 1990's era!

Daniel, The book, The story, The journey.

Written in the Author's truly unique and inimitable style, Daniel, The book, The life and The story purposefully conveys the innocence of Daniel, his brother and his friends in the brightly coloured political landscape of 1990's rural Essex. The book paints an intimate picture of the family's daily struggles, worries and triumphs.

The immersive topography of South East Essex is captured and recorded with great care, not only a joy to read for locals, but a peek into 1990's Essex for all.

Historical accuracy is of great importance to the Author in all of his works and this is no exception, with references that will bring nostalgia to anyone who experienced the 90's themselves.

A great read with something for all age groups.

Check out our Author Website (www.jjohnsonauthor.com).

We bring you through some of life's most important trials and tribulations, faced consequently within the injustice of things, that many parents and children struggle with today. To help you throughout this journey I will set forth an appraisal of guided steps we can take to better the chances of the relationship between child and parent. You may feel that the system is very one-sided when it comes to giving who has access to your children, with Social Services, Cafcass & Child Maintenance Services, with all those odds they would've taken a review and taken into account that the children reside with the opposing parent, which has left you feeling with lack of enthusiasm, lack of self-esteem, a failure as a parent. I like you, haven't given up my observations against all odds that humanity is up against, but believe my compassionate heart is led to believe I can give you a better understanding of how to guide you through this situation. You may or may not even be this close to setting forth an application to the courts yet. I will provide you, with every single bit of information that you desire to start to set things straight, both as a parent and for your children's sake.

www.jjohnsonauthor.com

Welcome to this book of prayers!

The author, Justin Johnson, has been on a journey throughout life and spirituality. Life brings a lot for all of us to deal with, sometimes the highs and sometimes the lows, but we all seek guidance and a sense of comfort along the way. I have collaborated with the author now for a few years on many publications, and his thoughts and beliefs are extremely profound and thought-provoking. He is a truly profound, inquisitive, analytical, spiritual, and religious person, who has studied the doctrines of many Religions and their beliefs and ethos.

In this publication, you are invited to read, absorb, and understand the prayers written. They cover all aspects, situations, and the doubts we all have in order to create some answers to the world in which we live, and the daily struggles we all encounter. You will find comfort in some, identify with many, and inspired to even to create your own. The range of prayers in this publication will take you on a journey from morning, throughout the day, and the feeling of hope at night.

Part, one focusses on Christian and Mormon prayers, celebrating not only the faiths themselves but also enlightening you into the true essence of what it is to be a Christian or Mormon. They deal with thoughts on daily struggles we all face and the comfort we seek from the Divine to make sense of and share our happiness, sadness, fears, and hope! We all need hope in order to function as a positive individual and to have the strength to carry on and enjoy the gift of life we have been given. Compassion to see the world as it is and through prayer seek to understand it and gain the empowerment to make a difference, day by day to truly flourish.

Part two focuses on the Jehovah's Witness faith, and the prayers encompass the religion. The prayers relate to Jehovah and what he has created for all of us, and how to celebrate his existence. Once again you will be taken on a full journey in this part of the book. This part provides an insight into the faith and what it truly means to follow. You will be intrigued and, am sure, inspired, by the collection of poems you encounter. The journey is there for all of us to read, reflect, and contemplate - for you will be able to identify your thoughts with many.

Part three focuses on children's prayers, and will be good to share with your children, or even take yourself to the nostalgia of your thoughts as a child.

These are truly thought-provoking and inspirational for the children as they grow and develop into the adults of the future and of our world.

Justin Johnson, academic integrity is arts and humanities, and has a love for writing fiction and non-fiction books, many published books on all major selling platforms

GENRE: Fiction

Blurb:

bringing you to the story and life of constant conflict that was running a feud between the Mods and Rockers through the late 1950s until the mid '60s, the sudden mayhem had begun as a rising panic through the British seaside towns, they were widely perceived as violent thugs, these rockers had worn black leather jackets jeans and motorcycle boots and they liked to listen to rock and roll music whereas the mod culture had centred their fashion with parker jackets and jeans and they had liked to listen to modern jazz, soul, Motown, and ska music, this was evident between the stark contrast between the Mods and Rockers. Conflicts and riots started to thrive throughout the seaside towns in 1964 especially throughout Clacton-On-Sea Essex area, throughout this story, we will be focusing on five casual Mod brothers that are still alive today 2024. But let me personally tell you this from this moment on, it is a fictional story as I am no witness to the events, but one thing I can say is I do know well. And three of them most certainly loved their scooters and motorcycles. These five brothers had become well known in the local area of Tendering and no doubt throughout the best part of Essex, as they had loved pubs, clubs, scooters, and five brothers, who wouldn't have loved to make some havoc? Mature teenage men with pure adrenalin and Ska music running through their veins, became the prime age to make a statement in the vicinity of their home territory. I mean what could possibly go wrong if they bumped into someone from a whole different culture, background, or group like the rockers, with their slick hair, leather jackets, and biker boots, they probably looked different, spoke different, and most certainly smelt different, with those leather jackets, smelt of leather and unpleasant Odor no doubt. The five Mod brothers and their clan weren't about to make up numbers they wanted to get known around the territory of Essex and anyone else that may want to cross paths with. A young teenage Mob had from the outset to Tread their mark throughout this era of the Mods and Rockers, and they would go to any lengths or heights to sabotage their rival's parties or local rally gatherings. The Mods were rising, so the Rockers knew they had to stand their territory, to stand and fight for what was right, their culture, rock n roll music, the black leather jackets, motorcycle boots, and slick back hair. They were fighting for their generation, they were fighting for their image, they were fighting for their differences, they were fighting for their right, they were fighting to become an icon. But we all know fighting is not necessarily the only answer for sorting out your differences, but when you get a herd of men arguing over a culture, it is fair to say it is like banging two large lumps of wood together. At the end of it all, you will still get the same response, two planks of wood, just like the two fighting cultures. The only thing that was left dented was their ego, their pride, and in the end, a depleted culture. With the passing of time, the novelty wears off, and cultures die out, facing all kinds of trials, illnesses, diseases, sickness, poverty, death, or imprisonment.

www.ingramcontent.com/pod-product-compliance
Ingram Content Group UK Ltd.
Pitfield, Milton Keynes, MK11 3LW, UK
UKHW041115280325
456815UK00001B/19

9 798230 247098